PRAISE FOR
Trouble Man

"Highly recommended—and y'all know I don't recommend much!"

—ERIC JEROME DICKEY,
author of *The Other Woman*

"Once again, Travis Hunter gives us unforgettable characters that move and touch us in a way very few authors have done. *Trouble Man* is full of surprises, and it shows that, with patience, love, and a willingness to look deep within our souls, we all have the capacity to grow and change for the better. This is fabulous work from a writer who has proven once again that he's here to stay."

—MARY J. JONES, PageTurner.net

"Travis Hunter continues to deliver entertaining, funny, true-to-life stories with his latest, *Trouble Man*, a novel about love, war, family, and people struggling to do the right thing. I felt that I knew these people."

—MALIK YOBA, actor and playwright

PRAISE FOR
Married but Still Looking

"Travis Hunter offers insight into the male psyche in ways that will captivate the reader, with stories that are both entertaining and compelling. There is a truth and boldness to his words that make him a noteworthy force in a new generation of fiction writers."

—LOLITA FILES, author of *Child of God*

"Despite its title, *Married but Still Looking* is about the sanctity of marriage, accepting responsibility for one's actions and understanding the consequences of bad choices. . . . [Hunter is] a good storyteller . . . readers are given solid, positive messages. . . . There's a lifetime of lessons in these pages."

—*The Dallas Morning News*

"An honest and multidimensional portrait of a self-centered player and his entourage, framed by the crooked consequences of his own indiscretions . . . a fast and appealing read, thanks in part to the authentic characterization of Genesis . . . his struggle is genuine and familiar, and yet his actions are unpredictable."

—**AALBC.com**

"The novel brings [Genesis Styles] and a handful of other characters . . . to understand that they can accept responsibilities as lovers and parents only when they have worked through the consequences of their parents' failings. Growing up means having the faith, and the conviction, to be better lovers and better parents to the next generation."

—*The Washington Post Book World*

"Hunter's writing is fluid and fast, and the dialogue is often raw and gritty yet comical."

—*Black Issues Book Review*

PRAISE FOR
The Hearts of Men

"Entertaining yet enlightening . . . Travis Hunter holds the reader hostage in his thought-provoking debut. Be prepared to laugh and cry as you examine *The Hearts of Men*."

—E. LYNN HARRIS, **author of** *A Love of My Own*

STRIVERS
ROW

During the 1920s and 1930s, around the time of the Harlem Renaissance, more than a quarter of a million African-Americans settled in Harlem, creating what was described at the time as "a cosmopolitan Negro capital which exert[ed] an influence over Negroes everywhere."

Nowhere was this more evident than on West 138th and 139th Streets between what are now Adam Clayton Powell and Frederick Douglass Boulevards, two blocks that came to be known as Strivers Row. These blocks attracted many of Harlem's African-American doctors, lawyers, and entertainers, among them Eubie Blake, Noble Sissle, and W. C. Handy, who were themselves striving to achieve America's middle-class dream.

With its mission of publishing quality African-American literature, Strivers Row emulates those "strivers," capturing that same spirit of hope, creativity, and promise.

TROUBLE MAN

TROUBLE

a novel

MAN

Travis Hunter

STRIVERS ROW / ONE WORLD

BALLANTINE BOOKS • NEW YORK

Strivers Row
An imprint of One World
Published by The Random House Publishing Group

www.striversrowbooks.com

Library of Congress Cataloging-in-Publication Data
Hunter, Travis.
Trouble man : a novel / Travis Hunter.
p. cm.
ISBN 0-8129-6651-1
1. African American men—Fiction. 2. Philadelphia (Pa.)—Fiction.
3. Life change events—Fiction. 4. Single fathers—Fiction.
5. Young men—Fiction. 6. Violence—Fiction. I. Title.
PS3558.U497T76 2003
813'.6—dc21
2003042274

Book design by Jennifer Ann Daddio

Manufactured in the United States of America

First Edition: August 2003
First Trade Paperback Edition: May 2004

4 6 8 9 7 5 3

To my son, Rashaad Hunter

TROUBLE MAN

Jermaine's Day

Jermaine Banks sat on the side of the bathtub as his three-year-old-son, Khalil, played in the sudsy water with a green-and-white plastic boat. The boat was one of the few toys that remained from Jermaine's own childhood. Khalil loved it and wouldn't take a bath without it. As Jermaine watched his child's carefree smile, he felt uneasy. He knew that, in order to keep that smile on his son's face, he was going to have to make some drastic changes in his life. But how? He was almost thirty years old with only a high school education and absolutely no work experience. Just as he got lost in his thoughts he looked up to see his pregnant girlfriend, Erin, in the doorway.

"Are you guys almost done?" Erin whined, crossing her arms.

"We just got in, Erin. Give us a minute," Jermaine said, shaking his head.

That girl wants everything on her time, he thought.

"I'm just checking, no need for the attitude," Erin said as she turned and stomped down the stairs to the living room.

Jermaine shook his head again and went back to washing his son. For the most part he loved Erin and she was a good woman. She had her ways, but who didn't? They had been together through a lot of thick and thin. Even when Jermaine had stepped out on her and got Khalil's mother, Amani, pregnant while Erin was completing her undergraduate work at Morgan State University down in Baltimore. But then again, that forgiveness had come with a price, and now that Jermaine was trying to take a more active role in Khalil's life, he was starting to notice that Erin was pretty ambivalent about her feelings toward his son. Sometimes she went overboard, trying to act as if Khalil were her best friend, like making sure he had a bedroom at her place, but whenever she was upset with Jermaine, her true feelings about Khalil surfaced.

The last few months had been pretty stressful for both of them: Erin getting used to the idea of being a *real* mom and Jermaine with the burden of becoming a daddy for the second time with no real plans for his future. Rightfully so, Jermaine seemed to be getting it the worst; it seemed as if every day someone was on his case about getting a real job and leaving his hustling days behind him. But just the thought of wearing one of those fast-food uniforms turned Jermaine's stomach. As far as he was concerned, those kinds of jobs were for high school kids and grown-up losers. Plus, he didn't see anything wrong with his current "job"—selling weed. As a matter of fact, he felt like he was doing Philadelphians a favor by providing a natural herb that helped folks calm the hell down.

"Jermaine. Jermaine," Khalil called out, with his arms outstretched toward his father.

"What's up, lil guy?"

"I'm ready to get out of the bathtub."

"Okay." Jermaine pulled the stopper and lifted his son onto the toilet seat. He toweled him dry, rubbed lotion all over his already soft skin, and helped him into his favorite Superman pajamas. The kind with the feet attached.

"You're all set, my man."

"Will you sleep with me?"

"You scared?"

"Yep," Khalil said with no shame.

"Man, how you gonna be a tough guy all day and a big baby at night?"

"I am tough." Khalil flexed his muscles for his father to examine. "But I still want you to sleep with me. Please." Khalil smiled.

Jermaine smiled too. He placed his hands on both sides of Khalil's face and looked down at his son. Khalil looked like a miniature version of himself. They shared the same caramel complexion and the same big brown eyes. Khalil even wore his hair in cornrow braids like his father.

As Jermaine stared into his child's eyes, he wondered if he had what it took to raise Khalil the way he deserved to be reared. An overwhelming fear came over him. Nothing else on God's green earth scared him like letting his son down.

"Yeah, I guess I can lay down with you for a minute. But you know what? I want you to stop calling me Jermaine and call me Daddy. Is that a'ight with you?"

"Yep," Khalil said, unaware of the powerful responsibility the word carried for his father.

Jermaine turned around and let Khalil jump on his back. He walked with him into his bedroom and laid him down on his bed.

"Jermaine, I mean Daddy. Miss Erin said I need to say my prayers."

"And Miss Erin is right. Let's do it."

They both got down on their knees and thanked God for his blessings. Once they were done, Jermaine lay down beside his son, and before a good five minutes were up, Khalil was snoring. Jermaine eased out of the bed and made the dreaded trip downstairs to have the same old tired conversation with Erin.

"So is he off to sleep?" Erin asked as she reached for the remote control to turn the television off.

"Sure is," Jermaine said, plopping down in the love seat across from her. "And I wish I could join him." Jermaine sighed, rubbing his temples.

"You can join him but you're going to have to face the truth about yourself one day, Jermaine."

"What truth?" Jermaine asked wearily. "I already know the truth about me, Erin. I live it every day. But what I don't need is for you to sit around all day figuring out ways to judge me."

"Nobody's judging you. But you need to get it together because we are having a baby and I'm not about to let you have my child around your drug-dealing friends while I'm at work. Now, you've let it be known that I can't tell you what to do when it comes to Khalil, but that line won't fly when the baby gets here because this child will be *my* responsibility."

"Baby, baby, baby. That's all you ever talk about. That and me turning into some kind of nerd. This pregnancy is still suspect."

"Suspect? What is that suppose to mean?"

"All of a sudden Erin just has to have a baby. For the life of me I can't understand why you feel like you need to compete with Amani."

"Compete with Amani?" Erin frowned. "Please! Trust me when I say that hood rat is no competition for me."

"Look at you. Always putting yourself up on some pedestal. If you were as high and mighty as you think you are, you wouldn't be trying to trap me with a baby."

Erin started laughing. Laughing so hard she had to hold her side.

"You must've fell and bumped your head. Jermaine, what is there about you that would make me want to trap you? You don't have a job. You got major baby-momma drama and there's a new police report out on you every month. Please! Now *you* need to come down off of your pedestal. If there's anybody that should be doing the trapping it's you."

"You crazy! Your family's got you thinking you're some kind of prize."

"Here we go," Erin said, huffing, leaning back against the sofa with her arms crossed.

"That's right, here we go. You didn't have a problem with where my money was coming from when it was paying for those expensive books that you needed for your bachelor's *and* your master's, which you only got so your mother could brag to her corny-ass friends, but that's another subject."

"Leave my mother out of this," Erin shot back.

"Whatever," Jermaine said, knowing how sensitive Erin was about her family. "Let's talk about that new car that you had to have, that brand-new Acura TL that my dirty money paid for, or what about when that dirty money paid your rent and all your other bills for two whole years so you could concentrate on school? But now you're straight and I'm the bad guy."

"I never told you or encouraged you to sell one dime bag. As a matter of fact, I begged you to stop and get a real job."

"Yeah, after you got everything you needed. Damn hypocrite!"

"That still doesn't change the fact that you need a job. And I can do without the name-calling."

"What kind of job do you want me to get? You want me to throw on a suit and tie and head down to Center City and walk up in one of those high-rises? Maybe then I'll be good enough for you, huh? You don't have a problem spending my dough but you got a problem with where it comes from."

"You know what, Jermaine? You are right. I didn't always have a problem with how you made your money, but I've grown up and you haven't. When are you going to grow up? You're still doing the same things you did when we were in high school. The only difference is you went from misdemeanors to felonies."

"So now I gotta operate on your schedule?"

"Just get a life," Erin said with a dismissive wave of her hand. She pushed the button on the remote control, letting Jermaine know that their conversation was over.

"You self-centered, arrogant bitch," Jermaine growled.

Erin's eyes widened and her creamy light face turned red as an apple. As thugged out as Jermaine was, he had never used profanity around her, never mind calling her that word.

She stood and screamed, "Get out of my house! Get your child and get out of my house!" Erin pointed toward the door.

Jermaine jumped to his feet and ran upstairs. He couldn't have thought of a better idea for the both of them, because at this point his blood was boiling and he couldn't stand the sight of Erin one more minute. He felt used and betrayed by the one woman he thought had his back. He knew he had his issues but she wasn't the one to talk. Here was a woman who wouldn't know how to cross the street if her mother didn't tell her, trying to tell him how to live his life. He raced into the room where Khalil was sleeping peacefully and quickly gathered his son and all of his belongings.

"Where we going?" Khalil asked sleepily.

"Go back to sleep, man."

He raced back downstairs and slightly bumped Erin as he passed her. She exaggeratedly grabbed her shoulder, acting like it was broken.

"Bye, Miss Erin." Khalil waved as his father carried him out to the street.

Erin sucked her teeth, rolled her eyes, and looked away.

Twenty minutes later, Jermaine parked his black BMW X5 on the street in front of his mother's row house and turned off the ignition. But before he could open his door there was a huge crash and broken glass went flying everywhere. Startled, he ducked down to avoid being hit by whatever else might be coming.

"Get outta this truck," an angry man's voice growled as he reached into the now open window, unlocked and opened the door. He grabbed Jermaine and pulled him to his feet, pushing a gun in his face. "I oughta kill yo' black ass right here, right now," the man growled.

The sound of the glass breaking woke Khalil, who had been sleeping peacefully in the backseat, and he let the entire neighborhood know of his displeasure by crying at the top of his lungs.

Once Jermaine got his bearings, he focused on the face in front of him. The bloodshot eyes, the dark skin with a mole on the tip of a pointed nose, and the eighties-style Jheri curl belonged to none other than Roscoe Jones, Erin's father. The hate subsided a little in Roscoe's red eyes when he heard Khalil's cries.

"You trynna make my baby girl have a miscarriage?" Roscoe whispered in a furious tone.

Slap! Punch! Slap!

"Man," Jermaine said, doubling over in pain. "What's your damn problem?"

"Didn't I tell you the next time you made my baby girl cry, I was gonna kill ya? You don't upset nobody that's pregnant. Babies come out all deformed and shit. Now take that boy in the house and come right back out here."

Jermaine touched his lip and looked at the blood on his hand. "Roscoe, have you lost your mind?"

Slap! "I told you to take that child in the house and bring yo' ass back." Slap! "I ain't playing wit' you," Roscoe said as he put his police-issue gun back into its holster.

Jermaine closed his eyes and took a couple of deep breaths. *I don't believe this broke-lookin' Barry White out here beating my ass,* he thought.

Jermaine walked around his truck and unbuckled Khalil from his car seat. He picked up his son and placed him on his shoulder, which was enough to quiet him.

"Hurry up, son. I ain't got all night," Roscoe said in his country accent, leaning against the hood of Jermaine's SUV.

Jermaine walked into his mother's house and sat Khalil down on the sofa.

"What's going on? Why is the police out there?" Nanette "Nettie" Banks asked her son, turning away from a rerun of *Sanford and Son*. "And why is your lip bleeding?"

"That's Roscoe," Jermaine said, trying to downplay the incident.

"Wait a minute. Roscoe hit you?" Without waiting on an answer Nettie went into a rage. "I don't play nobody puttin' they hands on my child. Who in the hell does Roscoe think he is?" Nettie hurried toward the kitchen, no doubt going for her gun. "I'll show that mother—"

"Hold up, Mom," Jermaine said, grabbing his mother's arm to stop her. He knew he had to come clean with his mother or in a matter of minutes Roscoe would be lying on his stomach in the back of an ambulance as the paramedics tried to remove a few .32-caliber slugs from his gluteus maximus. "Erin's pregnant. That's why he's tripping."

"Pregnant?" Mrs. Banks yelled, then reared back and planted one across Jermaine's face.

Slap!

Jermaine held his face and frowned. *Man, what is this? Slap the shit outta Jermaine day?*

"Boy, what is your problem? You barely can take care of this one here with his cute self." Nettie alternated from ranting to calm just as she always did when Khalil was around. "I'm getting too old to be takin' care of babies all the time."

"Who said you had to take care of my kids?" Jermaine said, still holding his face.

"Who else is going to take care of 'em, Jermaine? Not you. I know how you make your money. You ain't slick. Selling drugs ain't all that dependable, you know? And what makes you think you can get away forever doing something illegal? You need to stop being so damn lazy and get a job."

Here we go again, Jermaine thought.

"You've been getting slaps on the wrist all your life but one day one of those judges is going to put your butt in the penitentiary and I ain't sending you shit," Nettie said.

Jermaine ignored his mother just as he did every time she tried one of her scared-straight tactics. "Erin said she was on the pill."

"Oh, so it's Erin's fault, huh? How far along is she?"

"About five months, I guess."

"Five months?" Nettie yelled. "And when were you going to tell me? When the lil fucka graduated from pre-K?"

"Why you gotta cuss so much?"

"Why you gotta be trifling? Go on back outside. I should come out there and help Roscoe slap some sense into you."

Jermaine looked at his mother. "Mom, I'mma grown man and you're gonna have to figure out another way to get your point across besides hitting me," he said before walking back outside.

"Well, start acting like one then," Nettie said to her son, slamming her front door as he trotted down the steps and out toward the street.

Jermaine walked up to Roscoe, who was sitting on the hood of his truck smoking a cigar.

"Why you get my daughter pregnant without consulting me?" Roscoe asked as Jermaine walked up.

"Huh?" Jermaine frowned at the awkward question.

"You heard me, damn it. And don't make me get up again, cuz

I'm tired. I been arresting lil niggas like you all night," Roscoe said, shifting his weight to face Jermaine. "People ask fathers for their daughters' hands in marriage but nobody ask if they can get 'em pregnant. And that's ass backwards if you ask me. You can get a divorce and go on about your business but when a child is involved, ain't no going on about your life. Now, why didn't you ask me before you went and did the nasty with my daughter?"

"What do you want me to say, Roscoe? Me and Erin been to-gether forever, you didn't think we were having sex?"

Roscoe raised his eyebrows and looked as if he'd seen a ghost. "Hell no! Y'all ain't married."

"Come on, Roscoe. As much as you wanna think Erin is a little angel, she's still human," Jermaine said as he walked over beside Roscoe and leaned on the hood. They had never been friends. As a matter of fact, they didn't like each other at all; they simply toler-ated each other for Erin's sake.

"Jermaine, you know I don't like you. I can't stand yo' lil skinny ass. You ain't no good for my daughter. You ain't no good for black people in general. When white folks look at us, they think every one of us is like you."

"Roscoe, I couldn't care less what white people think about me."

"Ya see, that's why you ain't got nuttin' now. White people got all the power, boy, and to get a little bit you got to know how to deal with 'em. See, you're a part of that new dumb generation."

"And you are a part of that step-and-fetch-it generation."

"Shut up and listen. Some good people died just so you could have some opportunities in life, but do your ignorant ass take ad-vantage of it? Nah. You and your little wanna-be gangster friends run around here trying y'all best to screw things up worst than they were before."

"Oh, you think so?" Jermaine said, not trying to hear the ser-mon.

"I know so. Did you know that as a black man, I'm more likely to die at the hands of a nigga than any other natural force in this world? Tornadoes, hurricanes, any of that shit! I'm about nigga'd out."

Jermaine wanted to laugh at Roscoe but the more he thought about it, the more he realized that Roscoe was right. Every act of violence that he ever witnessed or participated in involved another black face.

"When was the last time you had a job?"

"That's not your business," Jermaine said defiantly.

"I'm making it my business. And you need to get a haircut."

"Roscoe, how you figure you can come over here breaking windows, throwing punches, and demanding haircuts? You got some weed in that cigar?"

"I love my wife," Roscoe said, ignoring Jermaine. "I really do. But I was the worst thing that could've ever happened to her. I wasn't worth a dirty nickel. Still ain't much better than I used to be. But she saw something in me and it screwed up her whole life. Before me, she was on the fast track to success. She was in her first year of law school and doing just fine for herself but then here I come trynna get some and she's never been the same. You see what I'm getting at?"

"No."

"You screwing up my daughter's life," Roscoe yelled.

"How you figure?" Jermaine responded calmly. He was getting used to Roscoe's rants.

"Cuz you ain't worth a damn! But you'll learn. Cuz you're taking care of Erin *and* that baby. Now, I got a friend who'll hire you at his car dealership. I already set everything up, all you have to do is go—"

"Hold up! Stop! I haven't said a thing about working at no car dealership. I'm my own man and I can get my own job."

"Either you can take your ass up there and try to make a legitimate buck or I'll have one of my men bust you every time you set a foot on the street. And I'm not mentioning what I'mma do to ya."

"Roscoe, I don't know what makes you think you can handle me like your child, but you need to stop pushing your luck. I'm really trynna to be respectful here because I don't let people put their hands on me."

"Jermaine, shut up."

"Okay, but you better act like you know."

"I don't better nothing but stay black and pay my taxes. Now, before you went and violated my daughter, I could ignore you and just hope you went away. Lord knows I prayed you would go away, but since you done *welcomed* yourself into my family, I gotta make sure you live a straight-and-narrow life cuz I don't want my grand-child around any foolishness."

"I guess you got it all figured out, Roscoe," Jermaine said. He knew there was no use arguing with Erin's father. He stood and walked over to the driver's side of his car. "Man, why you break my window?"

Roscoe stood and walked around to survey the damage. "You lucky I didn't break my foot off in yo' ass."

"Roscoe, you used up all of your hit-me-free cards. You raise your hands up again and I'mma knock yo' ass out," Jermaine said with a steely intensity that made Roscoe think twice about how old he really was.

"Okay, tough guy. Use some of your dope money to get your window fixed," Roscoe said as he walked over to his police car. He opened the driver's-side door and sat down, which caused the entire car to tilt to one side.

Who hired him as a police officer? You can walk and outrun him, Jermaine thought. *And how does everybody know I sell weed? I guess I do need to get a job.*

Calvin's Out

want a divorce," Calvin Sharpe said to his wife of sixteen years as he sat across from her at their breakfast table.

"Well, good morning to you too," Robin responded without looking up from her morning paper.

"I don't love you anymore, and I refuse to live the rest of my life like this."

Robin placed the paper on the table beside her plate and peered over her wire-rimmed glasses at her husband. "Just like that?"

"If you want to look at it like that, then fine, but I think you know I didn't come to this decision without a lot of thought," Calvin said.

"Forget working on our problems, huh? Let's just skip marriage counseling and go straight to the lawyers?" Robin said calmly, lifting her fork to finish off her vegetable omelet.

"We don't even need the lawyers." Calvin leaned in closer, placing both of his elbows on the table. "I'll make sure you are taken care of financially for the rest of your life. You can keep the house and your Mercedes. You can have full custody of C.J." Calvin looked away as if his son were an afterthought. "We'll work out a time frame for me to see him. I'll just take my personal belongings and you can have everything else. I'm not trying to take you through any more than you need to go through," Calvin said, satisfied with his offer.

Robin shook her head and went back to reading her paper.

"This has been on my mind for quite some time now, and like I said, I don't want to put you through any unnecessary drama."

"Well, that's very kind of you, Calvin, but I'm not giving you a divorce. And to me all this talk *is* unnecessary drama." Robin frowned and lifted her glass of orange juice to her lips.

"Oh, you'll give me one," Calvin insisted, raising his voice as he stood up from the table. "Or I'll make your life a living hell."

"Calvin, where have you been for the last few years? My life with you is already a living hell. But you made a commitment to me, and although I can't force you to be a man and stand by it, I'm certainly not going to let you weasel out of this marriage the way you do everything else."

"Robin, you don't make any sense. If your life with me is such hell, then why do you want to put yourself through this any longer? I don't love you and that's a fact."

"What does love have to do with it? I haven't been in love with you in I don't know how long, but that doesn't mean you can just up and run away. Sorry, but that's not what being married is all about. I'm not your girlfriend, someone you can just toss aside when the feeling hits you."

"I don't understand you, woman."

"Well, if you stopped running around trying to become the black Donald Trump, you might understand me a little better. I mean, how much money is enough?" Robin stood and took her plate to the sink.

"I'm not going to apologize for my wealth, and no matter what you say," Calvin stood and walked toward the kitchen door but turned around, "we're getting a divorce."

"No, we're not, and don't let my actions serve to further inflate your already bloated ego. It's not that I can't do without you. This is all about the vow we made before God," Robin said.

"Robin, please." Calvin softened his tone and decided to try a different approach. "You are a beautiful woman and you can have almost any man that you want. Why put us through this? Why put yourself through this? Come on, Robin, let's be reasonable."

"Calvin, I'm a woman of God and I'm a married woman so please don't insult me by associating me with any other man than the trifling one that's standing in front of me right now. Is that reasonable enough for you?"

"So you want to play hardball with me?" Calvin said, yelling again. "Okay, I tried to make this easy on you but you want to play hardball. Well, hardball it is. You'll be sorry that you wanted to go this route."

"No, it's you that'll be sorry. The only thing I'm sorry about is . . . well, you already know, don't you?" Robin said with a sad smile on her face.

Calvin left the kitchen without another word. He walked up the long, winding stairwell of their seven-bedroom, six-bathroom home and shook his head. His plan had already started to unravel. He walked into their spacious master bedroom and headed straight for his custom-made walk-in closet. Once inside he opened up a cabinet in his island and removed a Coach garment bag. As Calvin carefully placed his clothing in his suitcase, Robin walked in.

"Calvin, what are you doing?"

"I told you, I'm leaving you."

"Why?" Robin asked calmly.

"Robin, I'm tired. I'm tired of the monotony. I'm tired of not being appreciated. I'm tired of just existing with you and you can't even act like you're happy. I've given you this beautiful home, a brand-new Mercedes every year, and I've taken you all over the world. I even took you to Bethlehem so you could try to find Jesus himself, but did I get as much as a thank-you? No! And I'm just tired," Calvin said.

Robin stared at her husband, figuring there was more to this than he was letting on.

"Calvin, you do things just to say you did them. Nothing ever comes from the heart with you. I appreciate everything you've ever done for me but what do you want me to do? Jump up and kick my feet together just because we took a few vacations and you got me a car? I don't need all of this," Robin said, waving her hand, indicating the huge house. "This is you trying to impress your country club buddies, and that Mercedes doesn't mean a thing to me. And I'll have you know that every place we ever visited, I could've taken myself, so don't sit up here and act like you've done so much for me. And I don't know if you slept through Marriage 101 but we are a family and families do things together. We're *supposed* to broaden each other's horizons."

"Robin, it's not just that. You just . . . augh. Never mind. It doesn't matter, it's too late for talking."

"No! I'm just what?"

"Forget it."

"No, I don't want to forget it. Tell me why you want out of this marriage so bad."

"Robin, did you know that for the last few years I've been taking Viagra just to get it up for you? And I know nothing is wrong with me because I've seen a doctor about it. You're just boring the hell out of me and I'm through. You drain me. You make me sick," Calvin said, getting angrier with each word that left his lips.

"I didn't know you felt that way," Robin said as Calvin's harsh words tore into her already fragile heart.

"How could you not know? For the last six, seven years, our lives together have been one boring-ass ride, and this is where I get off the train. Now there is nothing you can do to change my mind. I'm leaving you."

Robin looked at the floor and tried to stop herself from crying. She would not let Calvin get to her. She nodded her head and smiled.

Calvin knew what the smile was about, but for some strange reason, unbeknownst to him, he didn't care. Maybe because he knew in his heart Robin wasn't the kind of woman who would blackmail him.

"You think this is funny?"

"Calvin, I really hate the day that I met you, you arrogant son of a bitch." Robin surprised herself with her outburst of profanity. She hadn't used such language in so long that she thought she had forgotten how to. But anger had taken over and there was no turning back now.

"You think you can just use people up and throw them away when you no longer have a use for them, don't you? Or worse, not even bother with them because they aren't of your social status," Robin said.

Calvin glared at her but Robin was on a roll.

"Not this sister. Oh, you're going to play by the rules with me." Robin started to raise her voice but calmed herself before continuing. "You see, let me explain it to you like this. You said you loved me, you asked my parents for my hand in marriage, I accepted, and that meant for better or worse. Not for when you no longer feel good about your situation. But more importantly, you gave my father your word. He asked you, while lying on his deathbed, to take care of his child. Well, you will honor my father's last wish."

"Robin, I said I would give you enough money to take care of you for the rest of your life; now, if that's not making your old man happy then I don't know what will. But I'll be damned if I spend one more minute as your husband. I'm fifty-one years old and more than likely I have more years behind me than I have in front of me so you can take what I offered you. Send your daddy a memo telling him that he raised a boring-ass daughter and I couldn't take no more so I owe him one. "

Robin walked over to Calvin and slapped him with as much force as her five feet three inches and 120 pounds had to offer.

"Don't you ever speak of my father in that tone! And as far as you leaving, you might as well unpack your bags because until death do us part. That's what I'm holding you to," Robin said, looking Calvin in the eye and almost breathing fire.

Calvin took a moment to gather himself. "Robin, if you ever touch me again I will kill you. And you better move out of my way and lower your damn voice in my house or you won't have to worry about a divorce because I will make sure you meet your Jesus," Calvin growled. "Now, I told you I'm leaving and you best move out of my way."

Unable to contain herself any longer, Robin screamed at the top of her lungs, "You wanna leave, then leave. Get out of my house." She raced over to Calvin's hanging shirts and slacks, reached up and grabbed a handful of tailor-made shirts and custom-made suits off wooden hangers, throwing them all over the closet.

Calvin stood back and watched his wife lose complete control of her faculties. Calvin decided she was too far gone to try and stop her so he leaned against the cherry-oak island with the black marble top and waited for her to calm down. Once she threw her last pair of shoes against the wall, Calvin decided it was his turn to act a fool.

"Now put everything back just the way you found it, damn it," Calvin said, standing over Robin as if he were scolding a child. "And this is not your house until I say it's your house. You can't afford this—you're a goddamn schoolteacher. Now pick up my damn clothes."

"You go to hell, you arrogant bastard," Robin said, rearing back and slapping Calvin again.

Calvin held his face and smiled. He growled something inaudible under his breath and grabbed Robin by her neck, pushing her petite body until her back was against the closet wall. He squeezed her until a vein showed in her forehead. He snapped out of his rage when he heard the sound of his son's voice.

"Dad! Dad," C.J. yelled as he took a deep breath and prepared himself to do what he had to do against his taller and heavier father. "Get your hands off of my mom. Now."

Calvin released his viselike grip from Robin's neck and grabbed his bag, not meeting his son's eye. He haphazardly threw a couple of items in his bag and made a quick exit. He pushed past C.J. as if he weren't even there.

Robin slid down the wall holding her throat, gasping for air. She was more shocked than hurt. In the sixteen years that they had spent as husband and wife, Calvin had never so much as threatened to lay a finger on her.

"I thought you said a real man wouldn't hit a woman," C.J. yelled at his father's back as he walked down the long hallway. He knew he was pressing his luck, but as far as he was concerned his mother was worth whatever abuse his father was willing to bring his way.

Calvin stopped and turned to his son. He looked at C.J. as if he could be next.

"Pull your pants up. You look like a damn thug," Calvin said before turning and walking out of the bedroom.

C.J. turned up his lip in disgust and hurried over to his mother's side. He wrapped her arm around his neck and helped her to her feet. Robin stood still holding her neck.

"Are you all right?" C.J. said, looking around the messy closet.

"I'm fine. What are you still doing here? I thought you left for school already," Robin said, trying to fight back tears.

"I forgot my tennis bag, and it's a good thing I did. Why were you guys fighting?"

"Your father wants a divorce."

"Good. He's hardly here anyway," C.J. said.

"It's not that simple."

"Mom, he doesn't want to be here, and when he is here you guys don't talk. Now he's hitting on you," C.J. said, shaking his head.

"It's not about that," Robin said, looking at her son, debating whether or not he was ready to handle one of the many secrets about his father.

"Then what is it about?"

"Follow me, I think it's time you learned the truth about your father."

3

One More Heartache

Jermaine was headed back to his house after his little altercation with Roscoe, when his cell phone rang.

"Hello."

"Yo, J, this Malik."

"What's the deal, homie?"

"Yo, where you at?"

"I'm on Stenton Ave on my way home, why?"

"I got some bad news."

"What else is new?"

"You sitting down?"

"Didn't I just tell you I was on my way home? How do you think
I'm getting there?"

"Come on, man, you don't have to get smart," Malik said.

"You should try it sometimes. Stop being stuck on stupid," Jermaine said, more frustrated with the entire night than he was with
Malik. "What's up, man?"

"Buster's dead."

"What?"

"He got shot."

Jermaine maneuvered around a few potholes and stopped his car in the middle of the street.

"Who shot him?"

"Some cats out in West Philly said he was moving in on their corner. Word is they knew he was your man and thought you were trying a takeover. Buster just got caught up in the wrong place at the wrong time."

"You gotta be kidding me. Them cowards know I don't get down like that," Jermaine said, slamming his balled fist against the steering wheel.

"Retaliation is a must. We can't let this ride. Buster was a civilian."

"Civilian? We ain't in no mob, nigga."

"I'm just saying, he wasn't even in the game like us."

"Meet me at my place the first thing in the morning. I need to think this thing out but I definitely got some drama for them faggots."

"You want me to bring a few soldiers?" Malik asked, still caught up in his gangster fantasy.

"Nah, just come by yourself," Jermaine ordered before ending the call.

Jermaine put his truck back in gear and drove in a trance. This couldn't be. Derek "Buster" Dorsey had been his best friend since they were small kids running the halls of Edmonds Elementary School. They had lost their virginity on the same day with the same girl in a coat closet at Leeds Middle School. And when Jermaine had decided to go to Dobbins High School, Buster took the trip every day with him over to Broad and Lehigh. But now he was gone. With the exception of his family, Jermaine hadn't known anyone on the face of this earth as long as he had known Buster. But if Malik's words were true, none of that mattered now; the mean streets of Philadelphia had snatched up another young brother, just thirty years old. People around him had been dying since he could remember, but death had never hit this close to home. Now here it was, staring him right in the face.

Shaken, Jermaine pulled his truck into the Sunoco parking lot at the corner of Broad and Stenton Avenue and pushed the button to the electric sunroof. He needed a direct view to the heavens above.

"God. What are You thinking about? I know I'm not supposed to question You, but why Buster? This world is full of fools. We got murderers, rapists, child molesters, and even a dumb-ass president. So why take one of the good ones?" Jermaine fought back the tears. "He never hurt a soul; even the times when he should've, he always walked away. You know, this is some foul sh—" Before Jermaine could finish his blasphemous sentence, there was a thunderous roar from the dark skies and all of a sudden it started raining, hard. Jermaine took that as a direct sign from God to shut up and stop minding His business, so he did what any sane person would do and pushed the sunroof button again to slide the black sheet back into place.

Jermaine sat in his truck trying to fight back the tears, but he was losing that fight. Oblivious to the rain coming into his truck from the broken window, drenching his left arm and leg, he stared straight ahead thinking about his best friend. He snapped out of his daze and opened the door to his truck, stepping out onto the wet pavement. He needed something to take his mind off his troubles, so he went into the store and purchased a forty-ounce bottle of Olde English Malt Liquor. He gave the cashier a ten-dollar bill and walked out of the store without waiting for his change. Once outside he looked up at the sky and let out a loud yell. He took a long swallow from the bottle, emptying almost half of it. Then, with all his might, he threw the remains across Broad Street. Jermaine opened the door and took a seat on the wet leather and wished he could take back his last conversation with Buster.

Over the years Jermaine had witnessed many of his childhood friends lose their lives. Some died the simultaneous slow death of drugs and prison while others were blessed enough to have a more swift and merciful ending and were sent straight to the coroner's office. But this was Buster, the good guy. He had just gotten married and had a brand-new baby girl for whom Jermaine stood godfather.

All Buster had ever tried to do was take care of the people he loved, and that's what he'd been trying to do when he had approached Jermaine a week earlier.

Buster had come to Jermaine frustrated with the violence and poor conditions of their neighborhood. He said he didn't feel comfortable leaving his baby girl and his wife alone while he worked. He told Jermaine that he was only two thousand dollars away from saving enough money to buy a home out in Germantown. Jermaine remembered teasing Buster about running away from his people. Then he said that he wasn't just going to give Buster the money— he would help him out. He paged Malik and had him bring Buster a pound of marijuana. Jermaine told him he could keep all the profits, which, depending on how he sold it, would give him more than enough money to move. Jermaine's mind was on money and generating more customers in Buster's corporate world. Buster was thinking about his family so, unknowingly, he stepped into another world. Jermaine's world. Now all Jermaine wanted was to take back that package and reach in his pocket and *make* Buster take that money.

Tears came by the pints and Jermaine didn't bother to wipe them away. He had never allowed himself to get that close to anyone, and up until this moment he hadn't realized that Buster meant that much to him. He knew he had mad love for Buster but not to the point where he would be feeling like this. Or was it guilt? Jermaine ended the chatter in his head, started his truck, and drove straight to his place.

Jermaine pulled into the alley beside his apartment and got out of his truck. Just as he was walking up the stairs he heard a familiar voice.

"Jermaine," Vera said, rolling up in her wheelchair. "Wait a minute. You wanna buy some pussy?"

Jermaine stopped and turned around to see a woman who was actually in her late twenties but looked to be at least twenty years older. Her once beautiful brown face now was riddled with acne, her once perfectly straight teeth now looked like a jack-o'-lantern's, and her hair stayed wrapped in a dirty bandanna. Through his sadness and anger, Vera was a welcome relief. He actually chuckled when he looked down at her. She was using her hands to open her legs.

"Vera, whatchu doing?"

"I'm trynna get paid. You gonna help me out or what? And I don't have time for one of your Malcolm X speeches tonight."

"So you trickin' now?"

"I do what I gotta do."

"Vera, you're too much work. You gotta have somebody lift you up out of the chair, then lay you down, then pick you back up and put you back in your chair. You picked the wrong profession for your medical condition," Jermaine said, shaking his head and turning to walk in his house.

"What about some head?" Vera said, pressing the issue.

"Vera, are you high? I know you know better than to come at me like that, and when did you start trickin'?"

"Man, give me a few dollars so I can go get my blast on," Vera asked, not wanting to go there with Jermaine.

"Listen," Jermaine said, shaking his head at his paraplegic friend's outburst. Then he thought, *Who is more resourceful than a crack head? Nobody!* "Vera, somebody broke my window in my truck. If you can go and find some plastic to put over the door to keep that rain out, I'll give you a few dollars. Better yet, since I know you'll be out here all night looking to get high, keep an eye on my whip for me and I'll give you fifty dollars in the morning."

"Okay, but give me twenty now," Vera said with her hand out.

"Vera, you know if I give you twenty dollars right now I won't see you until it's all smoked up. And you know I'll push your ass out of that wheelchair if you try to play me. So let's save both of us the drama and come on back with the plastic and I'll give you your money," Jermaine said as he placed his key into his door lock. "You need to roll up to one of them rehabs and check in."

"Why? I like getting high," Vera said as she rolled away in her wheelchair. "I'll be back in ten minutes and I want at least twenty dollars."

"Bye, Vera."

"Jermaine, don't make me have to shoot you. You know I don't play when it comes to my money," Vera said as she took off down the street.

"I know you don't, Vera." Jermaine stood and watched Vera roll down the avenue. He shook his head. *These streets ain't no joke.*

Jermaine walked into his apartment, which was furnished with the finest stolen goods the streets had to offer. There was a flat-screen plasma television hanging on the wall in the living room that he'd paid four hundred dollars for and a state-of-the-art entertainment system that he'd got for two pounds of weed. There was a leather sofa, wrought-iron-and-glass tables, honey-oak bookshelves with at least two hundred titles, custom-made art hanging on the walls, and all kinds of expensive but hot fixtures. The only thing he'd got out of a store was his and Khalil's bedroom sets, and even those were paid for with money he'd made selling weed.

Jermaine stopped when he saw a rat the size of a full-grown Chihuahua, sitting like a dog in the middle of the living room floor. He reached up to his bookshelf and threw a hardcover at the rodent, who looked at Jermaine before taking cover in a hole behind the wall.

"I'mma shoot my damn landlord. Got me in here living with rats with attitudes. Lil bastard acted like *I* was bothering *him*," Jermaine said as he ran to catch his ringing telephone.

"Hello."

"Jermaine. It's me," Erin's tearful voice said.

"What's up?"

"Can you come back over here so we can talk?"

"Erin, I'm not in the mood for all that right now. I just got a call from Malik telling me Buster was killed."

"Buster?" Erin asked, shocked. "What happened?"

"Don't know yet. I think he got caught up in the cross fire."

"What cross fire?" Erin blurted out. "Jermaine, what is going on?"

"Nothing. Let me call you in the morning."

"No, I want you to come over here right now."

"Erin, just let me have a moment. I need some time to myself. To get my head together, okay?"

"Jermaine, please don't go out and do what I think you're going to do."

"I'm not going anywhere."

"Jermaine, I know you. Let the police handle this. I need you. Khalil needs you and our baby needs you. So don't put yourself in a position to leave us."

"Where am I going?"

"Prison, the cemetery, I don't know, but I do know if you go out there trying to avenge your friend's death something will happen."

"I'm straight. Go to bed. I'll talk to you in the morning."

"Jermaine, I'm sorry for whatever it is that you think I've done."

"Yeah, okay," Jermaine said, shaking his head.

Jermaine hung up the phone and sat on the side of his bed. For whatever reason, he thought about his father, who lived on the other side of town but had managed to put Jermaine on his schedule only two or three times in the twenty-nine years that he'd been breathing. He wondered if his old man was even still alive. Then he wondered how different his life would be if he had grown up with his father out in the suburbs. The few times he had seen his father, he'd always been in some nice car and dressed in expensive suits.

Jermaine tossed the thoughts from his head and focused on the problems at hand. He debated whether he should call Buster's wife, then decided that he'd better check on her.

"Hello." The tearful voice cracked. Jermaine immediately wanted to hang up, but he knew they had caller ID.

"Sasha. This is Jermaine and I was just calling—"

"Ohhhhhh . . . Jermaine, he's gone. Why did they take my baby?" Sasha's words were barely audible as she sobbed. Her tears made Jermaine more determined than ever to make the killers pay. This pain was not supposed to happen.

"Sasha, I'm going to take care of the guys that did this."

"Is that going to bring my husband back? If you take care of those animals, will that give our daughter her father back? Jermaine, as much as I despise whoever did this to Derek, nothing will bring him back. I couldn't care less what happens to those fools. All I want is my husband back, my baaaaaby," Sasha wailed.

This was too much for Jermaine.

"Sasha, I'm sorry, and if you need anything, give me a call."

Sasha hung up the phone without responding.

Jermaine lay back on his bed, cradling the telephone receiver to his chest as if he were holding on to Buster himself.

It Takes Two

alvin paced the floor thinking about the drastic turn his life had taken in the last twelve hours, but he was satisfied with his decision to ask Robin for a divorce. Even though the reasons he'd given her were shallow, the truth was he was just tired of her. He knew that either Robin or C.J. was probably on the phone with his parents right now, as if he were a ten-year-old delinquent, and that it was only a matter of time before he would hear his mother's cries or his father's admonishments.

Calvin sat down on the bed and ran his hand through Kelly's long blond hair as his mistress slept peacefully. She opened her eyes and smiled up at him.

"Are you ready for round two?" she purred.

Calvin smiled at her and shook his head. "Can't, I gotta get going."

Kelly frowned like she always did when he left her, but it was one o'clock in the afternoon and Calvin knew another day of recklessly good sinning had come to an end. He stood and pulled his T-shirt over his head.

"I did it," he stated.

"Did what?" Kelly asked, sitting up and yawning.

"I asked Robin for a divorce," Calvin said with a smile.

"Why did you do that?" Kelly asked, taken aback.

"What do you mean, why did I do that? I did it for us."

"Us?" Kelly said without thinking. "I mean, Calvin, don't you think we should've talked about this before you made such a major decision?"

"What is there to talk about? I love you and I don't love Robin. Too many people waste their lives away being with someone they don't love and I'm not going to let that happen to us," Calvin said as he slid his feet into his wing tips.

"Wait a minute, I don't want to be the reason you walk out on your family."

"I'm not walking out on them. You make it sound like I'm leaving them to fend for themselves. Robin and C.J. will be well taken care of. Trust me on that."

"Calvin, I like you. I might even love you, but I don't want to be with anyone full-time. I enjoy my space," Kelly said, getting up and walking over to Calvin. She wrapped her arms around him. "You know what I mean?"

"Wait a minute. Are you the same woman that cries every time I have to leave you? This is certainly not the response I was expecting."

"What do you want me to say, Calvin? You just spring this news on me like this."

"I don't know. Maybe a little more excitement. We don't have to sneak around anymore. Isn't that your main complaint?"

"Yes, Calvin, but not like this. What about your son?"

"He's fifteen and he's off doing his own thing most of the time anyway," Calvin said, getting frustrated with the way this conversation was going. "Look, what's with the indecision?"

"I don't know," Kelly said, walking over to the window. "I guess I just need some time to figure this all out."

"What is there to figure out? Or was all that love talk just that? Talk!"

"I have a question for you and I want the truth. When was the last time you had sex with your wife?"

"Where did that come from?"

"I just want to know," Kelly said, crossing her arms.

"Look, we sleep in separate rooms and barely talk, let alone make love. And when we do talk it's only in reference to C.J. or something pertaining to the house. I already told you that."

"So your answer is . . ." Kelly said.

"Kelly, I can honestly tell you that it's been at least two years since I've laid a hand on that woman," Calvin lied. The truth was he had just made love to Robin the night before.

ast night, he had walked into their bedroom just as Robin came in from the bathroom naked as the day she was born. He had to admit after all these years she still looked good. No sagging breasts or pudgy midsection for his wife.

Robin turned and noticed her husband looking at her and covered herself as if she were a high school virgin. Calvin ignored her and walked into his closet to remove his business attire. He took a quick shower and crawled in the bed beside Robin.

"How was your day?" she asked.

"Bought two more buildings," he said nonchalantly.

"Uh-huh," Robin grunted, uninterested in her husband's part in gentrification.

"Why all the excitement?" Calvin said sarcastically.

"Does it matter what I think?"

"It matters," Calvin said, even though he knew he couldn't care less what she thought.

"Calvin, how would you like it if someone came and threw you out of your home just so they could make a few extra dollars off of your location? I mean, think about it, some of those people have nowhere else to go."

"Hey, don't drown me with your bleeding heart. I wasn't born with a silver spoon in my mouth. I worked for every dime I have and this country has too many programs for anyone to be living like savages," Calvin said, pulling the cover up over him. "If you ask me, I'm doing them a favor. You should've seen one of the places. It certainly wasn't fit for human occupancy."

Robin sighed. She prayed every night that God would place some kind of empathy in her husband's heart but God was truly working on His own time with Calvin.

"Then why don't you build some low-income housing?"

"There's no money in that," Calvin said, exasperated with his wife's naïveté.

"Calvin, please, will you do something for someone other than yourself sometime?"

"Robin, I'm not in the charity business."

"So what is this one going to be? A golf course?" Robin said.

"That's not a bad idea."

"Unbelievable," Robin said, looking at Calvin as if he were the Antichrist. "How can you sleep at night knowing you are uprooting families? And all so you and your moneygrubbing partners can make a freaking golf course."

Calvin really wasn't listening to Robin—he'd heard it all before, and he tuned her out. His mind was on the smooth chocolate he saw when she sashayed across their bedroom floor. It had been about two weeks since they had been intimate and it was time. Calvin visualized Robin riding him the way she did when they first started dating. He could still see her perky breasts bouncing up and down.

Calvin snapped out of his self-imposed trance and rolled over to face his wife. He wasn't sure how long he had spent on Fantasy Island, but she was now quietly reading a book. He reached over and removed her right breast from her silk nightgown and began massaging it. Calvin didn't notice the look of disgust on Robin's face because he was too busy sucking and licking her breast like it was ice cream on a cone. He kissed her neck and turned her head so that he could slide his tongue in her mouth, but Robin's teeth blocked his path to French land. Undeterred, Calvin moved his head back down to her breast and sucked like it was going out of style. Robin still didn't budge when he slid his hand between her legs and rubbed her dry vagina. Calvin tried and tried to get the juices flowing, but no such luck. Robin didn't even bother to close the book that she was reading when Calvin went down on her. She just lay there like a bump on a log. Calvin looked up from between her legs and stared at his wife.

What the hell is her problem? he thought, but kept it to himself.

Calvin shook his head and rolled out of bed. He walked into his private bathroom and slammed the door behind him. He dropped his underwear and took a seat on the oblong porcelain toilet seat and began his weekly masturbation ritual. As he closed his eyes and stroked his manhood up and down, he thought about Kelly. Then all of a sudden the thought that he was a married man popped into his head.

This is a bunch of BS. Robin will be performing her wifely duties tonight. I didn't get married to have to sit on a damn toilet stool to jerk off, Calvin thought as he turned on the cold water faucet and filled his mouthwash cup. He then opened his medicine cabinet and grabbed the silver bottle with "Centrum" on the label. He poured out a few vitamins in his hand and then removed two little blue tablets with a tiny *V* on them and placed the large white ones back in the bottle. He swallowed hard and said to himself, "It's a damn shame a man has to take Viagra in order to get it up for his own wife." Calvin opened the bathroom door and stared at Robin, who was still reading her book. He walked over to her and politely removed the novel from her hand. He turned the reading lamp off and climbed on top of his wife to have another night of uneventful yet satisfying sex.

s this really what you want, Calvin?" Kelly asked, smiling as she walked over to Calvin and sat on his lap. He ran his hands through her hair, looked into her blue eyes, and returned her smile.

"Of course it is."

"I thought that we would never be together," Kelly said. It was as if she had finally come to her senses.

"Why is that?"

"You know, with me being white and you being married. Too many obstacles."

"Baby, the only color that I fear is green, and the only reason I fear that one is not having it. And speaking of green, we have to tread lightly. Robin knows some things about me that could jeopardize everything that I've worked for."

"Things like what?"

"Never mind that. I'm just telling you so we don't get ahead of ourselves. I'll handle her; you just keep those real estate connections coming and before you know it, we'll have enough money to buy our own little Pleasure Island."

"O-kay," Kelly said as she walked over to her nightstand and picked up the telephone. She looked at Calvin as she dialed his home number.

Robin answered. "Hello?"

"Hi there. May I speak with Calvin Sharpe," Kelly asked.

"He's not here right now," Robin said, "but I can take a message. Who's calling?"

"My name is Lisa Cavalier, and I am the attorney that he has obtained to take care of his upcoming divorce proceedings. Do you know when he'll be home?"

"He doesn't live here anymore," Robin said, upset, as she slammed the phone down.

Calvin sat on the side of the bed and watched Kelly. Once she hung up she walked back over to him and smiled.

"So much for trust," Calvin said, shaking his head.

"I trust you now," Kelly said. "She sounded like she was crying."

"She'll be all right," Calvin said, leaning down to kiss Kelly. "It's about time she learns to live with a little disappointment."

"Calvin, you can be mighty cruel at times." Kelly laughed. "So when are you moving your things out?"

"Soon."

Skeletons

After Calvin had left, Robin grabbed C.J.'s hand and headed downstairs for Calvin's study.

"Sit down," Robin ordered as she took a seat in Calvin's high-back leather executive chair behind his massive cherry-oak desk. She turned and unlocked a drawer on the matching credenza. When she turned around she held a stack of yellow slips in her hand.

"What are those?" C.J. asked.

"These are receipts," Robin said, sighing deeply. Just the thought of what she held in her hand and the mind-set of her husband frustrated her to no end.

"Receipts for what?"

"Those receipts are for child support of your father's oldest son."

"Oldest son? Wait, I have a brother?" C.J. asked, stunned and confused. For as long as he could remember he'd wanted a brother and now his mother was sitting across from him holding what appeared to be proof that one had existed all along. He sat bewildered.

Robin's heart was beating rapidly as she watched her son. She knew how much this news was affecting him, but she felt he needed to know.

"Yes, you have a brother and his name is Jermaine Banks and this is all he ever meant to your father," Robin said, waving the thin yellow papers in front of her son's face. "He has chalked an entire human life up to a few dollars."

"Where does he live?" C.J. asked, totally focused on his brother.

"The last I heard he was right here in Philadelphia, but he's not a kid anymore. According to these documents he must be about twenty-eight, twenty-nine years old."

"I don't care. I want to meet him."

"You want to meet him?" Robin asked, shocked. She hadn't thought about the consequences of divulging this information. She sat still for a minute. She should've known this would be his reaction. C.J. was an all-or-nothing kind of kid; just knowing he had a brother would never be enough. Still, she tried to save her son's feelings. "Well, I don't know if that's a good idea."

"Why wouldn't it be? Don't you think he would want to know that he has a brother?"

"C.J., I don't know how he feels and I don't want you to get hurt if he doesn't want anything to do with you. I don't know what Jermaine's mother has told him about his father. All I know is what your father has told me and that's not much. I've only known about Jermaine for the last year and a half."

"How did you find out?" C.J. got excited when he thought about the fact that he had a brother. A real brother. Not the fake one that he had made up for years for his friends.

"One day this certified letter showed up from a child support enforcement agency for your father. I was being newsy-nosy and opened it up. It said your father was twenty-something thousand dollars in arrears for child support; well, of course I called him on it. At first he said it must be some kind of mix-up, but then I guess he found a conscience from somewhere and admitted that he had another son."

"But does Dad ever talk to my brother?"

"No, it's as if Jermaine doesn't even exist to him. I don't know how he does it, but he never says anything about him."

"So he's full of crap. All of that talk about being responsible for your actions doesn't mean a thing to him. He's bogus."

"C.J.! That's still your father."

"Yeah, whatever."

"Your father said he saw him a few times when Jermaine was small but stopped contact when Jermaine's mother wouldn't give him full custody."

"So he just walked away? Dad is an asshole!"

Robin threw her son a look but decided against admonishing him again because she couldn't agree more.

"He said that he didn't like the negative living conditions Jermaine was in and the way that Jermaine's mother carried herself."

"Don't try to justify his actions, Mom."

"I'm not, I just don't want you to hate your father. Nothing good can come from that."

"Well, too late."

"C.J. . . . ," Robin said.

"Have you ever seen my brother?"

"No, I've never seen him."

"Well, I'm going to find him. You said he might still live in Philly, right?"

"The last I heard he still lived here, but, like I said, he's a grown man now and I don't have any idea where he lives," Robin said. Although she was unsure of her feelings about her son's quest to seek out his half-brother, she felt that she had to let him do what his heart desired.

C.J. stood and walked around the desk to give his mother a hug. "Everything is going to be all right, Mom," he said, kissing her on the forehead before walking out of the room.

Robin swiveled around in the high-back leather chair for a long time. She couldn't believe that after sixteen years of marriage it had come to this. She placed the receipts back where she had got them and locked the credenza.

Robin got up and walked upstairs to begin her laundry. She walked into C.J.'s room and began emptying his hamper. As she went through his pants pockets looking for ink pens and other items that could ruin her entire load, she happened to come across a box of Trojan condoms. She counted them—one was missing.

Robin sat on her son's bed, dismayed. She stared at the little blue square box and couldn't believe her eyes. Her little baby was growing up and she didn't know how to take it. Robin stood and walked over to C.J.'s dresser and picked up a picture of him playing baseball. There he was, the only African-American boy on the team and, as always, the smallest one. A tear formed in the corner of her eye when she thought about how brave and fearless her son was.

When C.J. was five years old, he'd been diagnosed with polycystic kidney disease. The disease had slowed his physical growth but only increased his desire to live his life to the fullest.

Robin almost dropped the picture when the telephone rang. She placed the photo back in its place and walked over to C.J.'s desk to answer the phone.

"Hello."

"Happy birthday to you. Happy birthday to you. Haaaappy birthday to Robin, happy birthday to you. How ya doin', girl? With ya old ass," said Naomi, Robin's older sister.

"I'm fine, and have you forgotten who Momma and Daddy had first?" Robin said as she smiled for the first time today.

"What you got planned for your forty-fifth birthday?"

"Nothing. I took the day off, hoping I could get a grip before I lose it, but it doesn't look like that's going to happen."

"Let me take you to lunch. We'll talk about it."

"That sounds good. Where do you wanna go?"

"Oh, it's your day so you pick the spot and I'll pick up the tab."

"Let me think about that while I'm getting dressed."

"All right. Hey, how's my baby C.J. doing?"

"He's doing fine. A little too fine," Robin said, still holding the box of condoms. "You won't believe what I'm holding in my hand."

"What?"

"A box of condoms."

"I didn't know you still used those kinds of things once you were married."

"They're not mine. I'm in C.J.'s room."

"Why you snooping around the boy's room in the first place?"

"I wasn't snooping. I'm doing laundry."

"Laundry, what happened to the maid? Maria, or whatever her name is?"

"She's on vacation. But I just can't believe this boy," Robin said, still staring at the blue box.

"Ooooh, C.J.'s getting his groove on? Well, hell, at least he's being safe. The boy *is* fifteen years old, Robin."

"And you say that to say . . . ?"

"I'm saying leave him alone. Let him do his thing. Tell Calvin to give him a birds-and-bees talk. Well, at fifteen he'd be a little late, huh?"

"I just can't believe it. We're gonna have a little talk when he gets home. Out there dealing with those fast-behind little girls."

"Oh, you sound just like a mother. Blaming the girls. I'm sure whoever it is that C.J. is doing the nasty with tied his hands and feet together and made him do it," Naomi said sarcastically.

"I'm not saying anybody tied him up."

"Well, what are you saying? Even though being tied up ain't all that bad. Girl, have you ever been handcuffed to a bedpost and had the taste screwed outta your mouth? Oh, ain't nothing like it."

"Oh my God, I'm not having this conversation."

"I'm just telling the truth."

"You are a mess. How is Dominique doing?" Robin asked, changing the subject before her raunchy sister could really get started.

"Driving me up a wall. I thought when your kids moved out, they'd leave you the hell alone. That chick stays over here more now than when she lived here. I can't even sneak me a piece because she just pops her little ass up over here any time she wants."

"Girl, you're crazy."

"I ain't crazy. What did Calvin get you for your birthday? I know, Mr. Big Spender broke the bank."

"He didn't even spend enough time remembering. Neither did C.J.," Robin said, clearly hurt.

"Wait a minute. You mean to tell me neither one of those niggas remembered your birthday?"

"That's what I'm saying. Not so much as a card. And stop using that word."

"Okay, but wait a minute. How trifling can you get to forget your wife's birthday? And C.J. should know better."

"Unfortunately I'm getting used to it."

"Nah, that ain't something you should have to get used to."

"Well, such is life," Robin said as she peeked out the window and saw a white van pulling up. "Wait a minute. There is a 1-800-FLOWERS van pulling up now. Calvin's secretary probably remembered." Robin walked downstairs and opened the door and, sure enough, there was a large bouquet of roses with a card signed *Happy Birthday, MOM, Love, C.J.*

"I have roses," Robin said as she signed the paper for the delivery guy.

44 | TRAVIS HUNTER

"See, there you were about to get your panties all tied up."

"They're from C.J. I should've known my baby didn't forget about me," Robin said, feeling better about herself.

"Well, give Calvin some time, he might surprise you with something."

"He already did. He asked me for a divorce this morning."

"He did what?"

"He asked me for a divorce."

"That's what I thought you said. What's going on with y'all?"

"If I knew I'd tell you. But all I've ever done was try to be a good wife to Calvin." Robin fought back the tears.

"Oh, fuck him. Don't you get yourself all upset over that arrogant-ass nigga."

"Naomi, I don't know what to do. I don't believe in divorce."

"What, is Calvin going through some kind of midlife crisis or something?"

"I don't know, but he's not getting a divorce. I stood before God and made vows that I plan on honoring."

"Oh my, you're just full of surprises this morning, aren't you? Well, damn. You done got me depressed. That's why I don't have any married friends. Y'all too damn unhappy and I don't have time for all that misery. Call me when you've figured out where we're meeting, I'll cheer you up," Naomi said.

"I'll do that."

"You hang on in there. Everything will be just fine. I love you."

"I love you, too."

Sad Tomorrows

lose seven!"

Jermaine didn't budge as the large steel door to the cell block slammed shut. He just lay still on the thin mattress that separated him from the hard steel slab protruding from the wall and stared up at the dark gray paint chipping from the ceiling, thinking about the night that landed him at his new address: Seventh and Arch Street, the Federal Detention Center.

Jermaine and Malik had ridden out to West Philly in a stolen car. They'd had one mission in mind—to find Buster's murderer. They were riding down Lancaster Avenue when Jermaine spotted a tall, light-skinned guy with whom he'd had a few words one day while hanging out with Buster. When the tall guy saw Jermaine, he immediately took off running. That was all the confirmation Jermaine needed. Why else would he start running if he hadn't killed Buster or at least had something to do with it? Either way, he was breathing his last breath.

Malik slammed the gas pedal to the floor and they easily caught up to what was soon to be Philadelphia's latest murder statistic.

Jermaine got out of the car with his gun drawn. The dead man immediately started explaining: "I didn't mean to kill your boy. I was just busting at him to get him off my block, son. He was taking food out of my kids' mouths."

But Jermaine wasn't there for dialogue. He was there to avenge his best friend's murder and that's what he did. BAM! The explosion from the .40-caliber handgun interrupted the calm of the night.

Tall and Lanky's eyes registered disbelief as the reality that he was milliseconds away from dying hit home. Then the steel hollow-tip slug penetrated his cranium, cracking it into two equal halves, sending fragments of his frontal lobe flying in the air.

BAM! The second bullet caught him in the neck as the force from the first slug sent him rearing backward and crashing to the ground.

Jermaine didn't feel any joy or sorrow as he stood over the dead man. He pointed his pistol down at the corpse and fired a final shot into his chest.

"That's for Buster, you bitch," Jermaine growled as he slowly walked back to the car as Malik put it in gear and made a quick exit from the murder scene.

Jermaine's next memory was sitting in a cramped office at police headquarters as Malik turned snitch and pointed him out, no doubt saving his own butt. Jermaine visualized the courtroom, and he saw Erin holding her stomach, crying and shaking her head "I told you so." Next to her was his mother, who was crying her heart out. She was holding Khalil, who was reaching his little arms out for his daddy to pick him up. But Daddy was handcuffed to the table and was now considered the property of the state of Pennsylvania. And once the old, gray-haired judge slammed his gavel down right after sentencing him to fifty-five years without the possibility of parole, Jermaine realized that he would never see his son again as a free man. The thought crushed him, and he dropped his chin to his chest and cried for the first time since the police surrounded his house the day after the murder.

Prison was home now and Jermaine had come to the staggering realization that his freedom was gone. So he tried his best to block out all images of the outside world. All except those of Khalil. He was lucky enough to have his cell positioned where he could see out of a small window into the outside world. Every day, like clockwork, he would make sure that he was sitting at the window to see Amani walking hand in hand with Khalil to preschool.

Jermaine lost himself in dreams of playing ball with his son. Of watching him play quarterback for Germantown High School and standing in the bleachers as Khalil threw one touchdown pass after another, blowing Martin Luther King High out on yet another Thanksgiving Day game.

"Get up, nigga. That's my bed," Bulldog said as he stood over Jermaine.

Jermaine looked up at the leader of the white supremacist group the Aryan Brotherhood, and laughed. Before the last chuckle left his lips, Bulldog's hand came swinging down toward his face. Jermaine moved out of the way just in time and came up off the mattress swinging. Bulldog didn't stand a chance against Jermaine's superior hand speed and power, and blows rained down on his head and stomach. Within a matter of seconds Bulldog was sprawled out on the concrete floor, bleeding from his nose, head, and mouth. Jermaine gave Bulldog one last kick in the face for good measure before falling down on his bed to catch his breath.

"I don't care who you bastards send in here. I ain't taking no shit from nobody," Jermaine yelled out into the cell block to whoever was listening.

Jermaine calmed down after he looked at his watch and realized it was his window time. He stared out at the street and saw Khalil. Khalil was walking fast, his little book bag swaying from side to side on his back. Jermaine immediately wondered where Amani was and why was she letting their small son walk to school alone. Jermaine sat up and frowned as he saw his son walking toward a bunch of white bikers. All of the men were smiling at Khalil. Then one of the guys got off his Harley-Davidson and approached Khalil smiling while holding a candy bar in his hand. The man bent over at the waist so that he was eye level with Khalil. Jermaine stood up and ran toward his cell door but was stopped cold by the unforgiving steel bars. He turned back toward the window and yelled, "Khalil, run!" but Khalil was too far away and separated by too much concrete to hear his father's cries and kept talking to the stranger.

"Khalil, no, don't go with him," Jermaine yelled through the bars as the biker held Khalil's hand and led him into an alley.

Bulldog regained his consciousness and smiled at Jermaine. "He'll be dead soon and there's nothing you can do about it." He laughed before being kicked back into unconsciousness by Jermaine's steel-toe boot. . . .

Jermaine popped up in his bed like a jack-in-the-box, breathing like he'd just finished a marathon. He tried his best to catch his breath. His skin was covered with sweat. He looked around his bedroom, frantically trying to regain some sense of reality. Once he realized he was still a free man, he rolled over, grabbed the telephone, and dialed his mother's number.

"What?" Nettie snapped with major attitude.

"Mom, let me speak to Khalil," Jermaine said, still breathing hard from his nightmare.

"Boy, are you smoking some of that mess you've been selling? Khalil is asleep."

"Okay," Jermaine said, still breathing hard. "Sorry about that." Jermaine shook his head, trying his best to ease out of his bad dream.

"Jermaine, are you okay?"

"Yeah, I'm cool. I must've had a bad dream, that's all. Sorry to wake you up."

"It's all right. Do you want me to take Khalil with me to do my shopping or are you coming to get him?"

"I'll come and get him."

"Okay, and stop doing whatever it is that's causing you to have those nightmares."

"A'ight, Mom." Jermaine hung up and dialed Malik's number.

"What's the deal, J?" Malik said in a groggy voice. "It's six o'clock in the morning!"

"Yo, don't worry about coming over. I'll handle Buster's situation on my own," Jermaine said, deciding not to tell Malik what he was really feeling.

"You sure?"

"Yeah. I got this one. I'll holla at you later."

"Okay, J. I'll talk to you later, but if you need me, you know how to get me. Peace."

"I got you," Jermaine said before hanging up with his partner in crime.

Jermaine stood and walked toward his bathroom to relieve himself but stopped when he passed the mirror, taking a long, hard look at himself.

"Whatcha gone do with yourself, playa?" he asked himself before his eyes fell to a small framed picture of Khalil.

"Boy, you had me scared, but don't worry, little homie. Daddy's not gonna leave you out there like that."

Jermaine finished his bathroom business and returned to his bedroom. He sat on his bed and picked up the telephone to call his older cousin Prodigy, who lived in Atlanta.

"Good morning," a happy female's voice sang.

"Hey, Nina. How you doing?"

"Jermaine?"

"The one and only. How's life treating you and the family down in the dirty?"

"Oh, life is grand," Nina said.

"How are my boys doing?"

"Miles is growing like a weed and Blake thinks he's somebody daddy. Hold on. . . . Boy, sit back at that table and finish eating," Nina said, handling her motherly duties. "I hear you're getting a new addition to your family. Congratulations."

"My mom's got a big mouth. What she do, get on the family intercom?"

"You know she did." Nina laughed. "What are you doing up so early?"

"No particular reason."

"Oh, I thought you might've gotten a job or something."

"I need one," Jermaine said but decided to change the subject. "I'm going to have to get down there and see my boys. How old is Miles now?"

"Two going on twenty-three," Nina said.

"Time flies."

"Sure does. How's Prince Khalil doing with his handsome self?"

"He's good. I'm about to go and get him from my mom's."

"That's good. Well, give him a kiss for me. I'll get Prodigy for you. You take care of yourself, Jermaine."

"I will. Talk to you later, Nina."

Nina called out to her husband and a few seconds later he was on the line.

"What's the deal, youngsta?" Prodigy said. "Hold on, Jermaine. . . . Blake, I don't want to hear it. Eat your breakfast. I bet if that was a candy bar you'd be hungry."

"Leave that boy alone," Jermaine said with a chuckle.

"Man, Blake thinks he can grow up on candy and soda. What's up with you? Hold on a minute, let me go in another room before I slip up and cuss."

"Yeah, you do that, Ward Cleaver."

"Kiss my ass. What are you doing up this early?"

"Can't sleep."

"Did Uncle Herb get out of prison yet? I got a letter from him the other day."

"I don't think so. I haven't heard anything from him and I hope I don't."

"Why not?"

"The last time I spoke with him he was asking me to put him in touch with some knucklehead hustler. He's trying to go back to jail before he even gets out good."

"Just tell him no. Man, don't stress yourself out over something that two little letters can handle."

"P, you've been in the South too long, you sound country as hell," Jermaine said, chuckling.

"Hey, I live here now. I *am* country. What else is going on? How's Khalil?"

"Oh, he's straight but Erin's trippin', her father's trippin', and on top of that my man Buster just got killed."

"Whoa! I'm sorry to hear that. Buster was good people. What happened?"

"Wrong place at the wrong time," Jermaine said, not wanting to deal with the truth.

"Is there ever a right time to be at the wrong place?"

"I guess not."

"I've been thinking about you a lot lately. As a matter of fact, I was going to call you tonight when I got in."

"You still running that youth center?"

"Yeah, that and about fifty-five other projects. But listen, you know we're not getting any younger, so don't you think it's about time you started using some of the brains God gave you and leave that street life?"

"Man, you must be reading my mind. I was thinking about coming down there for a few weeks to get my head straight."

"You know you're always welcome, but I think you need to stay right there and handle your business. Aunt Nettie told me about the pressure Erin's father is putting on you, but you can't run away from your problems. You did that when Khalil was born, remember?"

"Yeah. Yo, you was out here one time, too, but now look at you. You're a straight-up businessman."

"Man, it's not how you start the race, it's how you finish. You are smart enough to know the final chapter of that life you're living. Look at Uncle Herb, fifty-something years old and starting over with nothing but a prison record."

"Stop preaching, nigga," Jermaine teased, but he knew his cousin was right. It was time to leave the game.

"Okay, but I want you to think about what I said. You might have the money but it won't do you or your kids a bit of good if you're locked up or dead. I don't want either one of those things to happen to you, brah. You're the closest thing I have to a little brother, so if I have to come up there and treat you like a little brother, then I will. I've been watching wrestling," Prodigy joked.

"Yo, P, let me ask you a question and then I'll let you go."

"Go ahead."

"What made you just quit the game and start a new life?"

"Man, I got lucky. I met this old man who gave me a crash course in Black Man 101. You remember Poppa Doc, don't you?"

"Yeah, the old dude that got you your first job. He died, didn't he?"

"Yeah, but he showed me the bigger picture when it came to life. I was trying to get that fast buck and wasn't thinking about the damage I was doing not only to me but to everybody around me. And I wasn't trying to be fifty years old and living from pillar to post or, worse, locked up somewhere. Then I married Nina, so I automatically had Blake looking up to me. Plus I didn't really like myself when I was out there hustling and that's bad when you don't like your own damn self. I mean lying about what you do for a living then forgetting the lie you told. My Moms wasn't proud of me. You know, it just got old. I realized I didn't have to play the hand that life gave me so I threw them cards in and decided to change the game."

"I feel you. Man, I want out but I don't have the slightest clue on how I'm going to do it. I can't do the McDonald's thing."

"Ain't no shame in paying the bills, playa, but I do feel you on the Mickey D's thing. Just find you some peace."

"Man, I got to do something drastic and quick."

"No doubt, but take your time and think it out."

"I might even go to college," Jermaine said, laughing.

"Go. Don't be afraid to break your own mold. If you want to go to college then go. I'm writing a book—"

"A book? Man, you're slipping off into true Nerdville. The brothers on the block ain't gonna believe this. Prodigy the author."

"You see, that's your problem. You always worried about what the wrong people are gonna say. Fuck them niggas on the block. Most of 'em hate themselves anyway, so you know they don't give a damn about you."

"I feel ya, Reverend."

"Amen."

"But on the real, I haven't picked up a textbook since I left high school."

"You barely picked one up then," Prodigy halfway joked.

"I know you ain't talking. You barely graduated. I walked with a three-point-six," Jermaine bragged.

"That's what I'm talking about. You got what it takes to make your paper the right way. You just got to step up and do it."

"Yo, I pass Temple University every day and I be seeing some fine-ass sistas out that piece."

"Listen to you, boy, you're crazy. Hold on a second," Prodigy said.

Jermaine could hear Prodigy talking to his stepson Blake, and he visualized a suburban life like that for himself and Khalil.

"Look here, Jermaine. I gotta get this boy off to school. He missed the bus again. Every time we get a new car he misses the bus all week. Ain't that something?"

"Ha-haaa. Blake said forget that cheese bus, I'm riding to school in style. What kind of car did you get?"

"Nina got a new little C-class Mercedes. I still got that gas-guzzling Range Rover. You know she thinks she needs a new car when the tires go bad."

"That's your fault, you got her spoiled."

"That's my baby."

"Well, at least she appreciates you. But that's another conversation for another day. Anyway, tell Blake and Miles I said what's up. How's Ariel doing?"

"She's good, she's here now."

"Boy, you got a houseful, don't you?"

"Wouldn't have it any other way. I love being a daddy," Prodigy said proudly.

"Me too. Man, I have so much fun with Khalil. That's why I gotta get it together," Jermaine said, thinking about his dream.

"You'll be a'ight, lil brah."

"You know it. Go ahead and handle your fatherly duties, we'll talk."

"Okay, but let me know how your journey to righteousness is going. But I'm sure you'll be straight."

"Yeah. I'll holla at you later. One!"

"Peace, lil brah."

Jermaine hung up the phone and took a deep breath. He closed his eyes and tried to come up with a master plan for the rest of his life. He didn't know what he was going to do or how he was going to go about it, but he could feel a change in the making.

Can I Get a Witness?

alvin pulled his black Mercedes sedan up his winding driveway and parked behind a navy blue Lincoln Town Car with a
rental-car sticker on the rear bumper. He wondered whose
car was blocking his path to the garage but figured it really didn't
matter. He was just there to pick up a few clothes and then he would
be on his way to a new life. He shifted into "park" and stepped out
of his car. But as Calvin walked up the ten steps leading to his front
door, something didn't seem right. He hesitated before putting his
key in the door but then decided whatever it was that was causing
his apprehension wasn't worth fretting over. Other than C.J., nothing in this house mattered anymore. As he stepped into the foyer he
looked into the living room and was shocked at the sight of his
mother, Edna Sharpe, from whom he had inherited his eyes and
mocha complexion, and his father, from whom he'd inherited everything else, sitting in the living room talking with Robin and C.J.

When his family saw him, whatever conversation they were having came to a screeching halt. The tension in the air was so thick it couldn't be cut with a chain saw, and if looks could kill, Calvin would've died three different deaths. The only set of eyes that appeared to care about him were his mother's, but that didn't surprise him. Robin was probably still upset because he was leaving her, C.J. was going through his own teenage thing, and nothing Calvin had ever done seemed to please his father.

"I see the gang's all here," Calvin said cautiously as he walked over and gave his mother a hug and a kiss on her cheek. "How are you, Mom?"

"I'm fine, son," Calvin's mother said as she returned her son's hug, although she remained sitting.

"Dad." Calvin nodded in his father's direction and reached out to shake his hand.

Louis Sharpe got up from the sofa and stood in front of Calvin. He stared at his only son as if they were two prizefighters preparing for battle. He looked down at Calvin's hand as if it were covered in feces. To say he was disappointed would've been an understatement. Calvin retracted his hand and put it in his pants pocket.

For as long as Calvin could remember, he had sought his father's approval but he never could do quite enough to please his old man. When he was younger Calvin played football not because he had a passion for the sport but because his father was a gridiron fanatic, and he did the same with baseball. When it came time for him to choose a college, he went to North Carolina A & T University, his father's alma mater, even though he truly wanted to go to Clark College in Atlanta. And now the man he wanted to impress the most was standing in his home looking at him as if he was the scum of the earth. Calvin realized that he had failed his father once again.

"Well, I guess Robin gave you the news. But first let me explain something to you. I guess I should've said this a long time ago, then maybe you'd realize that I'm my own man. The days of trying to win

Daddy's approval are long gone. Not a soul in this room can make me change my mind about my decision. Robin and I are history and that's pretty much the end of it," Calvin said with an air of arrogance.

"If that's what you want to do, then fine. But this has nothing to do with you and Robin. Although after seeing the manner in which you handle your affairs, I can't see why she would want to subject herself to you any longer than she has already endured. We're here about my grandson, a grandson that I just found out about," Louis growled, tossing the infamous stack of yellow receipts at Calvin. They hit him in the chest and fell all over the living room floor.

Calvin's heart hit the floor. He narrowed his eyes at Robin. *Why in the hell did you have to go and run your mouth?* he thought.

"Because you weren't man enough to handle your responsibilities as a father, you cheated everybody. Your mother and I were cheated out of a grandson, C.J. was cheated out of a big brother, and we're not going to even go into what you did to your son and all because you were too much of a punk to do the right thing. And Robin told me that deplorable excuse you gave for just sending a check. God knows I don't have the words to explain how I feel about you at this moment. I'm ashamed to be your father."

Calvin's heart sank a little deeper.

"Calvin, we didn't raise you to treat people like this, let alone your own child. And then I hear that you're running around with some white woman. Is that true?"

Calvin looked at Robin again, who only looked away and shook her head. He had no idea that Robin knew about Kelly. What else did she know?

"Is this how you repay me and your mother for all the sacrifices we've made?"

"You know what? I'm not about to stand here and be ridiculed in my own home. I can handle my own affairs, so if you'll excuse me,

I only came here to get some clothes," Calvin said as he exited the room in a hurry.

Louis threw his hands up in disbelief and walked toward the other side of the room.

"Calvin," Edna said softly as she stood and followed her son down the hallway. "What's going on? Why didn't you come to us about Jermaine? If you weren't prepared to take care of him, then we would've bent over backwards to help you. You know that." She placed her hands on his shoulders. "Now, I'm not going to lie to you and say I'm not disappointed by what I just learned, but you're still our son and I think you deserve a chance to tell your side of the story."

"Mom," Calvin said, dropping his head. He reached out and grabbed his mother's hand. "I don't know. Right now everything sounds weak, even to me."

"Just talk to me, son. I'm not here to judge you."

"First let me say that I understand how everyone feels because trust me when I say I feel ten times worse every time Jermaine crosses my mind, which is about a hundred times a day." Calvin cleared his throat and looked into his mother's compassionate eyes. "But at the time Jermaine's mother was not the kind of woman I wanted to spend any amount of time around. It was never Jermaine. I tried to get custody of him so many times but she just made things unnecessarily difficult. She was mad at me for not being with her and she made me pay for that by keeping Jermaine away from me. Back then I wasn't making very much money and she tried to take what little I had. It was just a bunch of mess. Then when she did allow me to see him I always had to go to her place, and that was torture. She always had a houseful of lowlifes drinking and playing cards and it killed me to see my son in that environment. And every time I left it broke me down to have to leave him over there, but she wouldn't let me take him so I decided that in order to keep my sanity I would just help her out financially and move on. I didn't know what else to do," Calvin said, embellishing his own truth.

"She was good enough for you to sleep with but not good enough for you to do what you had to do and help her raise your child, huh?" Louis barked from down the hallway, no longer concealing the fact that he was eavesdropping. "Sending a check ain't about nothing. Kids spell love *T-I-M-E*."

"Louis, that's enough," Edna admonished her husband. "Now this is Calvin's home, so please extend the same respect that you would demand in yours."

"No, Edna, this has to be said. And it has to be said the way I'm saying it. He needs to know the severity of what he has done. God only knows where my grandson is or what he's going through. Hell, he might even be dead for all we know," Louis barked, then closed his eyes and ran his hand through his hair.

Calvin had started walking up the stairs when he heard his father's voice but stopped in his tracks at the mention of his oldest son's mortality. He turned and started walking back down the stairs toward his father with fire in his eyes. "Everything that you are saying to me I've already said to myself. Don't you know that I'm tortured every day by the fact that I have a child walking around here who I wouldn't know if I passed him on the street? You have no idea what it feels like, so don't you stand here and pass judgment on me. I'm—"

"You damn right I don't have any idea because I raised mine," Louis shot back. "Obviously I didn't do that good of a job, but you never went without, and that much I know because I was man enough to see to it."

Calvin took a deep breath before continuing. "I did everything that I could to get my son," Calvin lied, but he felt under the circumstances he had no choice.

"That's a crock of shit and you know it," Louis shouted.

"Louis," Edna screamed. "That is enough."

"What do you want me to say, Dad? Do I regret it? Yes. Hell, yeah! If I could turn back the hands of time, I would kiss his mother's ass with every set of lips I could find just to see my son, but that can't happen, can it? I even tried to visit him when he got a little older but by that time his mother had him filled with so much hate that he wouldn't even come out of his room to see me. So trust me when I tell you that I have enough guilt to live with without y'all adding to it." Calvin turned on his heel and stormed up the stairs.

Edna gave her husband a scornful look. "Are you happy now?"

"Well, Edna, you just don't do things like that. Calvin knows better. I didn't walk out on him, so why on God's green earth would he do that to his own child? There is no excuse."

"Louis, I know that, but your bullying isn't going to make things better. Now, we didn't come all the way up here just for you to chastise Calvin. We came to try and find our grandson," Edna said as she followed Louis back into the living room.

C.J. spoke up for the first time since his father entered the house. "Grandma, I think I have my brother's mother's address. I found it on the Internet. I'm down to three people."

"Well, let's just pray that one of them is his," Mrs. Edna said.

"Yeah, and if it is, let's hope that he opens the door. I know if someone abandoned me, I wouldn't want anything to do with him or his family," Louis said.

"Well, I'm going to try and talk to Calvin before we leave. I hope he doesn't oppose us trying to locate our grandson."

"I wish he might. He's already cheated us for damn near thirty years. As a matter of fact, you can go and get in the car right now or I'm leaving you. Calvin has already proven himself unworthy of making proper decisions when it comes to Jermaine. That's my grandson and nobody's gonna stop me from seeing him. C.J., you riding?"

"Yes, sir." C.J. hopped up and headed to the door. "Come on, Grandma."

"Well, if you guys need anything, give me a call," Robin said. Then all of a sudden she thought about the violent side Calvin had shown earlier and opted against being in the house with him alone.

"Wait a minute. I'm going too," she said, not waiting for a response.

Sexual Healing

After hanging up with Prodigy, Jermaine decided against taking another chance with his subconscious, so he rolled out of bed and headed to the bathroom for a quick shower. He threw on a black Sean John jogging suit and some Timberland boots and then walked into the kitchen and poured himself a glass of orange juice.

It was almost seven o'clock in the morning and he couldn't remember the last time he'd been up this early. He walked down the front steps and noticed Vera sleeping beside his truck. She was slouched down in her wheelchair and was covered from her head to her knees in what looked to be a large plastic trash bag.

Jermaine removed the plastic from Vera's head.

"Vera. Vera. Vera," Jermaine said, shaking her.

"Huh! What? Where? Nigga, what?" Vera looked around, trying to locate what was left of her mind.

Jermaine shook his head at Vera's drama episode. "Girl, you trynna kill yourself?"

"Give me my money, Jermaine! You know damn well I couldn't get up your steps to knock on your door last night. Why weren't you watching out for me?"

"I asked you to get some plastic so I could put it over my window so my seats didn't get wet. Did you do that? Move out my way," Jermaine said as he opened the driver's-side door, where he saw another plastic bag covering his seat. He removed the plastic, balled it up, and threw it onto the already filthy street.

"Oh no, you ain't driving outta here without paying me. You're gonna give me my money. I stayed out here all night watching this ugly-ass truck. I ain't playing with you, Jermaine," Vera said, using her chair to block Jermaine from closing the car door.

"Who you talking to?" Jermaine snapped, even though he admired her tenacity. "And you need to watch that little mouth of yours."

"Jermaine, don't do me like that." Vera softened her tone.

Jermaine shook his head and took a seat in his truck.

"Vera, how'd you get turned out?"

"I ain't turned out. I'm fine," Vera said with her hand out for her payment.

"You used to be fine but now you look like the poster child for a crack commercial," Jermaine said, reaching in his pocket and pulling out a fifty-dollar bill. Vera reached for it but Jermaine held it away from her. "All jokes aside, what happened to you?"

"Jermaine, what goes on in my life is my business. Why should you care? Just leave it alone and give me my money. Please," she begged.

"Oh, you don't think I care about you? Do I need to start counting the things that I've done for you?"

"I never asked you for shit," Vera said, rolling her eyes at Jermaine.

"Girl, tell me why you rolling your little butt round here looking like you're already dead," Jermaine barked, tired of playing nice.

Vera crossed her arms and pulled her lips in.

"What, I hurt your feelings?" Jermaine said. "A'ight, I'm sorry," he said, softening Vera up a little.

"Jermaine, why you always walking around here like you're the king of the block? I see straight through you," Vera huffed.

"Oh yeah, what do you see, Vera?" Jermaine said with a smirk.

"You got a real big heart but for whatever reason you feel a need to walk around here playing the hard role. I mean, you can fight, but so what? You're almost thirty years old, and if you have to hang around people that you need to fight, then you need new friends."

"Look who's talking, Mrs. I'm Ready to Die."

"I have to be that way, you don't," Vera said, staring Jermaine straight in the eyes. "You remember that time I got some crack from this guy and didn't pay him?"

"How could I forget, he was about to push you in front of a SEPTA bus."

"That's right, the reason he didn't was because you talked to him. You didn't have to lay a hand on him."

"But the talking only worked, Vera, because he knew I would've laid hands on him. He just made a wise decision." Jermaine laughed.

"Maybe, but you underestimate yourself, Jermaine. I knew what I was doing because I knew you wouldn't let anything happen to me no matter what."

"Oh, so you played me!"

"No, I trusted you," Vera said. "I'm an addict, a paraplegic, who has all but given up. But you . . . you can do anything you wanna do if you stop taking life for granted. I used to do the same thing before I got in this chair and I honestly believe this was my punishment for taking life for granted."

"Well, trust me enough to tell me how you got the way you are and stop trying to change the subject."

"Jermaine, I don't wanna talk about that," Vera said, looking down.

"Why not?"

"Because it bothers me and I'm trying to forget about it."

"Well, I guess this goes back in my pocket." Jermaine smiled as he waved the fifty-dollar bill at her.

"I hate you," Vera said playfully, already calculating the amount of drugs she could buy with a half buck. "Okay. You know I was messing with that Ecstasy, right?"

"Nope."

"Well, I was. It was really this dude that I was kicking with. Old bastard. Anyway, he slipped one to me one night and it made me feel freaky as hell. And as ugly as his ass was, I needed all the help I could get. So every time I would get with him, he'd slip me some X then fuck the shit out of me. Well, to make a long story short, I guess my body had some kind of allergic reaction to it and I started tripping. I mean *really* tripping. One night I was running from him, don't ask me why, but I ran out in the street and got hit by a car. The doctors told me I'd never walk again and that was it. I just started getting high. I tried the rehab thing but these drugs got a mind of their own. One hit is too many and a thousand ain't enough. I needed something to look forward to every day because life in this chair is a little too depressing." Vera looked up at Jermaine and flashed a raggedy-tooth smile. "Are you satisfied now, Dr. Banks? Now give me my money so I can go get my blast on."

"Vera, that's a sad-ass story but you sound like a fool. There're plenty people out there living full lives in wheelchairs. You made a choice to get high because you lazy," Jermaine said as he handed Vera the fifty-dollar bill and pulled his legs into the truck before closing the door. "A'ight, baby girl. You stay out of trouble. And find yourself a bathtub and some deodorant—you smell like a dead dog."

"Go to hell, Jermaine," Vera said as she wheeled away.

ermaine drove to Erin's house with the weight of the world on his shoulders. He was hoping that she wasn't in one of her talking moods today because all he wanted was a little peace of mind.

He used his key to let himself in. Once inside her tastefully decorated apartment, he heard Erin's soulful voice singing an old Anita Baker song in the kitchen.

Operator, get my baby on the line. . . .

Jermaine sat on the arm of the love seat and listened as Erin gave Anita a run for her money.

Just the other night we had a horrible fight. . . .

Erin walked out of the kitchen and jumped back, holding her chest when she saw Jermaine.

"Whoa! Boy, you scared me. I didn't hear you come in." Erin smiled as she walked over to Jermaine. She reached out and wrapped her arms around his neck. She kissed him on his cheeks then his lips. She could feel the tension throughout his body. She held his face in her hands and stared into his eyes. Something was bothering him but she knew he'd never tell her.

"Everything is going to be all right, Jermaine."

"I know. I'm cool," Jermaine lied. Life was closing in on him and he felt as if he was on the verge of a nervous breakdown. "Will you do me a favor?"

"What?"

"Will you stay home from work today? I need to spend some time with you."

Erin smiled as Jermaine held her close and began removing her clothes. He pulled her shirt off, exposing a red lace bra that cupped her ample breasts, then he slid her skirt down and held it as she stepped out. Erin stood before Jermaine in only a bra and panties. Even with her pudgy midsection she was a sight to behold.

Jermaine stood up and kissed Erin on her forehead then pecked his way down her face until he reached her mouth. He slid his tongue between her moist lips and kissed her long and passionately.

Erin slid down to the floor and finished undressing while Jermaine stood over her, stepping out of his unlaced boots. He peeled off his jogging suit and lay down beside Erin. He rolled onto his back because he didn't want to put any pressure on his unborn child. She rolled on top of him and picked up the kiss where they'd left off. Erin slowly grinded her man to erection and reached down behind her and slid Jermaine's manhood inside of her. Their lovemaking was always something special.

When Erin woke up she was lying on the floor covered with a blanket. She looked up to see Jermaine fully dressed and fiddling around with her computer.

"What are you doing?" Erin smiled as she visualized Jermaine as some high-powered businessman. The thought turned her on.

"Yo, you're going to have to show me how to operate this thing. I might need it soon. I wanna learn how to surf the Net, or the Web—whatever you call it," Jermaine said.

Erin stood and walked over to Jermaine and took a seat on his lap.

"You're over here playing solitaire. I thought you were doing something."

"I'm not up on all this technology yet. But I'm about to get there."

"If I had a dime for every time I heard you say something like that, I'd be a rich woman."

"I'm for real this time."

"If you say so," Erin said, unconvinced.

"I need to call BMW to get my window fixed on my truck. Somebody broke it last night."

"I told you to move out of that neighborhood. It's a wonder you still have a truck."

"Don't start that. Plus, the clown that did it isn't even from around my way."

"Whatever," Erin said, uninterested in any details about Jermaine's thug life. That's why she didn't ask about Buster. She felt the less she talked about negative things with Jermaine, the quicker they would disappear and he would become the man she always knew he could be. "Let me go and shower up. Are you getting Khalil today?"

"Yeah." Jermaine looked at his watch. "I'm picking him up in a few so don't take all day."

Erin walked up the stairs to her bedroom. She walked over to her dresser and picked up a photograph of her and Jermaine that was taken when they were teenagers. She was riding on his back on the boardwalk in Atlantic City. She loved the snapshot because it was one of the few reminders she had of the innocence she once knew with Jermaine.

Erin sat down on her bed, when the telephone rang.

"Hello?"

"Hey, girl. What's going on?" Tosha, one of Erin's few girlfriends, asked.

"Nothing much."

"What are you doing home? I thought I was going to get your machine."

"I took the day off to hang out with Jermaine."

"That nigga still don't have a job?"

"Is the pope a Muslim?"

"Not the last time I checked," Tosha said.

"Well, a'ight then. What's up?"

"How's the baby coming along? You've been getting your prenatal checkups, right?"

"Of course!"

"That's good. Anyway, I called to hook you up with some money. And if you keep taking days off to hang out with other jobless people, your behind is going to be amongst the unemployed."

"Spare me, or do I need to hang up so you can leave your message?"

"Okay, you know I got a new boyfriend, right?"

"Who, Rafferty?"

"Yes! Well, his brother is moving to Philly and he's looking for a house. So I told Raff to ask him if he would mind using you as his real estate agent. You still doing that part-time, right?"

"Yeah. Thanks, love."

"Oh, and I need to warn you that he is fine as hell. I'm talking Morris Chestnut–, Denzel-fine."

"Tosha," Erin warned. "I'm pregnant, so he's going to have to be a desperate brother to want me. Plus, I'm not like you. I don't cheat."

"Whatever. Anyway, I told him that you would probably help him out with his house hunting. You might as well get that commission."

"That's cool. I appreciate you looking out for me."

"Girl, please. Okay, his name is Pembrook Washington."

"Pembrook?"

"I know, girl, don't blame him. Blame his parents because he has another brother named Inglebert."

"Well, a'ight then," Erin said, frowning.

"Tell me about it. Anyway, I gave him your cell phone number and your e-mail address. So be on the lookout for him."

"I will."

"Okay, girl. Well, some of us have to work," Tosha said sarcastically.

"Thanks, Tosha."

"Don't mention it, and tell Jermaine I said get a job. Bye," Tosha said, laughing.

Erin hung up the phone. Tosha was right about Jermaine; everyone was right about Jermaine. She was tired of having to lie when one of her colleagues asked her what her fiancé did for a living. She longed for the day she had a man she could take to job-related functions and not worry about him saying something ignorant. It was time to do something, because she had grown up and Jermaine was still doing the same things he did when they were younger. She rubbed her stomach and tears came to her eyes as she finally admitted to herself what everyone else had been telling her for years—she had outgrown Jermaine.

Distant Lover

"A re girls supposed to kiss other girls?" Khalil asked as his dad buckled him into his car seat.

Yeah, if you ain't slackin' on your mackin', but you're getting a little ahead of yourself, little soldier, Jermaine thought, smiling to himself.

"No, girls are not supposed to kiss other girls," Jermaine said.

"Then why does my mommy kiss Miss Tonya?"

"Sometimes girls peck each other on the cheek like I do you. That is, when you're not in front of your lil friends and wanna act tough," Jermaine said, tickling his son.

Khalil covered up laughing. "Unt-uh, my mommy kisses Miss Tonya on the lips for a long time."

Jermaine stopped harassing his son and stared at him. "What are you talking about, Khalil?"

"I saw Mommy and Miss Tonya kissing on the lips. They sleep in the same bed too."

"What? How long has your mommy and Miss Tonya been sleeping in the same bed? And where are you when all of this is going on?"

"Mommy makes me go in my room."

Jermaine thought about what he had just heard for a few seconds. He closed the rear door and walked around to the driver side.

"Did you hear that?" Jermaine asked Erin as he slid under the steering wheel and started his truck.

"Yeah," Erin said, looking confused. "What are you going to do?"

"I'mma break Amani's neck," Jermaine growled.

"Jermaine. And what will that solve? And stop talking like that in front of him."

"He didn't hear me." Jermaine snuck a peek in the rearview mirror, only to see Khalil looking directly at him.

"Daddy, don't hit my mommy."

"I'm not going to hit your mommy."

"But you said—"

"I said I'm not going to hit your mommy. Now be quiet."

"You shouldn't yell at him. You said it, so what do you expect him to think?"

"Erin, mind your business."

"I'm sick of you telling me that. How are we supposed to be a family if I can't speak up when it has something to do with Khalil or Amani?"

Jermaine turned the volume up on the radio and sighed, letting her know there would be no more conversation about that. They drove to the BMW dealership, ignoring each other. Once they arrived Jermaine asked Erin to give the service technician the details about his window, and he found a quiet place to make the call that he'd been itching to make since he heard that the mother of his son was bumping uglies with her best friend.

"Hello."

"Who is this?"

"Who is this?" the woman shot back.

"Put Amani on the phone," Jermaine ordered.

"I got it," Amani said on the other line. "You better learn some telephone etiquette, Jermaine, or you can stop calling my house. I don't know who you think you are."

"Amani, whatcha got going on over there?" Jermaine asked.

"What?"

"Don't play innocent. I heard you're a dyke now."

Amani was silent for a minute before finally opening her mouth. "Why are you so concerned with my personal life? As long as I'm not hurting Khalil, then you should keep your attention on Erin and worry about what she's doing because no matter how much you think you run things, I'm not your woman."

"Wrong answer! What you do does affect my son, and I'm not trying to have him around your freaky ass," Jermaine said, balling his hands into fists.

"Oh, you got a lot of nerve, Jermaine. Newsflash to superthug: you're a drug dealer. And no matter how you try to justify it, that's what you are, a predator. So save your judgment for the mirror."

"Whatever. Do you know what he just asked me?"

"No, and I don't care."

"He asked me if it was okay for two girls to kiss. Now, do you think I want him growing up thinking it's okay for him to stick his tongue in some man's mouth? That's disgusting."

"Don't knock it till you've tried it," Amani shot back.

"Oh, you think this is funny, you sick slut," Jermaine said, his temper starting to get the best of him.

"Your mother's a slut," Amani retaliated. "But you know what, Jermaine? I'm glad you've found out about us, but don't worry, we lock our door when we do our thing." Amani laughed. "If I thought you could handle it, I'd let you join us sometime, but you're not ready for that."

"Oh, I'm glad you can find some humor in this, but we'll see how funny you think it is when you don't see Khalil anymore."

"Oh, you'll have my son here by six o'clock this evening or I'll have every police in Philadelphia looking for your criminal ass. Have you forgotten who you're talking to? I got so much dirt on you, the cops would put you *under* the jail. I'll see you at six, but call before you come because I might be in the middle of something." Amani chuckled before hanging up the phone.

Jermaine stood with the phone in his hand, and it was then and there that he hated every crime he'd ever committed. If he were living a straight-and-narrow life, he would have a fighting chance of getting his son, but he knew no judge in his right mind would ever give him custody.

Erin walked over, holding Khalil's hand. "What's wrong?" she asked, reading the frown on Jermaine's face.

"You ain't gonna believe this. Amani *is* a dyke," Jermaine called himself whispering, but couldn't keep his voice down. "She be gettin' with women."

"Baby, that's what they do, they sleep with other women," Erin said, shaking her head.

"Don't get smart, Erin."

"And don't say 'dyke,' that's crude. She's a lesbian."

"I don't care what the politically correct term is. I don't want my son around that."

"Well, what are you going to do about it?" Erin asked calmly.

"I don't know right now but you need to stop downplaying it. This is serious."

"Why is it so serious? I mean, what difference does it make what she does or who she does it with?"

"Huh?" Jermaine asked, alarmed that Erin couldn't see the

wrong in what he'd just told her. "I can't believe you're asking me that. This is all the reason I need right here," Jermaine said, rubbing Khalil's head.

"What's so wrong about Khalil seeing two people who are in a loving and committed relationship? It shouldn't matter what sex they are," Erin said as she kneeled down and told Khalil to go and have a seat in the waiting area a few feet away from where they were standing. "The guy said they can have your window fixed in about three hours. Why don't we get a courtesy car and go and grab something to eat?"

"Wait a minute, I wanna know where you get that twisted mind from?"

"Twisted mind! Jermaine, grow up! This is the new millennium and it's perfectly all right to be gay if that's what you choose to do. They are plenty of same-sex couples who do quite well raising children."

"Did I ask you all of that? All I care about is Khalil and what he's being exposed to."

Erin narrowed her eyes at Jermaine as if to remind him that he was far from a saint but kept her thoughts to herself.

"God made Adam and Eve, not Adam and Steve. And since when did you become so pro-gay?" he asked.

"I'm not pro-gay. I just respect people's preferences. Khalil said he was hungry and I don't want to sit in here for three hours doing nothing on my day off. So snap out of that old-fashioned mind-set and let's enjoy our day," Erin said, ready to move on.

Jermaine looked at Erin in shock. *How can she be so nonchalant about this? And not only is she unalarmed, she seems to condone this,* Jermaine thought.

"So you into women too?"

Erin sucked her teeth and frowned at Jermaine.

"Nah, I *thought* I knew you, but since you jumped on the Elton John bandwagon I'm not sure anymore."

"No, I'm not attracted to women, never have and never will be, but it still doesn't change the fact that I respect a person's choice to be with whomever makes her or him happy," Erin said, walking back to the service area.

"I should've known something was wrong with that nut when she started buying all them Meshell Ndegéocello records," Jermaine said under his breath as he went over to where his son was sitting and plopped down beside him.

"Little man, how would you like to come and live with your daddy?"

"Yeah, when?" Khalil's eyes brightened up and he nodded his head vigorously. He was a daddy's boy.

"I got to work on some things but I'm gonna make it happen. Okay?"

"When?"

"I don't know yet."

Just then Erin walked over and took a seat on the other side of Khalil. "They will bring us the keys in a minute. What do you want to eat, Khalil, and don't say McDonald's?"

"Wendy's."

"Oh Lord. Why don't I pick the place today?"

"Miss Erin, why did Mr. Roscoe hit my daddy with his police gun?"

Erin looked at Jermaine with a question mark written all over her face.

"I didn't know that my father did that. When did this happen?"

"Last night at my grandma's house."

"Oh really?"

"Yeah, and he broke my daddy's car window. Why don't Mr. Roscoe like us anymore?"

"Khalil, I didn't know anything about that but I'm sure Mr. Roscoe still likes you and your daddy. That was some grown-folks stuff, okay?"

"Okay," Khalil said as he pulled a toy motorcycle out of his pocket and made *zoom-zoom* sounds.

"Miss Erin, are you coming to my birthday party?"

"Of course I am. What would you like for me to get you?" Erin asked, trying to fake excitement.

"I want a remote-control car."

"Boy, you have enough cars. Why don't I go to Toys 'R' Us and surprise you?"

"Okay," Khalil said and went back to playing with his motorcycle.

Erin stared at Jermaine while Khalil asked another fifty questions. Jermaine looked away. He didn't want to talk about what happened with Roscoe simply because in Erin's eyes, her father could do no wrong.

"So that's where that cut on your lip came from. I thought you ran into a wall. You're such a liar."

"It's your fault," Jermaine said as he stood up to greet a preppy-looking white guy.

"Mr. Banks, looks like we'll have to special-order that part for your window. So it's going to take a little longer than expected. Now, we have a few options here. You can leave the car with us and take a courtesy car or you can just bring your truck back when the part arrives. I suggest you leave it unless you park it in a garage."

"So, when do you expect the part to arrive?" Erin asked. Jermaine looked at her as if to say, "Sit your butt down and let me handle this." But instead of reprimanding her, he just looked at Mr. Preppy for an answer.

"Well, it could be a few days. But you can keep the courtesy car at no charge. We'll give you a call when the part comes in, and after that it's about a three-hour job."

"That's coo—" Jermaine started but was cut off by Erin.

"Will there be some kind of discount for our inconvenience?" Erin asked.

"Well, ma'am, that's why we give you a courtesy car, so that you won't be inconvenienced."

"Don't worry about it, my man." Jermaine saved Mr. Preppy from Miss Never Satisfied. "You have all my information so just hit me up when my joint is ready."

"Will do, Mr. Banks. Your car is the black 535 by the entrance. We put your child seat in the back already so you're all set," Mr. Preppy said, pointing toward the car and flashing Erin a look that said he didn't appreciate her trying to make his job hard.

"Is there a problem?" Erin asked Mr. Preppy.

"No, ma'am," he said and reached out and shook Jermaine's hand before walking off, shaking his head.

"I want to see a manager. I don't like his attitude," Erin said loudly, looking around for someone who looked important.

"Girl, come on. You're always making something out of nothing." Jermaine grabbed Khalil's hand and walked off, leaving Erin looking around.

"I hate when you don't support me," Erin said, walking up behind Jermaine.

"That's because you're always trying to get over," Jermaine said, opening the passenger-side door for her.

"I'm not trying to get over but if I feel a certain way about something, then I would expect my man to have my back. That's not asking too much, or is it?"

Jermaine buckled Khalil in and walked around to the driver's side, ignoring Erin. He asked Khalil what he wanted to eat and he said McDonald's.

"He doesn't need to eat that mess all the time, but I know. It's none of my business," Erin said, folding her arms.

Jermaine pulled into the nearest Mickey D's and ordered drive-through. He asked Erin if she wanted anything and she sucked her teeth and looked out the window. He took that as a no, so he paid for his son's Happy Meal and pulled into the gas station parking lot next door to the restaurant.

He got out of the car and returned with a bottle in a brown paper bag.

"Jermaine, are you about to drink and drive?"

"It's only a beer. Calm down."

Erin rolled her eyes and sighed. *I'm so sick of his ignorant ass.*

"So how is your lip my fault?" she asked him.

"If you didn't run whining to your whole damn family every time we had a slight difference of opinion, then maybe Mr. Chunky wouldn't be losing his mind."

"I don't tell my family all of our business."

Jermaine looked at Erin and twisted his lip. *Who does she think she's foolin'?* he wondered.

"Then how do they always know what's going on with us? I know it doesn't come from me."

"My mom is just being a mother, and if she asks me what's wrong then I'm going to tell her. Nothing is wrong with that," Erin said with a straight face.

"Yeah, if you're twelve years old, but you're thirty and still got your mommy and daddy fighting your battles."

"If I'm not allowed to get involved with Khalil and Amani then you need to keep my family's name out of your mouth," Erin shot back.

"I'll keep their names out of my mouth when they stop minding my business."

"You are going to have to stop drinking when the baby comes," Erin said, trying to change the subject. She hated when Jermaine talked about her parents.

"Why?"

"Because it's not good for you."

"Why do you feel a need to always tell me what's good for me?"

"Why is everything a battle with you?"

"You think it's a battle because I don't let you treat me like you see your mom treating your pop, but I'm not about to let some brat run my life just because you got a few degrees. Cuz when it comes to life, you're about as clueless as they come."

"Just take me home. And you will want to wait while I get your things, or I'm throwing them out in the street," Erin said, looking at Jermaine with pure contempt.

"You see what I mean? Every time you get mad, you start giving back everything I bought you. You give it back this time and I'm keeping it," Jermaine said, pissed. "That's the same shit you've been doing since high school. And you say *I'm* stuck in the past. I feel like I got two kids already."

"Just take me home, Jermaine," Erin said, staring out the window.

10

Pride and Joy

alvin drove around Philadelphia with a million thoughts flowing through his mind. *Why did Robin have to go and open her big mouth about Jermaine?* Jermaine was a painful chapter in his past that he didn't care to revisit. *How do you make right something that wrong? You can't, and unless you want to drive yourself completely insane, you find a way to move on,* he thought to himself.

Now that everything was in the open, Calvin didn't know how he was going to deal with it. His father had hit a nerve and now he was overwhelmed by guilt. He tried to block out the vision of Jermaine's young, innocent face as he walked out on his son for the last time, but it kept coming back. He cursed himself for being so weak and self-centered, because although everything he said to his mother was true, he knew deep down in his heart that Jermaine's mother's bark was much bigger than her bite, and if he had demanded to be in his son's life, she wouldn't have put up much of a fight. But the truth was he'd been too busy making money to be saddled down with the burden of raising a child.

Calvin sat with his hands gripping the wheel, trying to will himself to be strong, but his conscience was now in the devil's den and he was having evil thoughts. He pulled into the Cheltenham Mall's parking lot and shifted into "park." He stared across Cheltenham Avenue toward the state store. He could almost taste the burn of finely aged liquor as it flowed down his throat and into his chest. Calvin closed his eyes but couldn't bring himself to ask God to lighten his load. No, this was an anguish he needed to endure alone. He welcomed the grief because he knew he deserved it, yet it was too much to bear.

Calvin frowned and slammed his car back into gear and made a beeline to the state store. He pulled into the drive-through and asked the attendant for a fifth of Courvoisier. Once he paid for his poison, he put the bottle between his legs and drove off. His cell phone rang; Robin's name was on the caller ID screen, so he ignored the call.

"What the hell do you want?" Calvin said to the phone as it rang again, and tossed it onto the passenger seat. Robin was the last person on earth he wanted to talk to. He'd poured his heart out to her about his firstborn and she'd turned around and used it against him.

At a traffic light, his hands started to tremble as he slowly removed the cork from the bottle and took a whiff of the high-priced cognac. He closed his eyes as the intoxicating aroma filled his senses. Calvin took a long look at the bottle, knowing this one drink would take his entire life on a collision course with something very unpleasant. He put the cork back into the bottle and thought about his past battles.

hen Calvin graduated from college he was offered a job at a small real estate company in Philadelphia. He was in such a rush to prove his worthiness to his father that he accepted the company's first offer. He moved into a nice apartment in Center

City, but after a few months of living the high life he realized that his paychecks weren't growing as fast as his appetite for the finer things.

The last thing he wanted to do was move out of his lavish apartment, and there was no way he would ever ask his parents for money. That would be too much like admitting failure, and failure was not an option for him.

Just when Calvin was at the end of his rope he met Charlie Barzini. Barzini was a young upstart in the Mafia who was trying to buy an apartment building with cash. Calvin explained the auditing process to him and how making such a purchase would most certainly bring unwanted attention from the authorities. Barzini appreciated Calvin's knowledge of the real estate laws and thanked him by slipping him a roll of small bills. When Calvin got home he counted the money and realized that Charlie had given him a thousand dollars. Once Calvin got a taste of the easy money, he was in for good. Calvin helped Barzini and all of his associates create cover businesses for their unscrupulous practices. For his misdealings Calvin was always paid handsomely; he kept the paper trail clean, and he didn't ask any questions. But once you're in bed with snakes, it's hard to crawl out without getting bitten. One day Barzini came to Calvin's office and informed him that he was interested in selling his property. Calvin jumped at the opportunity to own his first rental unit. But he had bigger dreams, and in order to make them a reality he needed more capital. That's when he went into business with Gino Newman, a man rumored to be the head of a Mafia family.

Gino Newman was the only man Calvin knew who could drop fifty million without so much as blinking an eye, so he set up a meeting with the millionaire mobster and from that day forth, money was no longer an object.

Back then Calvin was going out to clubs almost every night,

looking for women with itchy kittens that he was more than willing to scratch. On one particular night he met a gorgeous lady named Nanette Banks; her friends called her Nettie. Calvin was trying to become one of those friends. He'd seen her on previous occasions but she always had some man trying to get her attention; however, that night she was sitting alone.

Calvin walked over and introduced himself. He offered to buy her a drink, and she said she didn't indulge and was only there to keep her sister, who was the barmaid, company.

Nettie had a contagious smile and a bubbly personality, and Calvin liked what he saw. They sat at the bar for hours, him drinking cognac and her drinking club sodas. Then Calvin popped his usual question: "Do you want to get out of here and go someplace a little more cozy?"

"Listen to you. I'd love to do that but not tonight. I just met you, you could be some kind of ax murderer or something," Nettie said, still smiling.

"Well, if that were true and I wanted to harm you, I could play the game of cat-and-mouse until you were comfortable and still chop you to little pieces."

"True, but you can't fake it forever. The true you is bound to come out. And that's a fact, so if you like me like you say you do, then we'll have plenty of time to get cozy."

Calvin was impressed. Finally a woman who respected herself enough not to jump in bed with the first guy that made her smile. Calvin stayed and talked with Nettie while her sister closed the bar. He walked her outside to her car, hoping for at least a peck on the cheek, but she only offered a handshake. They exchanged numbers and he was off into the night. He drove all the way home thinking about the lady with the pretty brown eyes and honey-colored skin. Conversation with her was more stimulating than any sex he'd ever encountered in his young adult life. The next day he called her and they had lunch at a deli in Germantown. Over the next six months they spent a lot of time together, but Nettie wasn't giving up the one thing that Calvin wanted the most and that was sex. She had been holding out and Calvin was determined to stay the course, at least until he could spread those long legs over his king-size at least once. Then on Christmas Eve, Calvin went over to Nettie's house with a present. She wasn't expecting anything because Christmas was always a sad time for her. Her mother and father had been tragically killed in a car accident on their way back from a Christmas Eve party. So ever since her parents' passing, Nettie and her siblings spent Christmastime in mourning.

Nettie was sitting on her living room sofa doing a crossword puzzle when Calvin rang the doorbell. She let him in, and he handed her a long, rectangular jewelry box. She opened it and found a sparkling two-carat diamond tennis bracelet. She was touched by the kind gesture, overwhelmed with emotion, and vulnerable. Calvin took full advantage of the moment. They made sweet love for the first time right there on the sofa. Nettie thought Calvin was a good man with values, and took a chance with her heart.

To Calvin's surprise, he started to catch feelings for Nettie. There he was biding his time, trying to get his groove on, and he actually fell in love. After that Christmas Eve night they were practically inseparable. Nettie moved in with Calvin and turned his bachelor pad into a real home. She enrolled in school to fulfill her dream of becoming a registered nurse, and Calvin was making his mark in the business world. They seemed to be perfect for each other. Then one day Nettie came home early from school not feeling well. She went to put her shoes in the closet and looked down and noticed a Polaroid of Calvin and two women doing things that would get them kicked off a triple-X porno set. The only thing Calvin wore was the watch that she had just bought for him. Nettie was crushed. After crying her eyes out for what seemed like hours, she pulled herself together and moved all of her things out of his place. She left him a note informing him she was pregnant and that she never wanted to see him again.

When Calvin found the note he felt like a wounded animal. He had never cried over a woman before, but Nettie was more than just a woman to him. She was his soul mate, his first real love. The pictures meant nothing to him, and since he could never bring himself to ask Nettie to help him fulfill his wild sexual fantasies, he called up a couple of women whom he cared absolutely nothing about to make it happen. Now he was asking himself why over and over, and since he couldn't come up with any answers on his own, he started searching for them in a bottle of Courvoisier.

Calvin stayed in his apartment for almost two weeks, only exiting to restock his liquor supply. A neighbor called the authorities after hearing a loud thump from Calvin's apartment and the police found him lying unconscious on his living room floor. Calvin stayed in the detoxification ward at Germantown Hospital for three weeks.

On the other side of town Nettie was searching for her own answers. All of her life she had saved herself for the perfect man, a man she thought she'd found in Calvin Sharpe. She made the dreaded trip to the clinic to abort their unborn child but couldn't bring herself to walk through the doors. Then she subconsciously tried to miscarry. She took her first drink, then her first puff of a cigarette during her first trimester. But every day she could feel the life forming inside her. She stopped drinking and smoking and decided that she would raise her child on her own.

A few days before Nettie stopped her self-destructive behavior, Calvin stopped by to visit her and she was drunk as a skunk. Having just heard everything that alcohol could do to the human body, especially a pregnant one, Calvin flew off the handle and tried to have her arrested. After that didn't work, Calvin told Nettie that he would be seeking full custody of his child the moment it was born.

Nettie removed a pistol from her purse and pointed it at Calvin and kindly asked him to stay the hell out of her life. Calvin liked his chances in court. He was rich, Nettie was pretty close to destitute; he lived in the affluent St. Ives, while her North Philadelphia neighborhood was starting to resemble a battle zone.

They didn't speak again until Calvin got an anonymous call informing him that he was the father of a baby boy. He had mixed emotions. He called Nettie a few days later and asked if he could see his son, only to have the phone slammed down in his ear. Calvin tried calling a few more times with the exact same result, so he decided to go over to her place. She was sitting out front of her house on the steps breast-feeding their child. He walked up and asked Nettie their son's name. She told him Jermaine Ceaser Banks. He wanted to ask why hadn't she given the baby his last name but decided that would be a waste of breath. Nettie stood and walked back in the house. Then Calvin heard a loud noise that sounded like some kids shooting firecrackers, but it was the middle of April.

"You better get out of here before you catch a stray," Nettie warned, as if gunshots were a normal thing.

Calvin looked around nervously and hurried in the house behind Nettie.

"Look, I don't want a child of mine to grow up around this nonsense. Why don't you let me get you another house? Someplace safer and more conducive to raising a child."

"And do what? Wait on you to throw me a bone every now and then. No sir. I'll pass."

"Nettie, I never wanted it to come to this, but I was serious about seeking custody. I won't have my child growing up with bullets going off around him like we're in some Third World country."

Nettie laughed, "You can write me a check for this month's expenses and get your bougie ass out of my house."

Nettie played the hard role to protect her feelings, but inside she wanted Calvin to fight for her. She knew she was worth that much.

Calvin never tried again to change her mind about moving. He would send a check and go on about his life.

Calvin cleared his head of thoughts from yesteryear when he heard a loud honking sound behind him. The traffic light had turned green, so he pulled off into a parking lot and took the cork back out of the bottle. He stared hard at the brown liquid before putting it to his lips. He took a long swallow and just like that erased fifteen years of sobriety.

11

Confused

Erin sat on her living room floor, leaning against the front of her love seat staring at her ringless left hand. Just yesterday there had been a platinum two-carat-diamond ring on her finger that had made people stop and stare, but now all that was left was the lightness of the skin that had sat beneath the beautiful ring.

Maybe it was the rain that had been falling off and on all day that sent Erin's mind back to the day Jermaine had asked her to marry him. As a matter of fact, every time it rained, she thought back to that day six months ago and her heart always began to beat a little faster.

It was a rainy September evening. Erin walked into her home after a long day of real estate classes. All she wanted to do was take a hot shower and cuddle up with the new Eric Jerome Dickey novel. But before she could get her purse off her shoulder there was a knock on her door. She walked over and looked in the peephole but didn't see anyone, and then there was another knock. She opened the door to see a little boy who couldn't have been any older than seven holding a dozen roses. The little boy held them up and smiled. Erin took the flowers, thanked the little boy, and asked him who they were from. The little boy hunched his shoulders and ran to get out of the rain. Just as she closed the door her phone rang, and Jermaine's voice was on the line.

"So you're cheating on me with a young boy now?"

"Jermaine, these roses are beautiful. Thank you, sweetie. What did you do? I know you are making up for something."

"Get dressed. I'm taking you out tonight."

"Where, I mean, what should I wear?"

"I don't know but I'm rockin' a suit. See you in an hour." Jermaine hung up before Erin could respond. *A suit? I forgot he owned one,* Erin thought.

Erin hung up then waited for a dial tone before calling her mother.

"Mom, is Daddy around?"

"What do you think?"

"Good."

"I guess this is about Jermaine. What did he do this time?"

"Mom," Erin whined. "This is a good call. I think he's going to ask me to marry him tonight. He just sent me a dozen roses, then he called and told me he wanted to take me out to dinner and he was wearing a suit. Mom, I think this is it."

"Well, congratulations to you, little girl. You know I always liked Jermaine. He gets on my nerves sometimes when y'all get into it but for the most part, I think he's a good boy."

"Oh . . . Mom, I'm so nervous. But wait . . . what if it's just dinner? I'm getting my hopes all up and maybe he just wants to take me out. I need to calm down. But something is telling me that this is it. Oh Mom, what should I do?"

"First you need to hang up this phone and get dressed, then you need to wait and see. Call me when you get in," Mrs. Jones said in what she hoped was an encouraging tone.

Erin was trying to find something to wear in her walk-in closet when her sister, Sharon, called. Sharon was ten years older than Erin and lived in North Carolina with her own family.

"Hey, girl. I heard the news," Sharon said.

"Dag, Momma can't hold water."

"You knew that when you called her, but what happened to my call? Or have you forgotten who helped raised you?"

"I didn't forget but I didn't want to tell you until it was official. How are Ben and the little one?"

"Everybody's fine. Ben had Reserves this weekend and we just got in from Joey's soccer game. So you think tonight is the night, huh?"

"I think so. But I'm trying not to get too excited."

"Well, it's about time. I don't know what Jermaine's been waiting on. He better realize what he has in you. You are a top-of-the-line chick."

"I don't know about all of that but I am getting a little tired of waiting around on him to make his move."

"Yeah, because you don't need to be waiting around on no man. They are not worth it. I can tell you that from experience."

"Well, let me go. He should be here in about forty-five minutes." Erin wasn't about to let her sister's opinions on men ruin her evening. "I'll call you."

"You need to call me as soon as you get in. Love you."

"I love you too," Erin said.

Erin decided on a sleek but elegant black evening gown. She slid diamond earrings in her lobes, wrapped a diamond necklace around her slender neck, and said a silent prayer that the diamonds she already wore would have a little company in the jewelry box before the night was over. As she applied the final touches of makeup, the doorbell rang. She grabbed her purse and ran to get the door. But it wasn't Jermaine on the other side of the door. Instead there was a tall white man wearing a black suit and a driver's hat.

"Ms. Jones, your car is waiting," the man said with a dramatic sweep of his arm, pointing to a black stretch limousine.

Erin took in the sight of the limo and almost fainted. Now she knew for sure that the time had come. She locked her front door and followed the man to the rear of the car. Once the man opened her door, she locked eyes with the smiling Jermaine. To her, at that moment, he was the most beautiful man this world had ever produced. She almost didn't recognize him; the only other times she had seen him in a suit were at funerals and court appearances. Erin stood paralyzed for a moment, basking in the beauty of her handsome and classy-looking man, whose honey-brown complexion seemed to glow. Erin was tempted to tip the driver and take Jermaine back into her house so she could rip all of his clothes off and make passionate love to him, but figured if things went the way she thought they were headed she'd have the rest of her life to do that.

Erin stood in the light drizzle staring at Jermaine, still unable to move, when he brought her back to reality.

"Girl, get your ass in this car before you catch a cold," he said, smiling.

"Shut up," Erin teased, taking a seat beside Jermaine. "Baby, you look nice," she said as she leaned over and kissed him on his cheek.

"You don't look so bad yourself," Jermaine said, and before the driver could get moving he was on one knee.

"Erin, I'm not into all that mushy stuff so let me get to the business at hand. You know we've been through a lot together and you've always had my back. We don't always see eye to eye but I know you love me and that's real. So if you'll have me, then I think it's time we make this official," Jermaine said, then opened up a burgundy jewelry box and almost blinded Erin.

"Oh my God," Erin said through tears as she reached for the ring.

"Wait," Jermaine said, pulling the ring away. "I asked you a question. Will you marry me?"

"Yes, yes, yes . . . oh, Jermaine, I love you so much." Erin reached out to hug Jermaine but the driver pulled off and she lost her balance and ended up knocking Jermaine onto the limo's floor. As he lay on his back with Erin on his chest, he looked into her eyes and told her, "I always want you in my life." And it was right there on the limo floor that Jermaine slid the ring on her finger.

Funny how feelings change, because now Erin rubbed her hand across her ever-growing belly and cried at the memory of her engagement. That had been six months ago. And now she was six months pregnant. The night Jermaine proposed was the first time they had ever made love without the company of Mr. Trojan. But now as she sat on the floor staring at her bare left hand, she realized what an enormous mistake that had been.

Erin stood and walked over to her window to close the shades. Maybe if she couldn't see the rain it would help to block Jermaine from her mind—but it didn't help. She could still hear the water pounding on her windowpane.

"Why can't he just grow up?" Erin asked no one in particular. She was so confused about everything. *Life* was kicking in and she didn't have a clue as to how to deal with it. Ever since Erin could remember, her mother had been giving her the answers to all of her problems, but now, at thirty years old, she was tired of going to Momma. She was tired of going to her sister but she didn't know what else to do. They had major drama in their own relationships. Her sister's husband, Ben, had been cheating for almost as long as they'd been married yet her sister acted as if they had the perfect marriage. She said she stayed for their son. And her father was even worse. Erin had gone to high school with girls she later found out were her half-sisters. But none of that mattered now; this was her life yet she didn't know how to manage it, so she did what she always did and picked up the phone.

"Momma, it's me," Erin sniffled.

"Hey, baby. Why are you crying?"

"It's Jermaine. I'm tired of him belittling me. I called him and tried to talk to him about our argument. You know, trying to take the high road."

"You can't take the high road with a lowlife, but what did he have to say?"

"He called me spoiled and self-centered. Talking about I think the world revolves around me. He has a lot of nerve. He's mad because I gave him back his ring and everything else he ever bought for me. I don't want anything of his. He can keep those evil spirits right over there in that ghetto that he seems to worship. He needs to grow up."

"That's right. I could've told you that a long time ago but your daddy seems to think I run my children's affairs, so I was trying to stay out of it," Mrs. Jones said. "But this is good. I know it don't seem like it right now but you don't need to be with anybody that's not going to treat you like the queen God meant for you to be. Jermaine must be out of his mind. He will be getting a call from me."

"Then," continued Erin, "he said just because I have a few degrees I think I'm better than everybody. I don't even act like that. That's his insecurity because he didn't go to college. I'm tired of him trying to make me apologize for making something of myself."

"Tell Jermaine to go to hell. Why wouldn't he want to be with a woman with an education? You don't need to talk to him no more. Just cut him off. You and the baby will be better off without him. Have I ever steered you wrong?"

"No, ma'am," Erin said through tears.

"Well, trust me when I tell you to cut your losses because it's not going to get better with him."

"I'm tired of all this drama. My hair is falling out, I'm taking

Tylenol by the family-size bottle, and I'm not sleeping well. And it's all because of him."

"Erin, you're thirty years old and it's just time you find yourself a real man, not some little boy. Do you want me to come and get you?"

"No, I have some work that I need to catch up on. But thanks for listening to me."

"That's what I'm here for. Now listen, I don't want you to have anything else to do with Jermaine. It's better to leave now while you still got your sanity."

"You're right. But what should I do when he calls?"

"Don't answer the phone and if he comes over, call the police and have a restraining order put on him. I'm going to call him and give him a piece of my mind. Your father and I have discussed it and we don't want you to have anything else to do with him," Mrs. Jones ordered.

"Okay," Erin obeyed.

"I love you. Now get you some rest and try to forget about that nutcase."

Erin hung up the phone with her mother with mixed emotions. On one hand she knew her mother only wanted her pain and anguish to stop, and that she really didn't have anything against Jermaine personally. But in her heart Erin still loved Jermaine and now she was more confused than before she had called her mother. Because she knew once her mother got off the phone with her that she would call her sister and after they hung up, they would get on a party line and have everyone in the family hating Jermaine. Erin wasn't sure if that's what she really wanted, but then again, she had never gone against her mother's wishes.

12

Life Is a Gamble

It was a little after midnight on a chilly March night and Jermaine found himself sitting on the front steps of his row house talking to his uncle Herb.

Herbert Banks was a nicely built man with smooth coffee-brown skin and salt-and-pepper dreadlocks framing his face and flowing smoothly down his back.

Herb sat on the concrete steps staring at the streetlights, treasuring his first night as a free man. It had been twenty long years since he'd inhaled the sexy yet polluted aroma of North Philadelphia's air.

"You spoke with your contact yet?" Herb asked Jermaine.

"I'm trying to get in touch with him but he's a hard man to catch," Jermaine lied. Herb had been hounding him all day about his drug connection. Jermaine figured he'd try to stall him out until he could come up with something better to tell him.

"This girl named Erin called you about ten times. I meant to tell you that."

"Oh yeah? Well, she can keep calling. I'm done with her."

"Is that the college chick that you were gonna marry?"

"Yep."

"Man, you better hold on to that educated woman."

"Education is all she has. Not that anything is wrong with that. She just doesn't have any common sense," Jermaine frowned and shook his head. "She's operating on a fifth-grade level when it comes to life. Every time she gets mad at me she gives me the engagement ring back."

Herb laughed.

"She done gave it back about five times," Jermaine said, shaking his head again.

"How long y'all been together?"

"Too long and I've had about enough of the drama. It's time to move on. Plus, I already got a mom. I can't lift my hand to show her somebody I know without her slapping my finger, telling me that pointing is rude. Can't have a decent meal without her frowning up at the way I chew my food." Jermaine sighed heavily. "I can't believe I dealt with her this long."

"That's a woman for ya, but hell, you get rid of this girl, don't think the next one is going to be perfect. Might as well stay with the one you're used to."

"Nah, it's like my man B.B. said: the thrill is gone. We stayed together so long because we're used to each other." Jermaine stared off in the distance. "I'm not going along just to get along. Fuck that!"

Herb stared at his nephew and shook his head. He knew Jermaine was trying to play the hard role but he could see the hurt in his eyes. He had seen that same pained expression on the faces of countless inmates during his twenty years in prison whenever the news came that the love they'd had when they got arrested wasn't loving them anymore.

"I guess you know better than me. But like I said, that's a woman for ya. Maybe I should say that's a black woman for you. I'mma get me a white girl so I don't have to put up with all that attitude and mouth. They know how to shut the hell up and let a man be a man."

Jermaine stared at his uncle, bamboozled. This from the mouth of a man who was once the leader of the Black Panther party.

"Prison sure has changed a brother."

"I haven't changed. I never hated white women. It's they husbands and daddies I got my problems with."

"You could at least have said a Puerto Rican."

"Oh, hell no! They're worse than black women. Plus those bitches'll cut ya and you can't hit 'em either. They got too many cousins. You'll be fighting somebody every time you change your drawls."

"Uncle Herb, you crazy." Jermaine laughed.

"Yeah," Herb said, exhaling. "Maybe I can make me some money doing stand-up, huh?"

"You'll give Bernie Mac a run."

"I gotta do something, nephew." Herb sighed heavily. "Cuz this ain't livin.' I'm a free man, but now I'm a financial slave."

Jermaine could only imagine how his uncle was feeling, and for a minute he seriously contemplated giving Herb his drug contact.

"I heard you got your car window shot out," Herb said.

"Who told you that?"

"Do you think it was the same guys that killed your friend?" Herb asked, ignoring the question.

"First of all, you need to stop listening to your sister. She doesn't let the facts confuse her."

"Don't you talk about my baby like that." Herb smiled.

"Yeah, well, tell your baby to stop gossiping so much. It was Erin's daddy."

"Whatcha do to him?"

"I got his daughter pregnant."

"How old is this Erin?"

"Thirty."

"Thirty? And her daddy's mad because she got pregnant? He should be happy, her biological clock is ticking."

"Oh, he ain't mad because she's pregnant. He's mad because she's pregnant by me."

"Oh well, in that case fuck him. If they all up in her business like that now, it won't get any better once you're married. You'll be marrying the whole family."

"Tell me about it. Yo, remind me to play you the message her Moms left me." Jermaine shook his head. He turned up his lips and mocked Erin's mother's voice: " 'Jermaine, you ain't shit. Leave Erin alone. If you got a problem with my daughter then call me. Now, I hope to God that you get it through your thick skull that Erin is done with you. I don't know what she ever saw in your skinny ass in the first place. What you need to do is take your ass down to the unemployment office and get a job. Don't call my daughter no more. Click!' "

Herb was holding his side, laughing.

"Count your blessings, nephew."

"Then her little anorexic-ass sister called with the same mess. I'm telling you, they some nuts."

So what does Erin say about her people being in y'all business like that?"

"Oh, she eats it up like candy."

"Damn."

"I don't know why, but I still miss that nut."

"I can tell," Herb said.

"Maybe not. I think I'm just used to having someone in my life, but me and that girl ain't gonna make it."

"Y'all youngsters will be a'ight. So what's up with them cats that did your friend in? They still breathing?"

"I don't know and don't really care. I'm about done with this gangsta life. Man, right about now, I'm just sick of everything," Jermaine said, sweeping his arms over all of North Philadelphia.

"You know I hate to sound selfish, nephew, but don't you quit before you do what we talked about," Herb said, not wanting to miss out on his hookup.

"I just need to get away. Take my little boy to the islands or someplace, then come home and get a nine-to-five."

"See, you can do that cuz you ain't in the system. All you got are misdemeanors, and I advise you to keep it that way. It ain't nothing nice behind them bars."

"If it's so bad, then why are you trynna go back?"

"Who said I'm trying to go back?"

"Uncle Herb, you've been trying to get me to hook you up with my connect all day, and the reason I keep stalling you out is because I don't want to see you end up back in the penitentiary."

Herb stood and walked a few paces down the block in silence. He turned around and walked back and sat real close to Jermaine.

"J-man, I've been poor all my life. Don't know why but that's just the way it's been, and for the last twenty years, I've been treated worse than an animal. Locked up twenty-three hours a day and the one hour I got out was in a cement box surrounded by razor wire. Now it's time that I get my piece of the so-called American pie. Reparations are due and I'm taking mine. You have no idea what prison does to a man. It can break you. Now I'm so-called free, but not really. I still have to live off of someone else.

"I don't want you to get me wrong, J-man. I'm not asking you to help me once I'm put on. All I need is the introduction to the man, then I'll be out of your hair. My back is against the wall, nephew. It's sink or swim for me, and this is the only way I know how to stay afloat. I'm fifty-three years old and I don't have a trade, so who's going to give me a decent job?"

"This is your first day out, Herb. You haven't even tried to get a job."

"Why do you think they have that little 'felony' box on job applications? I'll tell you: to keep my criminal ass out of their establishment. That's why. I'm saving myself the humiliation. I've been humiliated enough in prison. I'm in hustle mode."

Jermaine looked at his uncle and shook his head. Herb was right, he had no idea what prison could do to a man, and he wasn't trying to find out. That's why he was more determined to get his life in order.

Just as Jermaine was about to give in to his uncle's pleading eyes, his worker Dave walked up and handed him a thick envelope filled with cash. Dave was light-complexioned with curly hair. He said he was Puerto Rican but neither he nor anyone in his family could speak any Spanish.

"Dave, how's it going, my man?" Jermaine said, taking the package and putting in his jacket pocket without counting it. It was the same ten thousand he got from Dave every week.

"What's up, homes? I hear you setting up war plans to handle Buster's business."

"You heard wrong," Jermaine said, frowning at Dave.

"Okay," Dave said, not buying Jermaine's denial. Killers didn't broadcast. Dave looked at Herb and spoke. "What's up?"

"Oh, this is my uncle Herb. Herb, this is my man Dave," Jermaine said.

"What's up?" Herb said plainly.

"I'm cool. Where were you locked up?"

"How did you know I was locked up?"

"Just got that look," Dave said, smiling.

"Then this look should tell you to mind your business," Herb said before standing and walking back into Jermaine's house. "See you inside, nephew."

"I respect that," Dave said, nodding his head. "So J, what's been up?"

"Nothing, man, maintaining. What about you?"

"Same old two-step." Jermaine had a bright idea. Since Dave couldn't keep his mouth closed, he decided he'd let him know that he was getting out of the game and that way the entire city would know.

"Dave, I'm about to retire from the game."

"For real? Why? I mean, the police don't sweat you and it's easy money. You're moving pounds now so you don't even touch the stuff. All you do is collect your loot."

"Yeah, it is a sweet deal that I got going on, but some other forces are at work right now and it's just time to move on," Jermaine said, proud of himself for taking the first step to his new life.

"Move on to what?"

"Don't know."

"You crazy. What could be better than this?"

Jermaine ignored Dave.

"I knew something was going on with you. You just don't thug like you use to."

"How old are you, Dave?"

"Thirty-nine."

"Have you never gotten tired of this street life?"

"Naw, homes. I dropped out of high school, so what else is there for me to do?" Dave said with a smile. "You know how it is around here. People need an escape mechanism and all most of them can afford is a dream. So you can call me the ghetto dream maker. A ten-dollar rock will send some of these fools to a place no exotic island can touch."

Jermaine had known Dave all of his life, but tonight he looked at him differently. All of a sudden, he felt sorry for Dave. Sorry that everything Dave would ever be in this world would come at the expense of someone else's addiction.

"Hold on a minute." Jermaine got up and ran in his house to put the envelope away and returned. He walked past Dave and headed down his block. It was almost one o'clock in the morning and his block was crowded with addicts, pushers, prostitutes, and wannabe hustlers. He leaned against a light pole and took in the chaotic scenery North Philly was offering.

Dave walked up behind him. "J, you a'ight?"

"Yeah, I'm cool," Jermaine said as his eyes caught the face of a familiar young boy running across the street toward him. "Murphy, whatcha doing out here so late?" Jermaine asked the boy.

"Trynna get paid," Murphy said, desperation written all over his face.

Jermaine looked at Murphy's baby face and innocent eyes. It seemed like just yesterday, this same little boy was riding his Big Wheel on the sidewalk, living a child's carefree life, but here he was at one in the morning, giving in to the hopelessness of street life. He couldn't help but think that this could be Khalil. "Well, you better take it back in the house," Jermaine warned. "Don't you have to go to school in the morning?"

"I can't do the school thing right now. I gotta make some money. I'm hungry, my little sister is hungry, and my Moms is out here pippin'. I gotta do something, J," Murphy said, wiping his nose.

Just then a white Honda Accord pulled up and the passenger window rolled down.

"You guys got some crack?"

Murphy started toward the car but Jermaine snatched him back by his collar.

"Yo, my man. Just because you see some black men on the corner don't mean we hustling. Keep driving, faggot," Jermaine barked.

The car window rolled up and the driver sped off.

"Yo, J-man, why you blocking? I could've served him," Murphy pleaded.

"Yeah, and he would've served you right up to a judge Monday morning. That was a cop, stupid. How you gonna play the game if you don't know the players? Go in the house, Murphy, and I better see a book bag on your back in the morning. And I don't wanna hear nothing about being hungry because all you have to do is holla at me. And since that's your reason for being out here, your problems have been solved."

"Yo, J-man. I don't need no handout. I can get my own," Murphy said, opening his coat to show off the handle of a gun in his waistband. "Plus I got product," he said proudly.

"Oh, so you a man now, huh?" Dave asked as he quickly pulled the gun out of Murphy's pants before the little boy could react.

"Give me back my gun, Dave," Murphy pleaded.

"It's my gun now," Dave said, slipping the gun in his own pocket.

"Come on, Dave. I just got that," Murphy begged. "J, tell Dave to give me back my gun."

"Yo, Murphy. You don't make any sense. You got money for a gun *and* product but you're hungry? That ain't adding up to me," Jermaine said.

"I found the gun and somebody fronted me the work," Murphy explained.

"Who fronted you . . . ? Never mind." Jermaine was becoming angrier with each word that left Murphy's mouth. "Murphy, you really need to go in the house and when you come home from school tomorrow, I'm going to holla at Mr. White and ask him to give you a job cleaning his store or stocking shelves or something."

"And make what? A hundred dollars a week? I can clock that in an hour."

"I thought this was about you being hungry? I don't eat four hundred dollars' worth of groceries in a month. Bye, Murphy," Jermaine said, folding his arms.

"Can I have my gun back?"

"You believe this guy, J?" Dave said, shaking his head. "Hell no, you can't get it back. You're what, eleven, twelve years old? You know how many brothers are sitting up in prison wishing somebody would've taken their gun?" Dave said as he handed Jermaine the gun. "J, get rid of that for me. If I wasn't on probation I'd keep it myself."

"Man, y'all are buggin'. It ain't enough paper out here to share the wealth?" Murphy pouted.

"It's not about that. We're trying to do your young ass a favor. Stop being stupid and recognize the love," Dave said as he brushed Murphy away.

"I'mma be lookin' for you in the morning with that book bag," Jermaine said, cutting his eyes at Murphy.

Murphy didn't respond. He just looked at the ground, shrugged his shoulders.

"You know what, J? I can't figure you out."

"You don't need to figure me out," Jermaine shot back.

"But listen, I've seen you beat dudes up until they peed on themselves for selling drugs to pregnant women, but you hustle. I never even heard you say a cuss word, but you a thug."

"Murphy, stop stalling and take your ass in the house. You happy now? I cussed. Now give Dave that product."

Murphy shook his head, handed Dave a package, and jogged back toward his house.

"They're getting younger and younger," Jermaine said, sighing heavily.

"How long do you think he's going to stay in the house? When the streets come calling, most people answer."

"I know." Jermaine stared off in the distance. "Don't I know!"

"J, I gotta roll. I met this new young joint over at the gallery the other day. She claims she gives the best head in Philly and I'm about to be the judge of that."

"Handle your business," Jermaine said as he slapped Dave's hand and walked off.

As Jermaine walked back around the corner, he noticed Roscoe's police car sitting in front of his house. He cursed under his breath and slowly walked over to the driver's-side window.

"What's up?"

Roscoe got out of the driver's seat and slammed Jermaine against the hood of his car and frisked him from his neck to his toes. "Look what we have here," Roscoe said, pulling the gun from Jermaine's waistband.

"Man, I just took that gun from this little kid."

"Oh, I watched your big-brother moment unfold. But I still found the gun in your possession. So what should I do about this?" Roscoe said, waving the gun in Jermaine's face.

"Roscoe, man, why are you sweating me?"

"What happened with the job, Jermaine?"

"Man, I'm not standing on the highway wearing no gorilla outfit," Jermaine said, frowning.

Roscoe looked confused. "What are you talking about, boy?"

"Your man wanted me to wear a gorilla costume and hold a 'for sale' sign on the side of the highway and I'm not doing that."

Roscoe started laughing and stepped away from Jermaine. He tossed the gun in his car.

"Well, at least you went to check on it. I didn't know he was talking about that kind of sales. So what's going on with you and my daughter? Her momma ain't talking to me."

"We broke up."

"Good," Roscoe said, smiling. "But you still gonna take care of my grandbaby. And you're still getting a job."

Jermaine didn't respond. He was done arguing with Roscoe too. He didn't want anything to do with anyone in Erin's family. He would take care of his kid and maybe one day he and Erin would be friends, but for now he was just burnt out on her and everything that came with her.

Jermaine grunted then said, "Look, if you're done harassing me, I gotta go."

"Go ahead but I'll be in touch."

"I'm sure you will," Jermaine said as he jogged up the steps to his place without looking back. He walked into his apartment and wrinkled his nose at the smell. He looked down and his uncle was lying on his plush leather couch with his feet smelling like some old, stale corn chips.

"Oh my God, Uncle Herb, it smells like you soaked your feet in some shit."

Just as Jermaine hit the remote control to turn the television off, he heard a knock on his door.

"Oh, I'm too nice to these crack heads. They see your light on and think you want some company," Jermaine fussed as he stood and walked over to his door. He looked out the peephole but didn't recognize the old man standing on his steps. He opened the door.

"What's up?"

"Is this Jermaine Banks's house?"

"Who wants to know?"

"My name is Louis Sharpe and I'm his grandfather."

13

Ain't That Peculiar?

Jermaine stared at the old guy claiming to be his grandfather and knew that it was impossible for the man's words to be true. Even still, he tried to find a place in his memory bank to place the man, but nothing registered. Jermaine did a quick mental run through his family tree and came up with the fact that his mother's father had died before he was born and his own father had always been a no-show, so as far as he was concerned, it was impossible for him to have a grandfather.

"I think you have the wrong house, my man," Jermaine said, closing the door in the old man's face.

"Is your name Jermaine Banks?"

Jermaine stopped in midmotion.

"Who's asking?"

"All I need is a few minutes of your time."

"Look, I don't know what kind of hustle you're running but I'm not in a good mood. I don't have a grandfather," Jermaine said, and this time he slammed the door.

Louis stood on the stoop and tried to stop his hands from shaking. He had come too far and gone too long without his grandson, so Jermaine was going to have to do more than slam a door to keep him away. He knocked on the door again.

"What do you want, man?" Jermaine said, swinging the door open with attitude.

"Please," Louis pleaded. "Just give me five minutes of your time and I'll try to explain everything to you."

The man's persistence made Jermaine think. This old man had to be his father's father. And he didn't want anything to do with his father or the horse he rode in on. Anger took over, and even though this old man was not the direct cause of his anger, he would feel the brunt of Jermaine's wrath since he'd come calling.

"Listen. I'm twenty-nine years old and I'm really kind of over the wanting-a-grandfather thing. And how do you figure you can explain a lifetime of abandonment in five minutes?"

"I understand how you feel but—"

"Oh, do you?"

"I think I do," Louis said, staring intently in his grandson's eyes.

"Well, that's pretty fucked up because that could only mean that you had a deadbeat for a father too. Well, come on in here and let's talk about these bastard makers." Jermaine relented, stepping away from the door to let Louis Sharpe into his home.

Louis hadn't known what to expect when he'd set out to meet his grandson, but he certainly hadn't expected a war. He cautiously walked into his grandson's house as if he were entering a lion's den without a rifle.

"You'll have to excuse the smell, that's my uncle's feet," Jermaine said as he shook his uncle to wake him.

"Uncle Herb! Wake up. You can sleep in Khalil's room."

Herbert stood up on unstable legs and stared at Louis. He cocked his eye toward Jermaine to make sure everything was okay, and once he was satisfied that this stranger meant no harm, he continued on his way.

Jermaine went into the hallway bathroom and exited with a can of Lysol. He sprayed the stench away before taking a seat on his soft red leather chair.

"Okay, Mr. Sharpe, have a seat but don't get too comfortable. Your clock is ticking."

"Well, I really don't know where to start." Louis took a seat on the plush leather sofa. He looked around and took in the impressive decor. The inside of the house certainly didn't match the outside or the neighborhood, but who was he to judge? It didn't matter anyway, because the minute Jermaine opened the door he could see a strong family resemblance. The high cheekbones and dark eyes couldn't be denied even if a DNA expert testified differently. "All of this is still new to me. I'm still trying to let it sink in," he said.

Jermaine propped his feet up on the matching ottoman and frowned at the statement.

"I just found out about you early this morning, and I've been trying to find you ever since. I used every contact I could think of to locate you."

"Mission completed. Now what do you want?"

"My son, your father, kept you from us."

"I don't have a father," Jermaine stated bluntly.

"Okay," Louis paused. *He sure isn't making this easy,* he thought. "Well, I'll just call him Calvin. God only knows why he kept you from us but that's what he did. So when I said I understood how you felt, what I meant was that when I heard the news that I had a full-grown grandson, I almost died. I felt cheated, and to be honest with you I felt abandoned myself. Because my own son didn't think enough of me as a father to share the greatest gift ever created with me." Louis looked over at the fireplace and noticed an eight-by-ten framed photograph of a little boy with big brown eyes sitting on Jermaine's lap.

He stood and walked over to the mantel. He looked at Jermaine. "Do you mind?"

"Help yourself."

Louis lifted the picture and stared at the bright-eyed little boy.

"Is this your son?" he asked, but knew right away that the little guy was his great-grandson.

Jermaine stared at Louis but didn't answer. Intruding on his life was one thing, but to even mention his son was crossing the line. Yet there was something about the old man with the bald dome and graying sides that calmed him. Jermaine didn't fully understand what was going on inside of him, but he wasn't angry anymore. Louis seemed sincere, and as Jermaine watched him gaze at the picture of him and his son, he heard a sniffle and saw the old man shake his head to choke back his emotion. Louis pulled a white handkerchief from his suit coat pocket and wiped his eyes and nose before looking at Jermaine.

"That's my son. His name is Khalil."

"Khalil! What a powerful name," Louis said, and this time he didn't bother to wipe away his tears.

"It's Arabic for 'companion,' " Jermaine said.

"Are you a Muslim?"

"Nah, but I read the Koran from time to time."

Louis ran his hand across the picture as if it were Khalil's and Jermaine's actual faces.

"Son—" Louis stared at Jermaine as if he'd made a mistake. "Do you mind if I call you that?"

Jermaine hunched his shoulders and shook his head. "I've been called worse," he said, and they shared a smile.

"You have no idea how terrible I feel about the choice my son made."

"It was probably for the best."

"Somewhere along the line I feel like I failed him, had to for him to walk away from his own flesh and blood. Now, I'm far from being God, but to me, when you abandon your bloodline that's the worst sin a man could ever commit. And there is no way I could ever make up for the twenty-nine years, but I'd like to try," Louis said, staring hard at Jermaine for any kind of sign of hope.

Jermaine exhaled, looked around, and rubbed his hands together. "You know what? I don't have anything against you, Mr. Sharpe."

"Please, call me Louis."

"Mr. Louis, I don't have anything against you. You seem to be a nice-enough man, and I apologize for the way I treated you earlier, but it's not every day a man comes knocking on my door claiming to be my grandfather. As a matter of fact, that has never happened. My mother's parents were killed before I was born so I never experienced that grandparent thing. They say you can't miss what you never had, but that's a lie. I always wanted a father and a grandfather, but for whatever reason, that wasn't in the cards for me. So I'll tell you what. I'm going to make a deal with you. You can come over and visit me anytime you like and I'll even let you meet my son, but I don't, under any circumstances, want to see your son. Don't get me wrong, I don't hate him, I don't know him well enough to hate him, but I do have some very ill feelings toward him. So you can hang around and try to get to know me and my son, but you have to keep him away. That's the deal, take it or leave it." In his heart, Jermaine was hoping the old man would take the deal.

"I'll take it. My son has his own crosses to bear. But there is one more thing that I need to ask of you," Louis said. He knew he was reaching but this was just as important.

"Let's hear it."

"You have a little brother. And once again my son kept you from him too." He shook his head.

"Yeah, it wasn't hard to figure out that I didn't exist to him," Jermaine said. All of a sudden his heart sank. What was there about him that was so bad that his father chose to abandon him and take care of another child?

"I'm so sorry about that," Louis said, reading Jermaine's expression.

"It's not your fault. You should never apologize for another man's shortcomings even if he's your son. But go on, you were saying something about a little brother."

"Yes. He would love to meet you. He's fifteen years old and ever since he's found out about you, he's been talking about you nonstop. It would mean so much to him if he could meet you. He wanted to come tonight but he got sick and had to go to the hospital."

"Is he all right?"

"Well, he has kidney problems, so we're prayerful that he'll be fine."

Jermaine nodded his head. "Yeah, tell him I'd like to meet him too."

"That's great," Louis said, nodding his head and smiling. He had achieved his goal of meeting his grandson. Now he knew that he'd never let Jermaine out of his life.

"Well, son, I really hate to leave you but my wife is over at the hospital with C.J. and she's waiting on me."

"C.J.?" Jermaine said thoughtfully. "Is that short for Calvin Junior?"

"Yes," Louis said, dropping his head apologetically. "That's normally a name for the first son."

Jermaine picked up on his grandfather's mood change and decided to clear things up.

"Oh, don't worry about that. I wouldn't want the name of a coward. I'm cool with the one I have. Let me write my numbers down so you can stay in touch."

"That would be great. Here is my card with all my info on it as well."

"Oh, you live in North Carolina," Jermaine said, reading the thick white card.

"Yes, we only came up here to find you."

"We?"

"Yes. Me and my wife. Her name is Edna and she's gonna pass out when she hears that I found you." Louis smiled from ear to ear.

"Hey, I'll meet the whole gang in due time. Everyone except the coward. Is that cool?" Jermaine smiled.

Life in the streets dictated that he show no weakness, but he couldn't lie to himself, it felt good to be wanted, to connect the dots to his existence.

"That's fine with me," Louis said.

"Wait just a second," Jermaine said as he walked over to the mantel and removed the picture that had choked Louis up. "Take this. I don't know you that well but something tells me you a'ight."

"Yeah, I'm all right," Louis said, smiling, as he reached out, almost snatching the photo from Jermaine. "We're family and you're a good man, Jermaine."

"Give yourself some time to get to know me before you say that." Jermaine smiled.

"Oh no. I can tell you have a lot of character. Hey, I've been dying to get me a Philly cheese steak. You know any good places?"

"No doubt. Maybe I can take you to lunch before you go back to North Carolina. There's a place out in Mt. Airy on Ogantz Avenue called Pagonnos. They've been keeping me full since I was a kid."

"That would be great. Well, I must say that this has been one of the best nights of my life," Louis said as he reached for Jermaine's hand.

Jermaine shook his grandfather's hand. He could tell the old man wanted a hug but didn't know how to go about asking, so he just pulled Louis to him.

Louis hugged his flesh and blood and didn't want to let go.

"You've done well for yourself, Jermaine. I'm proud of you. No matter what, I'm proud of you," he said before walking out toward his rented automobile.

Jermaine stood in the doorway watching his newfound grand-father get in his car. Once the old guy drove off, Jermaine closed and locked the doors. He plopped down in the leather chair and ran his fingers over his braided hair. He closed his eyes and thought about what had just transpired. He reached over to the end table and picked up another picture of Khalil.

"Little man, looks like you got yourself a great-granddaddy."

14

Got to Give It Up

alvin felt like someone was pounding his head with a pair of
brass knuckles. He squinted his eyes and looked around.

"Mister," the hotel's security guard said, looking in Calvin's car window. "Are you all right?"

"Yeah umm," Calvin stuttered. "I'm fine."

"You're either going to have to check into a room or move on.
You can't stay out here all night."

Calvin looked at his watch. It was almost one o'clock in the
morning and his mouth felt like someone had filled it with cotton.
He heard his cell phone ringing but couldn't find it. He searched
around the car and located it beside the empty cognac bottle wedged
between the passenger seat and the door. He fumbled around with
the little gadget until he saw the caller ID; it was Robin again. He
pushed the "talk" key and barked, "What the hell do you want?"

"Calvin, this is your mother," Edna said.

"Oh, I'm sorry about that, Mom. I thought you were Robin."

"We've been trying to call you all night. Where have you been?"

"I had a few meetings that ran over," he lied.

"Son, do you always keep hours like this?"

"I try not to make a habit of it but sometimes I have to."

"I was calling you to tell you that C.J. had to go to the hospital tonight. He's at Chestnut Hill. I think Robin said it was on Germantown Avenue."

"Yeah, I know where it is," Calvin said, unalarmed; this wasn't a new occurrence. "What happened?"

"He said he wasn't feeling well, then his eyes started to swell a little so we just took him up there. They're going to keep him overnight for observation."

"Okay. Where is Dad?"

"He went looking for Jermaine."

Calvin paused. Just the mention of his son's name sent chills down his spine.

"I'm going to run by the hospital, then I'll probably check into a hotel."

"Okay, I just wanted to let you know."

"Thanks, Mom."

"Calvin?"

"Yes."

"Are you going to be okay?"

"Yes, everything is fine, Mom. C.J.'s been in and out of the hospital so many times that I pretty much know what to expect."

"I'm not talking about C.J. I'm talking about you," Mrs. Sharpe said.

"I'm making it."

"We all make mistakes but it's not the end of the world."

"I know. I'll talk to you tomorrow, Mom," Calvin said, cutting his mother off.

Calvin didn't want his mother to try and make it better this time.

He hung up the phone and started his car. He drove straight to Chestnut Hill Memorial and parked in the emergency parking lot.

Calvin walked in and asked the Information nurse where his son was and she pointed to a room that was directly behind him. He thanked her and turned on his heel. He walked in the room and saw Robin sleeping in a chair in the corner. C.J. was awake and staring straight ahead at a television. He acknowledged his father's presence by shifting his weight to let him know that he was already bothering him. Calvin eased in the door and walked over to the side of his son's bed.

"How are you doing, C.J.?"

C.J. ignored him and changed the channel.

"Are you feeling any better?"

C.J. cut his eyes at his father then returned them to the television.

"I guess you don't feel like talking and I understand. Well, get you some rest and if you need anything, I'll be right outside the door," Calvin said. He didn't particularly like the treatment he was getting from his son, and under normal circumstances he would've chastised him. But Robin's big mouth had changed things. So now he had to eat a little crow to get back in his son's good graces.

"Leave. I don't want you outside the door. I don't want anything from you. You lied to me and you put your hands on my mom."

"I didn't lie to you about Jermaine. I just didn't tell you."

"Oh, that makes it better." C.J. frowned.

"C.J., maybe one day you'll understand why I never told you about Jermaine, but right now you need to focus on getting your health back. Don't you have a big match coming up?" Calvin said, trying to distract his son.

"Now you wanna act like you're interested in my matches?" C.J. huffed and rolled over onto his side.

Calvin nodded. He didn't know what else to say so he walked

over to his son and placed his hand on his shoulder, which tensed up the moment of Calvin's touch, then he turned and walked out of the room, never even glancing in Robin's direction.

Calvin stepped out into the corridor and almost bumped into his father. Even at two o'clock in the morning, Louis Sharpe was still wearing a three-piece suit with his tie in a full Windsor.

"How's he doing?" Louis asked.

"I don't know. I was about to go and find his doctor," Calvin said cautiously. He knew he wasn't on his father's list of favorite people right about now.

"Son, don't get lost after you speak with C.J.'s doctor. We need to talk."

"Can it wait until tomorrow? I have a big meeting in the morning and I have to get some rest."

"No, it can't! It's a family issue. You do understand the importance of family, don't you?"

"I'll be in the lobby," Calvin relented.

"Good," Louis said, and without another word, he walked into C.J.'s room.

Calvin walked over to the nurse's station and asked for the doctor who was treating his son. The nurse looked up from her romance novel and pointed to a young white male who looked to be in his late teens. Calvin wanted to ask the rude lady if she could talk but instead he just gave her a look to let her know that she could use a few customer relations classes. The young doctor informed Calvin that one of C.J.'s kidneys wasn't functioning properly and they would be holding him until all of his test results came back from the laboratory.

Calvin thanked the doctor and headed to the waiting room, where he joined a grungy-looking white boy wearing torn jeans and a Jimi Hendrix T-shirt. He was lying on the floor pulling on his long spiked green hair.

"Are you C.J.'s dad?" Spiked Hair asked.

"Yes, I am. Who might you be?"

"Kevin. I'm a friend of C.J.'s."

"Is that right? Don't you have school in the morning?"

"Yeah, but I'm going to camp out here tonight to make sure my dude is okay."

"And your parents don't have a problem with that?"

"My father's zapped out. He doesn't even know where *he* is."

"So who takes care of you?"

"Mrs. Sharpe helps me out from time to time. A few months back I stayed in your basement for sixty days straight. But I pretty much take care of myself."

Calvin stared at Kevin and realized how far out of touch with his family he'd become. Louis entered the room and stood before Calvin.

"Calvin, I want you to know that I'm very disappointed in you."

Calvin grunted to clear his throat then stood to face his father. They were almost nose to nose when Calvin spoke.

"I'm sorry to hear that but I'm past reproach. I've made some bad decisions, none worse than the one I made not to be in Jermaine's life, but I'm still my own man. Now, if that's what you wanted to talk about, you can save it, because I refuse to be a part of it," Calvin said as he turned to leave.

"Calvin, have a seat," Louis said, realizing that his son was right, and from the looks of him, he'd beaten himself up enough.

Calvin stopped but remained standing.

"I met Jermaine tonight," Louis said, removing the picture of Jermaine and Khalil from his briefcase.

Calvin's heart palpitated when he laid eyes on the photograph of his son and a child who was obviously his grandson. Then his legs took on a mind of their own and he had no choice but to take a seat.

"He's such a wonderful young man. He looks just like me."

Louis smiled proudly to himself. "We're having lunch before I go back."

Calvin sat stunned. He was at a loss for words. He dropped his head into his hands and began to sob. First they were subtle sobs, then all the years of neglect and guilt came crashing down on him like a boulder. He could no longer keep his emotions in check and he no longer tried. Calvin started to tremble and his heart rate increased. He began to rock back and forth, moaned something inaudible, then he let out a soul-wrenching howl.

Kevin, who had fallen asleep, jumped up and ran toward the exit door but stopped when he noticed Calvin and Louis still sitting.

"Dude, are you okay?"

Louis waved a hand at Kevin to let him know that all was well.

"I know he hates me," Calvin said through sniffles and tears.

Louis didn't feel the least bit of sympathy for his son. He sat back in his chair with his arms folded and watched Calvin purge himself of guilt.

"You're right about that," Louis said plainly.

"I wish I could do it all over but it's too late."

"It's never too late. He's a helluva guy. It was pretty rough going at first but we ended up having a wonderful conversation."

"Where does he live?"

"Can't say! He asked me not to tell you and I can't break my word to my grandson."

"Come on, Dad. This is my son we're talking about," Calvin snapped.

"Wait a minute. Don't you raise your voice at me. I found him and I don't even live here. Put forth a little effort," Louis barked back.

"Even if I found him, I doubt if I'd get the same welcome that you got."

"Something tells me he's a bigger man than even he knows."

Calvin looked at the picture. "What's my grandson's name?"

"Khalil." Louis smiled. "And he looks like me too."

Calvin took a deep breath and blew out a week's worth of frustration.

"What am I going to do?"

"Son, you can only reap what you sow, and all you've sowed in Jermaine's heart are the seeds of hatred. You got your work cut out for you."

"I gotta figure out a way to make this right," Calvin said, wiping his eyes with the handkerchief his father casually handed to him.

"You are a smart man and if you want to make it right then you'll figure out a way. Like I said, he's a good man. He has that Sharpe blood running through his veins." Louis couldn't stop smiling.

Calvin stood. "Dad, I need some time to figure things out. I'll be honest with you. If you and Mom hadn't come up here then I probably would've gone on forever without trying to locate Jermaine. I just dealt with it by not dealing with it, but there's something about seeing him in this picture that won't allow me to live that lie anymore. I'll make this right if it's the last thing I do."

"I hope so, son. I really hope so," Louis said, standing and reaching out to shake his son's hand. "Give me a call in the morning. We're staying at your place."

Calvin shook his father's hand and hurried out of the hospital.

15

Moving On

ooooo, nooooo! God, please don't do this to me! Not my baby, Lord!" Brenda Dorsey screamed as the pastor closed the casket on her youngest son. "Send him back to me, Lord, please!" she begged before passing out.

Brenda's screams brought Jermaine back to reality. Before his best friend's mom lost complete control of her faculties, he had sat calmly in the overheated church, letting his mind wander to a place he used to call home. Philadelphia was once a place of peace and tranquillity. At least it was in March 1973, when he'd elbowed, pushed, and kicked his way into this world. Jermaine reminisced about running around his neighborhood of one-way streets and row houses without the fear of a stray bullet piercing his skin. Crack wasn't a factor back then, so the neighborhood had managed to escape all of the violence and treachery that became kin to the perilous drug, but the good times hadn't lasted for long. Now, the Philly he knew was a battle zone where only the so-called strong survived.

The days of handling your differences with your fists were replaced by Uzis and AR-15's issuing out final justice. Youngsters were acting out their ghetto fantasies with real guns, taking real lives, and filling up Pennsylvania's prisons in the process. He couldn't help but wonder how much a part he played in the new Philadelphia.

Jermaine rushed over to help a few people lift Buster's mother off the floor and take her out of the church. Once she was situated in the funeral home's limousine, he walked back into the sanctuary and took his place as a pallbearer. Standing there holding the steel tube encasing his friend's lifeless body made Jermaine think about his own mortality. Why wasn't it him lying there? He had certainly fired his own gun and been fired upon enough times for his ticket to have been punched over and over again.

Just the thought of Buster's senseless demise sent Jermaine into retaliation mode. He had battled with thoughts of revenge but always talked himself out of it, but now all he wanted was the shooter's head on a platter. Words alone simply could not describe what the triggerman had done. Jermaine felt helpless thinking about it. What could he do to help ease the pain from the loss? What could he do? So far he had managed to keep all of his workers in check but he knew one day soon someone would take matters into his own hands. That was just the way of the ghetto: You take one of mine, I'll take two of yours. Trouble was, no matter what decision he made, Jermaine knew he'd end up paying for it the rest of his life. If he walked away, he'd lose the respect of the street, and if he took action, he would have a murder on his conscience. For most people the decision would have been an easy one, but not for Jermaine.

Jermaine's legs felt weak as he and the other pallbearers took coordinated strides, carrying the casket down the aisle. As Jermaine walked he caught the eye of Buster's wife, Sasha. She looked right through him. Tears threatened to fall but Jermaine held them back because in his heart he knew that death was the one thing beyond his control, and no amount of tears could ever bring back his best friend.

Once the casket was in the back of the hearse and the door closed, Jermaine could not take anymore.

"Willie, can you get someone else to take my spot?" Jermaine asked Mrs. Dorsey's boyfriend.

"Yeah, man, you a'ight?"

"Naw, not at all. I can't watch them put him in the ground."

"I understand. You going home?"

"Yeah," Jermaine said as his voice cracked.

"J-man, at least come by the house. I know Brenda wants to see you," Willie said.

Jermaine nodded but he knew he didn't have any plans to go over to the projects where Mrs. Dorsey lived and deal with all the drunks and addicts who were sure to show up for a free meal.

Just as he was about to walk away, he saw Sasha walking his way with her eyes set on him.

"This is all your fault," she screamed.

"Sasha, calm down," Willie said as he tried to grab her arm.

"Get your hands off of me, Willie." Sasha turned to Jermaine, breathing fire. "You know, Jermaine, I begged my husband to stay away from you. I knew from the moment I met you that you were nothing but trouble, but no, he insisted on being your friend. Well, being your friend has cost him his life."

Jermaine didn't say anything, but Sasha's words cut like a sword.

"This is all your doing, Jermaine. You think I don't know what went down? I know. You're the reason that my husband is gone. It's your fault that my daughter has to grow up without her father. Jermaine, I don't wish death on anybody but I swear to God I wish that was you lying in that coffin." Sasha lunged and started swinging wildly, hitting Jermaine in the face, chest, and arms. "I hate you! I hate you, Jermaine!"

Willie had seen and heard enough. He grabbed Sasha and pulled her away. All the while she screamed, "I hate you, Jermaine. I hate you."

Jermaine stood there with his suit wrinkled and his heart beating fast. He knew he didn't deserve everything that Sasha was putting on him, but he did feel a certain responsibility for Buster's demise.

"Are you okay?" Erin asked as she walked up a second after Sasha was led away.

"Yeah," Jermaine said, still trying to figure out what had just happened to him.

"She's just grieving. She probably didn't mean any of that," Erin said, trying her best to console Jermaine.

Jermaine nodded his head and walked toward the bus stop.

"Jermaine, where are you going?"

"I took SEPTA."

"I'll give you a ride." Erin pleaded with her eyes. She wanted to be there for him.

Jermaine turned and followed her back toward the parking lot.

"How have you been?" Jermaine asked, wanting to take his mind elsewhere.

"We're okay. I haven't heard from you. I expected a call, even it was just to check on the baby."

"I'm sorry about that. I've had a lot on my mind lately. How is my little man coming along?" Jermaine said, his mind still on Sasha.

"Your daughter is doing just fine."

"Daughter, huh?"

"That's right." Erin smiled. "She's been kicking a lot lately."

Erin could see sadness written all over Jermaine's face. And even though they weren't on the best of terms, she still felt his pain.

"I think we need to talk," Erin said.

Jermaine didn't respond.

On the ride home, Jermaine stared at Erin. She was truly a beautiful woman. He had to get his mind off Buster and Sasha, so he thought of more pleasant times. Like when he'd first met Erin.

Jermaine had been sitting on a swing in the playground in the projects where they lived, reading Claude Brown's *Manchild in the Promised Land*, when Erin had walked over and snatched the book out of his hand. She read the back cover and nodded.

"How old are you?" she'd asked with her hand on her hip.

"Fifteen. Why?"

"Just asked," she'd said before handing him back his book. "Are you reading that for school?"

"No, I just like reading."

"You're weird. I never seen anybody your age read just to be reading."

"Oh," Jermaine had said, simply because he didn't know what else to say.

"May I read it when you're done?"

"Yeah. How old are you?"

"Older than you," Erin had said as she walked off.

Jermaine had wanted to ask her name but had been way too shy for that. He'd sat for a minute, staring at her slim figure until she'd disappeared around the corner of his building. He was in love. She had the prettiest, smoothest skin he'd ever seen. And there was something mesmerizing about her honey-colored eyes. He couldn't put his finger on what had happened in the short time that they had spoken that had his nose so open, but whatever it was had left him with a smile and a hard-on.

re you going home or over to Mrs. Brenda's?" Erin asked, snapping Jermaine back from memory lane.

"Home," Jermaine said.

"I know this is not a good time, but you know we need to talk, right?"

"I know."

"Jermaine, how are we going to move from here?"

"I thought you said you knew this wasn't a good time."

"Jermaine," Erin whined, as a tear made its way down her cheek, "I'm tired and I don't know what to do."

"Erin, can we talk about this later?"

"We don't talk anymore. So when do you plan on discussing this?"

"Anytime but right now."

"Why does everything always have to be on your terms?"

"Erin, please. I just buried my best friend."

"Jermaine," Erin huffed.

"What is there to talk about? You've been pretty clear about how you feel about me. And what I've come up with is that if I don't live my life the way you think I should, then we'll always have problems."

"Jermaine, I've been with you through all kinds of hell. You got another woman pregnant, been in and out of jail I don't know how many times. And for my loyalty, what have I gotten in return? Nothing," Erin said through a river of tears. "Don't I deserve more?"

Jermaine sat quietly on the passenger side of Erin's car staring out the window.

When Erin pulled up in front of Jermaine's house on the corner of Thirty-second and Diamond Street, he opened the door and got out without a word, letting Erin know she was not invited in.

Jermaine heard his front door open then close. Erin sniffled a few times, then he heard her footsteps coming toward his bedroom. She stuck her head in his bedroom.

"Jermaine, I'm sorry that things have come to this," Erin said, taking a seat beside him on his bed.

"Erin, we've been through this too many times. It's so played. Just do what you have to do," Jermaine said plainly.

"I just kept holding on, hoping you'd come around but you keep letting me down."

"Come around and do what? Be the person that you and your wannabe uppity family wants me to be? I told you a million times, if I'm not what you want then you're free to go and find it," Jermaine yelled as he stood and walked into the bathroom, slamming the door behind him.

Erin closed her eyes and ran ten fingers through her hair. She removed Jermaine's house keys from her key ring and left them on the bed.

16

What's Going On

As he drove around Philadelphia, Calvin couldn't stop thinking about the photo his father had shown him of Jermaine and his grandson. He had traveled from North Philly to South Philly to West Philly and back to North again, asking at least ten people in each area if they could help him find Jermaine, but all he got for his efforts was the runaround.

"Yeah, I know Jermaine, but how much is it worth to you?" one guy said as Calvin gave him ten dollars for what turned out to be erroneous information.

"Oh, Jermaine Banks? Yeah, he moved out to West Philly with his girlfriend," another stranger said to Calvin.

"Jermaine works at a place out in South Philly by the airport," another said.

Frustrated, Calvin pulled into a package store and purchased a fresh bottle of cognac. Just as he pulled out onto the street, his two-way pager went off.

It was a message from Kelly reminding him of a one o'clock business meeting in the Blue Cross/Blue Shield building. He looked at his watch and cringed when he realized he didn't have time for a good drink, and then he cursed himself for allowing the cravings back into his life.

An hour later, Calvin sat at his enormous conference table across from Kelly going over some last-minute details in his proposal for yet another real estate takeover. He pushed back from his large leather chair and walked over to the window overlooking the City of Brotherly Love. Calvin couldn't help but think of how far he had come, but then his guilty conscience asked him, *But at what cost?* Once again his mind drifted to Jermaine and his grandson. He shook the images from his head and tried to focus on the business at hand.

Calvin buzzed his secretary. "Sylvia, will you get that private investigator, Jacobi, on the line for me? I need to know if he has any information yet."

"I thought these guys were already willing to sell," Kelly asked.

"It's not that. This is a personal matter."

"Too personal for me to know about it?"

"We'll talk about it later," Calvin said, still staring out the window.

Jacobi was a private investigator whom Calvin used on a regular basis to find skeletons in the closets of potential sellers. A little dirt always seemed to help make their decision to sell their property to Calvin a little easier.

As he stared down at the people hurrying to their destinations, he thought about how he wanted to rebuild a relationship with his sons and his parents.

Just as Calvin turned away from the window he heard a commotion outside his office door. He saw Sylvia backing into his office as two large Italian men effortlessly pushed her tiny frame out of their paths.

"Mr. Sharpe, I tried to stop them but . . . ," Sylvia glared at the men. "Would you like for me to call the police?"

"That won't be necessary, Sylvia. Please close the door behind you," Calvin said as he stared at Bruno and Big Luckie DiBella, Mr. Newman's personal bodyguards.

"Calvin, we need a minute of your time. Would you kindly ask your guest to leave?"

"Kelly, go on to the meeting," Calvin said nervously.

"Is everything okay?" Kelly looked around anxiously.

Bruno slid Kelly's chair back and nodded toward the office door.

"I'm fine," Calvin said but his fear was obvious.

Kelly gathered her paperwork and headed out. She looked back at Calvin but he nodded his head for her to go on.

Calvin stared at the DiBella brothers. He had no idea why Mr. Newman's bodyguards were there but the thought alone caused him to shiver. Calvin moved toward his desk but stopped dead in his tracks when Big Luckie cleared his throat. That was all it took. These men had reputations of destruction. Calvin had no intentions of being added to their list of the disappeared and maimed, so he slid his hands in his pockets and waited for instructions.

Mr. Gino Newman entered the room walking with his cane and holding his hat in his hand. He was a small man with an olive complexion and he was always handsomely dressed.

"Calvin, my friend," Gino said, reaching out for an embrace. "Why do you look as if you seen a ghost?"

"Mr. Newman, I'm just surprised to see you, that's all. To what do I owe the pleasure?" Calvin stammered before taking a seat behind his desk.

"Calvin, I hate to barge in on you like this but some issues have arisen that we must deal with."

"Okay," Calvin said cautiously.

"Do you watch a lot of television? Are you a movie buff?"

"No and no," Calvin said, relaxing a little. Mr. Newman's presence meant there would be no acts of violence. He was much too smart a man to be at the scene of any crime.

"You know, a lot of people watch television and come up with all kinds of negative images of Italian people. They get all these perceptions of the so-called Mafia," Mr. Newman said, easing into a chair across from Calvin.

"Okay," Calvin said, unsure of where Mr. Newman was headed.

"Movies like *The Godfather, GoodFellas*, you know? Do you believe that's real life or Hollywood?"

"I assume it's a bit of both."

Mr. Newman smiled. "Well, the jury is still out on that one. Calvin, my friend, I've been in this wonderful country of ours for forty-five years and there's no place I'd rather be. Where else on earth could a ten-year-old immigrant boy land on the docks with only the clothes on his back and three dollars in coins and make enough money within two months to bring his mother and father from Sicily? I've lived an astonishing life, Calvin, but nothing ever came easy. My family's name is Corleone. I'm very proud of that name, but do you know what kind of weight that name carries in this country? And all because a man wrote a book that became a popular movie. When I carried my family's name, I was indicted by the federal government twenty-one times. And you thought your people had it bad. Now I want you to ask me how many times I have been convicted of any crime."

Calvin looked at him with questioning eyes.

"Not once. The boys in blue can't even make a single parking ticket stick. But I don't blame the cops. Those poor schmucks are just trying to make a living like everyone else. No, I blame that stupid idiot box and guys like you."

Calvin jerked back as if he had been slapped.

"Guys like me?"

"I was paid a visit from some of your new friends. They said some very disturbing things that could've only come from you, Calvin." Mr. Newman pointed an accusing finger at Calvin.

"Mr. Newman, I don't have any new friends. Someone is playing games with you."

"Do I look like the kind of man that people play with?"

"Do these new friends have a name?"

"They use initials. Three of them. FBI."

"Mr. Newman, you have the wrong man," Calvin said, relaxing slightly. He knew that he hadn't had any contact with anyone from the FBI, nor could he think of anything that they would want to talk to him about. He made sure that he was squeaky clean.

Mr. Newman stared hard at Calvin. He had a knack for uncovering lies.

"I'm going to take you at your word for now, but if I find out that you're double-dealing with me, then . . . well, you know the rest of that story, I'm sure." Mr. Newman stood and headed toward the door. "Calvin, it wouldn't be wise to cross me, but please try to enjoy the rest of your day."

Once Mr. Newman and his goons had cleared the office, Calvin ran to the bathroom to throw up. What in the world was happening to his life?

17

Inner-City Blues

nce Jermaine was sure that Erin had left, he came out of the bathroom and lay across his bed. A million thoughts ran through his mind, about his life, his son, his child on the way, Erin, but the most pressing thing was Sasha. Sasha's assault had taken him by surprise, but deep down he felt as if he'd got off easy. How could he ever fix that situation? He and Buster had made childhood oaths that if something happened to one of them, then the other would always take care of the other's family. But now it seemed that oath would go unfulfilled, if Sasha had anything to say about it. Jermaine rolled over onto his back and stared at the water-stained ceiling. He reached for his cordless telephone to call Sasha but stopped. Maybe now was not a good time. Maybe she needed a few more days to calm down. Just as he felt as if his head were about to explode, his telephone rang.

"Hello."

"Is this the home of Jermaine Banks?" an eager young voice said.

"Who wants to know?"

"My name is C.J. and I'm your little brother." Excitement was dripping from his voice.

"Oh yeah?" Jermaine said, smiling to himself. "How you doing, C.J. my little brother?"

"Hey, I want to meet you," C.J. said anxiously.

"I heard, but I also hear you're in the hospital, or has that changed?" Jermaine said, taking in the very proper accent of his little brother. *Must've gone to a private school,* he thought.

"Unfortunately that hasn't changed, but I still want to see you," C.J. pressed on.

"Okay, that's cool. Which hospital are you in?"

"Chestnut Hill," he said almost before Jermaine could finish asking the location.

"A'ight, I need to get out of this house anyway. Give me a few minutes to get myself together and I'll come down there and check you out. What's your room number?"

"It's 6212. Are you coming for real?" C.J. asked excitedly.

"Yeah. I'll see you in about an hour. Do you need anything?"

"Oh man. This is great. I hate to ask you for something the first time I see you, but I would sacrifice a goat for a Butterscotch Krimpet."

Jermaine chuckled. He remembered when he'd had his little spell of getting locked up once a month, a stop at the local corner store to pick up a Butterscotch Krimpet had always been his first move. "Are you supposed to have those?"

"No one told me I couldn't have any. But I'm tired of this nasty hospital food. I need something to see if my taste buds still work."

Jermaine laughed. "A'ight, my man. I'll grab you a few packs."

"Thanks."

"No problem. I'll see you in a few," Jermaine said before pausing. "Yo, is your father there? Because if he is, I'll have to catch you another time."

"No, he's not here and I'm not expecting him. As far as I'm concerned, he's not welcome."

"Okay, I'll see you in about an hour."

Jermaine hung up the phone and stood up. He tried to stretch away the stress that had been weighing him down lately. He thought about his little brother's voice and how excited he sounded. He couldn't put a finger on how he felt about these new family members, but he'd give them a shot.

He peeled away his heavily starched white shirt and black slacks and tossed them in a pile behind his bedroom door. He walked over to his closet for something a little more comfortable. After going through about ten different outfits he settled on a baby blue Phat Farm terry-cloth warm-up suit. Jermaine walked into his kitchen, did his ceremonial stomping of the roaches, and opened the cabinet.

"What the . . . ," Jermaine said, jumping back.

It was his enemy, the rat.

"How did you get yo' fat ass all the way up there?"

Jermaine eased away from the cabinet door and went to the hall closet to retrieve his Louisville Slugger. He walked back over to the cabinet and noticed the rat staring back at him, as if to say, "What do you want?"

"Oh, you ain't even trynna run, huh," Jermaine said as he commenced swinging. He swung three times, missing the rat every time. Then it went through a big hole in the back panel. "Oh, this is a joke." He frowned before slamming the cabinet door so hard that it flew right back open.

"That's it. I'm out of here. The last thing I need is for this little bastard to bite my son. Then I'll be in jail for murdering my landlord," Jermaine said to himself as he headed back to his bedroom. He threw the bat on the floor and took a seat on the bed. He rubbed his temples and took a deep breath and before he could exhale, his telephone rang again.

He looked at his caller ID and didn't recognize the name. Dana Kelly.

"Whatever you selling I ain't buying," Jermaine said, ignoring the call. But as soon as the phone finished ringing, it started up again. Jermaine reached over and grabbed the phone.

"Hello," he said with attitude.

"May I speak to Jermaine?"

"Who is this?"

"My name is Dana. Umm, we met about two weeks ago at—"

"A Brave New World. How you doin', gorgeous?" Jermaine said, smiling.

It's amazing how a beautiful woman can change your mood in a matter of seconds, he thought.

"I'm fine. How've you been?"

"Been better but it's all good."

"Man, I'm beginning to think it's me. When we met you were having problems with your girlfriend. Y'all still going at it?"

"Oh no, we're history. One of my homeboys got killed and I just left his funeral."

"I'm sorry to hear that. Should I call you another time?"

"Nah, you good. What's up?"

"I remembered you said you like poetry so I was calling to invite you out to a poetry reading tomorrow night at Gloria's."

"The last time I went to an open-mike everybody was horrible. Are you a poet?"

"I don't know if you would call me that but I do a lil something from time to time."

"You're a lawyer, right?"

"For now."

"For now?"

"Yeah. I hate my job. I did this for the prestige but I'm so over that. Life is too short to be title searching."

"I hear ya." Jermaine smiled as he thought about the chocolate-flavored sister with the mini-dreadlocks on the line. He remembered her confidence and reassuring eyes. The one thing that stuck out in his mind was what she hadn't done. She hadn't turned up her nose when he'd told her where he lived or that he didn't have a real job. But then when he hadn't heard from her in the days following their meeting, he'd chalked her up as just another cute face in the club.

"I've been thinking about you off and on since we met but I misplaced your number. I was also wondering why you haven't called."

"I didn't think a girl like you wanted a guy like me calling you. I figured you for the suit-and-tie type."

"If I didn't want you to call, I wouldn't have given you my number, my home number at that."

"True," Jermaine said with a chuckle. "I apologize."

"Don't let it happen again," Dana joked. "Or I'll have to make my dog bite you."

"What kind of dog do you have?"

"A mutt. I got him from the pound. But he's just as cute as he can be, isn't that right, Gumball?" Dana said, obviously playing with her pet. "So, you sure it's over with that girl?"

"Oh yeah."

"Good. You didn't seem all that happy with her anyway. Relationships should make you smile not cry."

"I wasn't crying."

"Not on the outside," Dana said softly.

"Where do you live?"

"Why?"

"Because I'm looking for a new place. I have a rat that's the size of a damn poodle running around here."

"Oh my God," Dana said, laughing. "That's what I like about you, Jermaine, you keep it real. Most guys would be too embarrassed to tell a woman that he had a rat in his place."

"It is what it is. It's not like I invited him in." Jermaine also laughed. "And he has a bad attitude. Just be staring at me. At least act like you scared. Jog away or something."

Dana couldn't stop laughing.

"Boy, you're crazy."

"A brother needs a new place with the quickness."

"I see. I live in the Art Museum district. Eighteenth and Spring Garden."

"How do you like it out there?"

"It's cool. Kind of artsy!" Dana chuckled.

"Man, I need to move like yesterday."

"I love house hunting, so if you need a woman's opinion on that, let me know."

"I'm going to take you up on that. Maybe you can transfer some of that good taste over to my house hunting."

"You're such a charmer. What kind of place are you looking for? I mean an apartment, town house, condo, what?"

"I don't care. Just away from here."

"I'm not a real estate agent or anything like that, but I'm sure if we put our heads together we can find you a place where you and your son will be comfortable. What was his name again?"

"Khalil." Jermaine smiled, impressed that she remembered he had a son.

"Yeah, that's right. How is he doing?"

"He's good," Jermaine said proudly. "What kind of law do you practice? And what were you doing up at the club?"

"I'm a civil rights attorney and one of my colleagues invited me out for drinks, but then he tried to get a little too familiar so I had to dismiss him, which was why I was alone when you saw me."

"I see, but you can't really blame the man, now can you? You're a good-looking woman."

"Thanks, but the feeling has to be mutual, plus I don't date where I work."

"So where is your boyfriend?"

"Out there in the universe somewhere," Dana said, laughing. "Have you had any luck with your job search?"

"Nah, not yet. I've only filled out a few applications but I'm about to get back on it. My mind has been someplace else lately."

"Wait a minute. How are you going to get an apartment without a job?"

"Money talks, or do they speak a different language out there?"

"No, it still speaks the loudest. Okay, Jermaine, when will this house hunting take place?"

"You tell me, I have nothing but time. I'm jobless, remember?"

"Well, let me get back to you. I'm wrapping up a case."

"Busy lady, huh?"

"Yes, but the case that I am working on is almost settled so now I might be able to have some kind of life. I like to get out early now. I usually hit the gym around six."

"Oh, I'm usually just going to bed around that time. But I'll adjust my schedule for you."

"Cool. It was nice talking to you, Jermaine."

"Oh, no doubt. Same here, baby, but before you go, do you know anyone that might be able to help me out with a custody case?"

"Boy, you're just making all kinds of moves, huh?"

"If you only knew."

"I could probably help you out with that but I'll tell you now, you will need to be employed. So that's the first order of business. It's pretty hard for men to get custody unless the mother is just totally unfit."

"She is."

"Well, let's take care of the job issue first, then we can move forward. Okay?"

"A'ight. Well, I'll see you tomorrow."

"Yep. That's the plan."

"Okay, take care."

"Bye, Jermaine," Dana said.

Jermaine hung up the phone. He walked into his closet and carefully moved ten size-eleven shoe boxes and peeled back his carpet. He removed the floorboard and reached his hand in the sub-flooring, feeling for his stash of money. When he felt nothing, he panicked. He stood and yanked the entire carpet from the floor. Timberland boots and Nike sneakers went flying everywhere. He reached up to his top shelf and retrieved his flashlight. With the light leading the way, Jermaine searched frantically for his stash of thirty thousand dollars in cash; when he didn't find it, his mind went directly to his uncle Herb.

"I'mma kill that nigga," Jermaine said as he threw the flashlight against the wall, smashing it into tiny pieces. He rushed back into his bedroom and threw his bed onto its side. He kneeled down and tore a piece of baseboard from the wall. He reached his hand in the wall and felt the plastic bag that contained his other stash. He quickly pulled the bag from the wall and emptied its contents. It looked to be all there but he wasn't taking any chances. He ran his fingers across the ends and flipped the stacks to make sure they weren't filled with paper only. Once he checked the authenticity of the bills, he did a quick count and realized that the entire fifty thousand dollars was still there.

Jermaine leaned against the wall to catch his breath. He reached up to his nightstand and grabbed his cordless telephone.

"Hello," Nettie answered.

"I'mma kill your brother. I let him in my crib, and he robbed me."

"What are you talking about?"

"Uncle Herb robbed me. He got me for thirty G's."

"Jermaine, I don't even want to hear that. Why do you have thirty thousand dollars in your house anyway?"

"I'm trying to make some moves and this nigga trynna keep me from making 'em."

"Jermaine, calm down. Now this may be God's way of telling you that you don't need to make those moves that you are talking about."

"You know what? I'm not even going to go there," Jermaine said, frustrated that the only thoughts his own mother could associate with him were negative.

"I haven't seen Herb, but if I do I'll talk to him."

"Nah, don't tell him a thing. He'll get the message when I put a spark to him. I'll talk to you later."

"Jermaine, don't you let Herbert get you into any trouble."

"I don't appreciate him stealing from me."

"Well, who *would* appreciate someone stealing from them, but you need to find some kind of lesson in this and move on. Herbert doesn't have anything to lose. You, on the other hand, have a son and another baby on the way. Don't you get caught up in that foolishness."

"Yeah, whatever," Jermaine said.

"Don't 'whatever' me. Let it go. Just let it go. Herbert will get his."

"That's easy for you to say. You wasn't robbed."

"You weren't either if you wanna get technical. You got that money just as illegal as Herb did."

"I gotta go."

"All right," Nettie said, having spoken her piece. "When are you getting Khalil again?"

"I don't know. Amani is acting up because I told her that I was filing for full custody."

"Oh Lord. When did this come about?"

"A few days ago. She's a dyke."

"A what?"

"A lesbian. She's bumping uglies with some bald-head joint and I don't want Khalil around that."

"My Lord. What is that girl thinking about? Hold on a minute."

"Just call me back," Jermaine said but was too slow. His mother had already clicked over to answer her other line. A few minutes later she came back to Jermaine.

"Well, that was your uncle. He said he was sorry that he had to take your money but babbled something about he was going to pay you back."

"Where is he?"

"He didn't say and my caller ID said 'out of area,' but he sounded high."

Jermaine blew out all of his frustration. "High! On what?"

"When he was in prison I know he had problems with heroin."

"This is a joke," Jermaine said, frustrated.

"Jermaine, I know you don't want to hear this right now but life is passing you by. I don't like seeing you throw your life away out there in those streets. Walk away from Herb. You'll be all right, and I know that's not all the money you have. These little stumbling blocks you're running into are just challenges to see what you're made of."

"I hear you. Now will you please let me go? I gotta go to the hospital to meet somebody."

"Bye, boy. I can't even have a heart-to-heart with you without you rushing me off the phone."

"Man, I'm too old for all that mushy mess."

"Bye, boy."

"Hey, Mom," Jermaine called out.

"What?"

"I love ya," he said, realizing it had been a while since he had said those three words to his mother.

"Now look who's getting mushy. I love you too."

ermaine called Dave.

"Yo, you remember my uncle that you met the other night?"

"Yeah, what about him?"

"I need him found with the quickness. He got me for about thirty G's and he's on heroin."

"Oh yeah, that money won't last long."

"Exactly. He's probably around one of the shoot-up spots around here."

"I'm on it. How far do you want me to take this thing?"

"As far as you need to," Jermaine said, gritting his teeth. He hated a thief. All Herb had to do was ask him for some money and Jermaine would've given it to him. Especially after what just happened to Buster.

"On second thought, that's my mother's brother, so don't go there. Just call me when you find him," Jermaine said, hanging up.

18

I'll Be Doggone

R obin sat with her legs folded under her in a recliner next to C.J.'s hospital bed. She was leafing through a two-month-old issue of *Essence* magazine when she heard a light knock on the door.

A tall, honey-brown man with cornrow braids eased his way through the door.

"Does this room belong to a guy named C.J.?"

"Yes, it does," Robin said, looking at the man strangely.

"How you doin'?" Jermaine said, walking into the room.

"I'm fine," Robin said cautiously.

"I'm his brother."

Robin wrinkled her brow. "His brother? I'm his mother," she said, looking at the man wearily.

"Okay," Jermaine said, reaching out to shake her hand. "My name is Jermaine Banks. We have the same umm . . . umm . . ." He was unable to bring himself to call Calvin his father.

"Oh Jermaine," Robin said, sucking her teeth and fanning away her momentary memory loss. She stood and reached out to hug Jermaine. "How are you doing, baby? My mind is just completely gone."

"Oh no, you're a'ight," Jermaine said, and he lightly hugged this stranger.

"It's so nice to meet you. You're like a celebrity around here."

"Is that right?"

"God, yes."

"I guess there are worse things I could be, so I'll take that," Jermaine said, walking over to his brother's bedside.

"C.J. fell asleep about an hour ago. They keep him so drugged up when he's here. I hope you can stay awhile."

"Yeah, that's no problem."

"Good, have a seat. I can't tell you how happy I am that you are here. C.J.'s been talking about you so much you'd think that you guys were long-lost identical twins."

"He seems like a cool kid." Jermaine walked over to the window. He stole a glance over at his sleeping younger brother and smiled. He had always wanted a little brother, and now that he was standing here looking at him, he didn't know what to think. "He's a good-looking youngster."

"Thank you. You guys have a lot of the same features," Robin said, marveling at their resemblance to each other.

"So what's wrong with him?" Jermaine said, finally taking a seat beside Robin.

"He has a very rare kidney disease and we're waiting on a specialist to come in from California to advise us of our options."

"I'm sorry to hear that."

"Thank you, but all we can do is pray for the best," Robin said, looking like she was about to cry.

Jermaine picked up on it and decided to change the subject.

"C.J. asked me to bring him these." Jermaine pulled out the Tasty-cakes Butterscotch Krimpet and handed them to Robin.

"Oh no, he didn't. That boy knows he's not supposed to have anything like this," Robin said, taking one of the cakes from the bag and tearing open the package.

Jermaine chuckled as Robin took a bite of the sponge cake. "Help yourself."

Robin laughed at herself and offered Jermaine a pack.

"No thanks. I ate one coming over here."

"Oh, this is good. I haven't had one of these things in ages. So, Jermaine, tell me about yourself."

"Not much to tell," Jermaine said, hunching his shoulders. "Just trynna survive. One day at a time."

"Aren't we all? So what do you do for a living?"

"Right now I'm looking for a job."

"Oh yeah. What's your field?"

"At this point anything I can get outside of a fast-food spot. I have a son and I'm trying to get custody of him but—" Jermaine caught himself. He didn't really know this woman.

"Yes, my father-in-law showed me a picture of you and your son and I must tell you that he is absolutely adorable," Robin said. "His name is Khalil, right?"

"Yep, that's my little man," Jermaine said, showing all thirty-two.

"Look at you. Such a proud daddy. That's the only way to be, Jermaine. You should be commended for taking an interest in your son's life like you do. Not enough black men feel that strongly about their kids these days, and if you ask me, it's shameful."

"You don't have to tell me."

"What kind of work are you looking for? I might be able to help," Robin said, changing the subject, realizing her conversation was headed into territory that she wasn't ready to visit.

"I don't know," Jermaine said, feeling a little awkward. "I've never really worked before."

"You've never worked? How old are you?" Robin almost screamed. She found it hard to believe that this man had lived almost thirty years and never worked. But the look on Jermaine's face told her that he didn't appreciate her judging him.

"I didn't ask for your help," Jermaine said calmly. "Who are you to sit here and look at me crazy?"

Robin averted her eyes, embarrassed that he'd read her so easily.

Jermaine stood and walked toward the door and paused, turning to face Robin. "You don't know me, lady, and maybe that's a good thing. Tell C.J. that I came by." Then he was gone.

Robin's heart pounded as Jermaine's daggerlike words pinned her to her seat and made her head swirl. She closed her eyes and took a deep breath before standing to run after him.

"Jermaine," Robin called out as he kept walking. "Jermaine. Please stop."

Jermaine stopped and slowly turned to face her.

"I'm sorry. I didn't mean you any harm."

Jermaine just stared at her with a blank expression on his face.

"I'm a mother and my first instinct is to help ease whatever pain my child is in. That's just the way I am."

"But you're not my mother," Jermaine growled.

"I know, and I apologize if I crossed the line. I'll admit sometimes I speak before I think, and for that I'm sorry."

"It's no problem," Jermaine said and continued walking toward the exit.

"You said you could stick around for C.J.," Robin said desperately.

"I think I'll scratch this little family meeting. Tell C.J. to hang on in there."

Jermaine kept walking but Robin wouldn't be denied. "Wait, please wait," she said, running after him. She grabbed his arm tight. Tight enough to let Jermaine know that she wasn't letting go until she was heard. "Maybe we can start over," Robin said, extending her hand. "I'm Robin, C.J.'s mother."

Jermaine stared at her hand, sighed, and shook his head.

"Why are you trying so hard, lady?"

"Because you're family."

"Family? It takes a little more than biology to use that term with me."

"We all really want to be a part of your life. Even if it's just as a friend. I promise I won't ever judge you again," Robin said, rubbing her hands together nervously.

"If what my new grandfather said is true, you guys didn't even know I existed. I'm sure y'all will get over the newness. Besides, you can't miss what you never had."

"I knew," Robin said shamefully.

Jermaine could see the regret in Robin's eyes. "It's all good, lady, take care," he said, walking off again.

"Look, you've been out of everyone's life for far too long and all because your father is a first-class asshole, but please don't make your little brother and your grandparents suffer any longer. All they want is your company. That's all. To get to know you. I'm begging you, please don't walk away," Robin said, walking beside Jermaine.

Jermaine stopped and stared at Robin strangely. He was trying hard to find something in her eyes that would allow him to hate her and be done with this whole get-together, but he found nothing but compassion, desperation, the look of a woman who seemed genuinely concerned about him.

"Okay, Mrs. Lady," Jermaine said, extending his hand. "You win."

Robin couldn't contain her excitement; she almost jumped into his arms. The last thing she ever wanted to do was be the cause of Jermaine not being a part of their lives again. "Thank you, thank you, thank you. You are a good man," she said, still hugging Jermaine's neck.

"I don't know about all that."

"Oh, but you are. You don't owe any of us a thing. It's us that owe you, but you've found it in your heart to stay and that says a lot about you."

"If you say so. But now I have a question for you. What's a nice woman like you doing with a dude like my . . . umm, I don't even know what to call him . . . Calvin."

"Now you're asking questions that only God could answer, but one day maybe we'll talk about it."

Robin returned to C.J.'s room with Jermaine on her heels.

C.J. was awake. His eyes grew wide and full of life when he saw his brother for the first time. "Hey, big bro," C.J. said, smiling.

"How did you know this was me?" Jermaine said, smiling down at his younger sibling.

"Brother's intuition."

"Is that right?" Jermaine walked over and shook C.J.'s hand.

"How long you been here?"

"Not long. How you holdin' up?"

C.J. placed his other hand on Jermaine's; he was all smiles.

"I feel like crap," C.J. said.

"C.J. Watch your mouth," Robin admonished.

"Sorry, Mom, but I do," C.J. said, frowning before turning back to Jermaine. "I'm glad you made it. You look just like me except you got braids."

"Nah, you look like me. Let's not forget who's the oldest here."

"Hey, did you bring my Tastycakes?"

"I don't know why you had Jermaine waste his money on those things. You know you can't have stuff like that," Robin piped in.

"Mom, do you have anything else you need to do?"

"Oh, excuse me. I'll leave you two gentlemen to your male bonding or whatever it is that you do," Robin said, shaking her head and gathering her magazines before exiting the room.

"I hate for our first meeting to be like this, Jermaine," C.J. said. "You know, with me being all laid up in the hospital."

"I'm sure you didn't plan to be here. It's all good."

"You play tennis?"

"Nah, brah, ain't no tennis courts where I'm from."

"Are you from the ghetto?" C.J. asked with amazement.

"You could call it that."

"Cool," C.J. said.

"I don't know what's so cool about it. It's kind of messed up if you ask me."

"Will you take me over there sometime?"

"Yeah," Jermaine said, looking at his brother strangely.

"I mean, I've seen the inner city before. Just not up close and personal."

"You ain't missing a thing. Where do you live?"

"Gladwyne! We're two properties over from Allen Iverson. He gets a bad rap. Actually, he's a pretty cool guy."

"Oh yeah?" Jermaine said. "So are you any good with that tennis racket?"

"Pretty good. I'm the number-two player in the state right now."

"Sounds like more than pretty good. Maybe you can hook me up with Serena Williams one day."

"You like her?" C.J. said, frowning. "I'm more of an Anna Kournikova fan."

"Who is that?"

"You don't know her? She's only on every magazine cover every month. She's beautiful."

"I'm not really a tennis fan, but I do watch when Serena's playing. I keep waiting on one of those little tight shirts to pop open."

C.J. cracked up laughing. "Man, you're crazy. Do you golf?"

"No sir," Jermaine said.

"Oh man, I'll show you how to play. You'll love it."

"If you say so. It just doesn't seem all that sporty to me."

"I won't even ask about lacrosse."

"Don't. I don't even know what that looks like."

"I'm really not into it that heavy yet. Tennis is my sport."

"I'm going to have to come and check you out sometime."

"Yeah, if I can get my kidney to act right. This is a real crappy time for me to get sick. I have a match on Friday and if I don't play, I lose my ranking."

"Tennis ain't going nowhere. Don't you think you need to focus on your health right now, little soldier?"

"I guess you're right."

Jermaine smiled at his little brother's easygoing persona and was about to take a seat when the door swung open and in walked Louis Sharpe and a very pretty older woman.

"Hey there, big man," Louis said, surprised to see Jermaine as he walked over to him and shook his hand.

"Oh my God," Edna said, losing the fight with her tears as she ran over and grabbed Jermaine before being properly introduced.

Jermaine smiled. "I guess you would be my grandmother."

"Oh my God, I can't believe this. You are beautiful," Edna said, finally releasing her grandson, holding him at arm's length to get a better look at him. "My name is Edna Sharpe but please call me Grandma. That's if you don't mind."

"I don't mind at all, Grandma," Jermaine said with a smile that caused Edna to cover her face again with both hands, trying to stop the tears.

Damn, these are some affectionate people, Jermaine thought.

"So how you holding up, Jermaine?" Louis asked.

"I'm making it. How's everything with you?"

"Oh, couldn't be better. I got my two boys here with me. What more could an old man ask for? C.J. you doin' all right?"

"Yes sir," C.J. replied.

There was a knock on the door before it swung open. In walked a white-haired doctor carrying a clipboard and a stack of folders.

"Dr. Talmage," the man said, extending his hand to no one in particular. "I'm the specialist that will be taking care of this young man from this point on."

"Louis Sharpe," Louis said, shaking the doctor's hand.

"Are you the patient's father?"

"No, I'm his grandfather."

"Are you his legal guardian?"

"No, but let me try to find his mother for you," Louis said.

"Thank you," Dr. Talmage said as he walked over and checked C.J.'s vitals.

"C.J., I'll be right back," Louis said. "Jermaine, don't you run off now."

"I do have to run. I have a few things I need to take care of, but I'll stop by tomorrow and I'll try to bring my son for y'all to meet."

"I got a nephew?" C.J. said excitedly.

"Yeah, and he *thinks* he can play basketball," Jermaine joked.

"That's so cool. Are you sure you have to leave?"

"Yeah, I do, but I'll be back tomorrow."

"So soon? But we just got here," Edna said, still crying.

"I'll try to make it back up here tomorrow about this same time, but if not I'll definitely make it tomorrow night," Jermaine said as he reached out to hug his grandmother.

"Oh," Edna said, closing her eyes and hugging Jermaine. "I understand you're probably busy. I'm so happy to see you and please try to bring my great-grand with you."

"No problem, Grandma." Jermaine smiled as the title came out easier than he expected. "And it was nice meeting you. I'm sorry I gotta rush off like this, but I really gotta take care of some business."

"I understand. But please come back tomorrow."

"That's a promise," Jermaine said before saying his good-byes.

"Jermaine, I'll walk you out and I'll find his mother for you, Doc," Louis said.

As Jermaine and Louis walked out to the parking lot, they noticed a rough-looking man walking toward them. Louis stopped and stiffened. His face read shock and disappointment. *What the hell has happened to him?* Louis thought. *He looks like a homeless person.*

"Not now, Dad," Calvin said as he raced by his father, hoping Louis wouldn't smell the alcohol on his breath. He hurried into the hospital without looking back.

"Dad?" Jermaine said. "I guess that was Calvin, huh?"

"Unfortunately," Louis said, staring at Calvin's back as he disappeared through the hospital's glass doors.

Life Is a Gamble

Calvin stood by the picture window in an expensive hotel room overlooking downtown Philadelphia. He held a bottle of cognac in one hand and a .38 revolver in his other.

He took a long swig from the bottle and steadied his hand long enough to place the gun to his temple. He took what was to be his final breath.

"Awwww," he screamed, squeezing his eyes shut before pulling the trigger.

Click! The hammer hit the empty cylinder of the rusty gun he'd purchased off the street for fifteen dollars.

Fear and anxiety overwhelmed him as he dropped the firearm and collapsed to the floor. He rolled over on his hands and knees and tried to breathe deeply. His arms could barely hold his body weight, so he rolled onto his back and tried again to regain control. His hands wouldn't stop shaking.

Calvin got it together long enough to stand and run to the bathroom and throw his head in the toilet. He held on to the porcelain god as he threw up the expensive steak dinner he had ordered from room service. His heart felt like it was beating outside of his chest.

There was only one bullet in his gun and he figured it was only a matter of time before the one round that he had placed in the cylinder would make its way to the chamber, and he would no longer be guilt-ridden but in a safe place where he would not be judged. Calvin fought back the tears as he replayed the day over and over in his head.

After his meeting with Mr. Newman, Calvin made it to the IBC building on Nineteenth and Market Street, parked, and ran inside. He hurried over to the elevators and stabbed the "up" arrow and paced back and forth as he listened to the dings and watched as the highlighted numbers made their slow descent. He looked at his watch and realized that he was twenty-three minutes late for what had turned into the meeting that would give Jermaine his first piece of real estate.

Calvin had decided that he would put Jermaine's name down as the official purchaser of the deed to the half-million-dollar property. He knew that the gesture could never make up for what he had done, but it was the least he could do. Robin and C.J. would be set for life if something were to ever happen to him, and he figured Jermaine had been left out of the fold for far too long.

Calvin couldn't wait another second so he ran toward the back of the building and hit the stairwell running.

His meeting was on the tenth floor and he was already breathing hard, even though he'd just cleared the fifth level. He paused to catch his breath and made a silent promise to himself that he would no longer let his gym membership go to waste. He continued running until he reached the tenth floor, then he leaned his back against the door until his breathing returned to normal.

Just as he caught his wind he heard a commanding voice telling someone to keep their hands behind their heads. Calvin eased open the heavy door and saw two men in suits being led down the hall in handcuffs by two more men in navy blue windbreakers with the letters "FBI" stenciled across their backs in bright yellow. There were a few news cameras in the hallway. Then he remembered Mr. Newman saying he'd been visited by the FBI, so Calvin closed the door softly and ran up ten more flights of stairs. This time, adrenaline forced all fatigue out of his mind. He stopped when he reached the top of the building and opened the door leading to the rooftop.

Calvin walked over to the ledge overlooking the parking lot and noticed several FBI agents walking around his car. They were talking on handheld radios and looking around, obviously for him. But what did they want? he wondered. Calvin waited until the men had left, then pulled out his cell phone and called Kelly. She answered after a few rings.

"Hello," Kelly said.

"How are you?"

"Just waiting on you. Where are you?" Kelly tried to sound normal but there was an obvious uneasiness in her voice. Calvin picked up on it.

"I'm running a little late. Is everything all right?" Calvin said, still trying to figure out what was going on.

"Sure, we're just waiting on you. Everything is in place."

"Okay, I'll see you shortly."

"Are you in the building?"

"I'm about fifteen minutes away," Calvin said, closing his cellular phone.

All of a sudden things became crystal clear. Kelly was trying to set him up. He remembered the look on her face when he told her about divorcing Robin. Something wasn't right. Calvin eased back away from the ledge.

What in the hell is going on? Think fast.

He removed his suit coat, tie, and then his crisp white button-down until all he wore was an undershirt, slacks, and shoes. Calvin ripped the sleeves off his custom-made dress shirt and wiped them along the smut-covered poles that were protruding out of the building and washed his face with it.

He walked around until he found some black tar, then reached down and grabbed a fingerload and ran it across his teeth. The taste was almost unbearable but he just frowned and dealt with it. Next Calvin removed his seven-hundred-dollar shoes and turned them over so that he could scuff the soft leather against the hard rooftop. They had to look old and tattered, so he scuffed some more until there was a hole in the top sole. His heart was beating on overdrive and he was moving at a breakneck pace. Next came his pants. He turned them inside out and put them back on. He slid his feet back in his shoes and looked down at himself. In a matter of minutes he had transformed himself from a good-looking CEO of a Fortune 500 company to an undesirable homeless man who had seen better days.

Satisfied with his new appearance, Calvin walked back over to the ledge and peered down. The agents were still out in force. He heard his cell phone ringing and answered on the first ring.

"Hello," Calvin said.

"Calvin, this is Solomon. We've got trouble," Calvin's lawyer said in a hurried tone.

"I know, but you wanna tell me what's going on?"

"The FBI has a warrant for your arrest."

"For what?"

"I'd rather not speak about this over the phone. Now, I've arranged a time for you to turn yourself in but—"

"Wait just a goddamn minute. What is all this about?"

"Calvin, they have a laundry list. Improper accounting procedures, securities fraud, and tax evasion are the ones that we'll have trouble with! Everything else they added is just to make it look good in the media."

Media? Calvin's mind went straight to his mother and what she would think seeing her son paraded in front of CNN's news cameras in handcuffs. That would never happen, he told himself.

"Now keep in mind this is nothing that I can't handle. Ever since investors started losing their shirts, the feds feel like they need to do some spin control and haul in a few CEOs for their dog-and-pony show. I've already filed most of the paperwork to make this thing go away but—"

"I have to go. I'll call you later." Calvin hung up without waiting to hear whatever his lawyer had to say.

He walked over to the roof door leading to the stairwell and eased his way down the stairs and out the service exit.

As soon as he turned the corner he was met by a tall blond man wearing one of those blue windbreakers. The man took one look and kept walking but another man kept staring. Calvin nodded then flashed a rotten-tooth smile. "Do you have any loose change?" he asked the man in a groggy voice.

The agent frowned, shook his head. "Get a fuckin' job," he said before hurrying down the sidewalk.

Calvin closed his eyes and blew out a week's worth of frustration. He was still a free man, for now.

Calvin got up off his knees and took a seat on the side of the bed. He pulled out his wallet and removed two pictures, one old and one in fairly good condition. The old one was a picture of Jermaine when he was about seven years old; the other was C.J. in his tennis outfit.

"I never meant for our lives to be this way, Jermaine," Calvin said as a tear made its way down his cheek and fell onto the picture. He quickly wiped the picture clean. "You are my own blood, for God's sake, but time just kept on ticking and before long there was no turning back," he said as he opened the cylinder of the gun and checked to make sure the bullet was still there.

"C.J., I'm not worried about you, you're already a man. More man than I'll ever be." Calvin closed the gun's cylinder and placed the barrel in his mouth but stopped when he visualized himself slouched over in the hotel bed with his brains splattered all over the wall. His palms began to sweat and his stomach felt queasy. He quickly removed the gun from his mouth and ran to the closet for a fresh suit.

Calvin grabbed his cell phone and called his lawyer back.

"Solomon Dash."

"Solomon, this is Calvin Sharpe."

"Calvin, where are you?"

"How do you think this whole thing will pan out?" Calvin said, skipping the formalities. "Be straight with me. No BS."

Solomon took a deep breath before speaking. "Well, Calvin, I can take care of most of these charges. The tax evasion will only carry the actual taxes, a fine, and a few penalties; the improper accounting procedure might be a little tricky, but the real problem is the securities fraud. That could bring some prison time. But you need to come down to my office so we can turn you in, man. The quicker you do that, the sooner we can get this thing behind us," he pleaded.

"Will they offer bail?"

"Yeah, but it's going to be high. You are looking at around ten million dollars. And they've frozen your assets so it can't come from you. Do you have any friends with that kind of money who would be willing to help you out?"

"I don't know. I've never been in this situation before."

"Calvin, I'm going to do the best I can for you on this but you really need to turn yourself in."

"I will but not right now. I have to take care of some personal matters first."

20

Deep

Beep. Beep. Beep. Beeeeeeeeeeeeeep.

Jermaine opened his eyes and stared at the clock as if it were a foreign object. He reached over and hit the snooze button. Fifteen minutes later it went off again.

Beep. Beep. Beep. Beeeeeeeeeeeeeep.

This time Jermaine reached over to his nightstand, grabbed the clock, and threw it against the wall, forever silencing the electronic interrupter of his nasty dream with Janet Jackson. But the flying clock hit a framed picture, crashing it to the hardwood floor and breaking the glass.

"Awwww, damn," Jermaine said as threw the covers off and sat up. "Janet was just about to get on top," he said as he switched on the table lamp.

He turned and looked into a pair of eyes that were looking at him as if he were crazy.

"Who is Janet?"

"It's time to get up," Jermaine said before standing and dragging himself to the bathroom.

The bathroom door crept open while he was relieving himself of his morning water.

"Uh-oh," Jermaine said, squeezing his stomach muscles, trying hard to empty his bladder but to no avail. Khalil was already on him and aiming in every direction except the toilet bowl. Jermaine jumped back, causing his own water to hit the back of the seat.

"Hey, hey! Watch out, man." Jermaine frowned. "Augh, I *hate* when you pee on me."

"You peed on me too," Khalil said, looking up at his father with innocent eyes.

"That's cuz I was trying to move out of the way of your pee."

"Sorry, Daddy."

"Yeah, you gonna be sorry if you don't learn how to control your little dick. Now take off those pissy draws so you can get in the shower."

"Where we going?" Khalil asked, stepping out of his underwear.

"You're going to day care and I'm going to a job interview. Now let's get a move on, youngsta."

After they showered, Jermaine got Khalil dressed. His mind flashed back to yesterday, when his father had walked right past him without even recognizing him. Even though he really hadn't expected Calvin to know him, it bothered him. Jermaine shook the thought from his head and flicked on the television to keep Khalil occupied while he got himself dressed.

He walked to his closet and grabbed the Italian navy blue suit that he'd purchased yesterday from some guy selling them out of the back of a van. After dressing he walked over to his wall-length mirror and frowned at his own reflection.

"Daddy, can I get a haircut like yours?"

"Why? I like your braids."

"But I want to look like you."

"Man, *I* don't even wanna look like me," Jermaine said as he ran his hand across his new, very short, conservative style. "If I didn't have to get a job, I definitely wouldn't be sporting the supernerd look."

"So can I get one?"

"If you want one."

"Yeaah." Khalil pumped his fist before turning back to the cartoons.

Jermaine paused and watched his son. The little guy loved him. Now all Jermaine had to do was not let him down.

"Come on, lil fella. Let's eat."

Jermaine walked into the kitchen and turned the light switch on, saw the roaches scatter, and turned it right back off.

"We're doin' McDonald's."

The telephone rang and Jermaine walked over to check the caller ID. It was Erin calling from her cell phone. They hadn't spoken in a little over a week. He let the call go to his voice mail and grabbed Khalil's book bag.

Jermaine decided he'd call Erin after his job interview. Whatever she wanted, which was probably nothing, could wait.

Jermaine and his son ate a drive-through breakfast before pulling up to Khalil's day care.

"A'ight, lil man. No fighting today. If that teacher tells me that you raised your hand one time, I'm spanking that lil butt. Comprende?"

"I thought you told me I could punch 'em in the lip," Khalil said, making a fist.

"I know what I said, but now I'm saying no fighting. Got that? Now give me a hug."

"Okay," Khalil said as he reached over and gave his daddy a tight hug.

Just as Khalil got out of the car he was met by Mrs. Jackson, the day care's director.

"Mr. Banks, may I have a minute of your time?" she asked, holding Khalil's hand and leaning into the window.

"What's up?"

"Khalil's day care fees haven't been paid in two months. Now I understand how finances can get sometimes, but we can't keep doing this month after month."

"Month after month?" Jermaine asked, perplexed. "How much is it?"

Mrs. Jackson handed Jermaine a printout. Khalil's bill was a little over eight hundred dollars.

"Okay, I don't have this money on me but I could bring it back to you around noon," Jermaine said, wondering what Amani was doing with the thousand dollars he was giving her every month.

"I'm sorry, Mr. Banks, but we can't keep him until the bill is paid," Mrs. Jackson said, as if she'd heard this line too many times.

"You kidding me? I have a job interview in fifteen minutes. I don't have time to take him to my mother's. Can you please do me this favor? I promise you I'll have his bill caught up before twelve o'clock today."

"I'm sorry Mr. Banks, but we have rules," Mrs. Jackson said, opening the SUV's door for Khalil to climb in.

"Damn," Jermaine said, his mind racing, trying to think of someplace he could take Khalil.

"Mr. Banks, I'm really sorry, but this is the third time you guys have been two months past due. We can't operate a business like that."

"Okay, from now on I want the bill sent to me."

"That's fine. And again, I'm sorry," Mrs. Jackson said, walking back toward the facility.

Ten minutes later, Jermaine and Khalil arrived at the twenty-story mirrored-glass building in downtown Philadelphia where Pace Financial conducted their business. He walked up to the receptionist and was greeted by a cute sister with dreads and a pretty smile.

"How you doin'? My name is Jermaine Banks and I'm here to see Semi Nible about a collections position."

"Was it automobile collections?"

"I think so," Jermaine said to the smiling lady.

"I'm Carla. How are you doing this morning? And who might this cute little fella be?"

"This is my son, Khalil. I know I'm not supposed to bring him here but his mom didn't pay his day care bill and I just found out about it when I tried to drop him off, and by that time it was too late to find someone to watch him. I need this job so I couldn't be late."

"Hey, calm down. Things happen. Let me call my girlfriend and see if she can watch him right quick. You don't want Mr. Nible to find out you brought your child in here. We have arguments all the time about the differences between Africans and African-Americans. He thinks we're always up to some kind of scheme. I think they're all arrogant and full of it. But you didn't hear that from me." Carla winked as she dialed a few numbers then spoke into her headset.

A few minutes later a familiar brown-skinned sister walked in. She wore a nicely fitted business suit. It was Dana.

"Why, hello there, little guy," Dana said as she leaned down to speak with Khalil.

"Hello to you, Mrs. Lady," Jermaine said.

Dana looked up and squinted her eyes. She put her hand over her face to hide her embarrassment. "I didn't recognize you with all your hair gone."

"I take it you two know each other?" said Carla.

"Yes, this is the guy I was telling you about," Dana said, giving Carla some kind of homegirl eye contact.

"Ohhhh," Carla said, nodding her approval.

"What are you doing here?" Dana asked.

"Job interview."

"You weren't playing, huh? Let me give you a bit of advice. You need to get a sitter the next time you go on an interview," Dana whispered, as if she were giving away some great big secret.

"I know that; this was out of my control. His mother didn't pay—"

"I'm just kidding. Carla already told me," Dana said, waving Jermaine down. "This cute fella must be Khalil?"

"Hi," Khalil said, smiling.

"Khalil, do you want to go back to my office with me? I have television in there and you can watch cartoons."

"Daddy, can I go with her?"

"You have no choice," Jermaine said, smiling. "Thanks, Dana."

"No problem. Carla will show you where we are when you're done. Smooches." Dana waved and she was gone.

Jermaine watched as Dana's long and shapely figure made its way through the glass doors, holding Khalil's hand.

"Small world, huh," Carla said. "She was telling me how fine you were. I just don't see it," she joked.

"Hey, leave me alone."

"Here, fill out this information so that we can get you drug-tested." Carla smiled and asked Jermaine with her eyes if he thought that he'd pass the test.

"Oh, I'm straight," Jermaine said.

Carla smiled. "This company doesn't pay that much but the benefits package is unbelievable. And being that I have two little ones, I need the insurance a little more right now."

"I hear you."

"Go ahead and have a seat and Mr. Nible will be with you in a minute."

Jermaine did so, and filled out the drug-test request form. His cell rang and just as he was about to answer, he heard his name being called by a tall dark-skinned man with distinct African features. He sent the call to his voice mail and turned the phone off. Jermaine stood and followed the man back into his office.

"Have a seat," Mr. Nible said with a slight African accent as he sat down behind his large glass desk. "So this is your first job?"

"You can say that."

"Were you in school?"

"No, I was in my family's business."

"What kind of business is that?"

"Construction," Jermaine lied.

"So have you ever done collections before?"

"I think we all have at one point and time."

Mr. Nible smiled.

"Have you ever done formal collections before?"

"No, I haven't, but with some training I feel I can do a good job for you," Jermaine said confidently, but inside he felt like he was begging and he knew that if he got this job, it would be strictly temporary. But for now he silently told himself to do what he needed to do to get the job. Khalil's custody depended on it.

"I'm sure you will. Now, Jermaine, are you willing to stay late if you have to?"

"That wouldn't be a problem."

"Okay, I'm not going to drag this out. We need to fill a position and you need a job. So, pending a clean drug test, you have a job. There will be a thirty-day probation period. If you're late for any reason other than things beyond your control, you'll be terminated. After thirty days your work will be evaluated and you will either be offered a permanent position or given one last chance at another thirty days to prove yourself. It's pretty demanding work and it's not for everyone. If you have any problems I have an open-door policy.

Work hours are from eight to five with an hour lunch break and two fifteen-minute breaks. That's it. Any questions, concerns, or comments?"

"When do I start?"

"Drug-test results normally take a few days to come back. If there are no problems, then I'll see you bright and early on Monday. Dress code is business casual. Similar to what I'm wearing," Mr. Nible said as he stood and modeled his polo shirt and khakis.

"Carla will show you where you need to go for your test. Good luck." Mr. Nible walked around his desk and reached out to shake Jermaine's hand.

"Thanks a lot. I appreciate the opportunity," Jermaine said, reciprocating the handshake.

"Good enough," Mr. Nible said, walking Jermaine to the door.

They only give these tests to the brothers," Carla whispered to Jermaine as she handed him a pass that looked like a credit card.

"Hey, I need a job. I don't care about the politics right now."

"Just letting you know. After you're done there, come on back down here and I'll show you where Dana's office is."

"When do you think I'll hear something?" Jermaine said, all of a sudden getting paranoid. He was thinking about the many times he'd been around his friends, inhaling secondhand marijuana smoke.

"Could be as soon as this afternoon. You want me to call you when they come in?"

"Oh yeah." Jermaine wrote his number on a Post-it. "Call me on my cell."

"You better be glad Dana done snatched you up or I would use this number myself," Carla flirted.

"I thought you said I was ugly."

"You are."

"Whatever." Jermaine smiled at his new friend. "Yo, it was nice meeting you, Carla." He reached across the desk and shook her hand.

"You too, Jermaine. So I'll be seeing you around, right?" she asked as she raised her eyebrows and pointed at the drug-testing form.

"No doubt."

Jermaine went up to the third floor and gave a man, wearing eyeliner, lip liner, and something red on his cheeks, his form.

"I'm here for a drug test."

"What company?" Mr. Lady said in a high-pitched voice.

"Pace Financial."

"Oh, I work there part-time."

"Good."

"Will you be working day or night?"

"Don't know."

"Well, I know the girls in the office will be happy to see you coming," Mr. Lady said, handing Jermaine a small plastic bottle. "And some of the guys," he whispered under his breath.

"What was that?"

"Nothing. You'll have to wait until the supervisor gets back. He'll have to monitor you."

"Monitor me?"

"Yes, honey. Guys be coming in here using their three- and four-year-old-kids' urine. They keep it in travel lotion bottles and condoms and things," Mr. Lady said, shaking his head.

"That's a little too much information for me."

"But you look like a nice, clean-cut guy, so I'll give you a break. Use that bathroom right there."

Jermaine completed his test and made a quick exit. He caught the elevator back down and, after finding Carla away from her desk, searched the hallway until he found a sign for Dana's office.

"I'm here to see Dana Kelly," Jermaine said to the stranger sitting behind a desk.

"We have two of them."

"Two Dana Kellys? The one I'm talking about was with a little boy about this high." Jermaine held his hand right at his waist.

"Dana Kelly the attorney. I'll ring her."

A few minutes later, Jermaine walked into Dana's spacious office. Khalil was playing on the floor with a couple of silver balls.

"Hey, thanks for watching my little man for me. I think you helped me get a job."

"You got it?" Dana asked, as if she was happier than Jermaine.

"I think so. Gotta wait on the drug test."

"Oh, is that going to be a problem?"

"Nah, it shouldn't be," Jermaine said, turning his attention to his son. "Hey, man, did you talk Miss Dana's ear off?"

"No, he was great. Isn't that right, Khalil?"

"Yes," Khalil said without looking up from the balls.

Jermaine's cell phone rang. He didn't recognize the number so he sent it to his voice mail.

"We've held you up long enough. Thanks again for watching my little man for me. I'll give you a call tonight."

"I'll be waiting by the phone," Dana said, reaching over to give Jermaine a quick hug.

Once he was outside the building, Jermaine grabbed his cell phone to see whose call he'd missed. He didn't recognize the number so he pushed "redial."

"Hello, did somebody call Jermaine?"

"Jermaine, get yo' ass down here right now. Erin having complications with the baby," Roscoe yelled.

"Where y'all at?"

"Germantown Memorial."

"I'm on my way," Jermaine said as he hung up the phone.

As Jermaine drove down Broad Street, he caught sight of a man who looked just like his uncle Herb. He squinted his eyes and once his suspicions were confirmed, he whipped his truck around and pulled up on the curve and slammed on the brakes. Herb took off running. Jermaine opened his door and reached under his seat for his Glock .40 handgun. He rested his arm on the hood of his truck and aimed at Herb's back. Just as he was about to pull the trigger, something held him back. He cursed whatever it was that kept him from shooting his thieving uncle and got back in his SUV.

"Daddy, what are you doing?" Khalil asked.

"Nothing. I thought I knew that guy," Jermaine said, trying to conceal the weapon from his son as he got back in his truck.

Jermaine sat still for a few minutes trying to let his anger subside. Then he heard his mother's words.

Leave that foolishness alone.

21

Sick and Tired

Jermaine dropped Khalil off at his mother's house and headed straight to the hospital to check on Erin. He didn't miss her or her drama in the least, but he hoped she was all right.

At the reception area, Jermaine was told that Erin was on the third floor in room 3622. When he walked into the room, to his surprise, he saw some light-skinned guy in wire-rimmed glasses standing beside Erin's bed. He was rubbing her forehead.

"What's up?" Jermaine said, nodding at Erin.

"Nothing," Erin said as she shifted her weight, giving away her discomfort at being caught between her past and present.

"I see," Jermaine said, moving his gaze to the new guy. "Will you excuse us for a minute, homie?"

"I'm not your homie," Glasses said, with all the nerd attitude he could muster.

Jermaine smiled. "Erin, will you ask your friend to give us a minute, please?"

"You don't scare me."

Jermaine looked surprised at his comment. *What has Erin been telling this guy?* he thought.

"I'm not trying to scare you. I'm just trying to get a minute alone with the mother of my child. Do you mind?"

"She doesn't want to talk to you," Glasses said, still rubbing Erin's head.

"Listen, man. I'm not here for any trouble. Now I've asked you nicely, will you give us a minute?"

"No," Glasses said, standing his ground.

"Man, get your ass out of here before I crack those fuckin' glasses," Jermaine barked, losing his battle with politeness.

"Wait a minute," Erin said, pulling herself up in the bed. She knew Jermaine couldn't play the cool role for long. "Pembrook, will you give us a minute."

"Pembrook! What kind of name is that for a brother?" Jermaine said.

"Erin, I'm not afraid of him. I can protect you."

Jermaine dropped his head, laughing.

"It's okay, honey. I'll be fine," Erin said, rubbing Pembrook's hand.

"Yeah, she'll be fine," Jermaine said, still laughing.

"Don't underestimate me. You thug," Pembrook said.

"Yeah, I'm sure you're a fantastic fighter. Now get the hell out," Jermaine said with a straight face.

Pembrook stared at Jermaine as he walked by. "Honey, if you need me I'll be right outside the door."

Jermaine flinched at him and Pembrook almost stumbled over himself trying to cover up. Jermaine laughed as Bill Gates's black twin hurried out the door.

"He walks like something's stuck in his butt."

"Jermaine, please," Erin said, trying to hold back her laughter.

"'I can protect you, honey,'" Jermaine mocked Pembrook. "So that's your new man?"

"No, he's just a friend."

"Looks like more than that to me, but hey, who am I? Y'all make a good pair, just perfect for each other."

"What do you mean by that, Jermaine?"

"That's who you wanted me to be."

"That's not true, but he's nice. And he treats me good *and* he has a career."

"Whupdie-damn-do."

"Are you jealous?"

"Please, you giving yourself too much credit."

Erin sighed. "What's with the haircut and suit? You look nice," she said.

"Yeah, I got a job with Pace Financial so you know I got to play the corporate game for a minute," Jermaine said as he took a seat on the edge of the bed.

"Job? Maybe you're the one that needs to be in this bed. Are you okay?" Erin reached up to feel Jermaine's head.

"Stop playing."

"Man, you look about ten years younger with your hair like that."

"You like it?"

"Yeah, you look good. How long have I been asking you to get a haircut?"

"I'm sorta immune to the things you wanna change about me now."

"Why is that?"

"Because that's all you ever try to do."

"That's not true."

"Whatever. You don't look bad yourself."

"You're crazy, I'm fat."

"Nah, you're just glowing."

"Yeah, okay!"

They sat in silence for a few seconds then Erin spoke: "Jermaine, I'm scared. I've been throwing up and bleeding a lot."

"Bleeding?" Jermaine said with a frown. "How long has this been going on?"

"A few weeks."

"And you're just getting around to coming to the doctor? What's up with that?"

"I thought it would pass. I called the midwife and she told me that some discharge was normal and we all know that everybody throws up when they're pregnant. So I didn't think too much of it."

"Well, what are these doctors saying?"

"They ran some tests so now we wait."

"Well, a'ight. How long have you been here?"

"A few hours. I called you this morning before I left my house but I got your machine. I guess you were at work," Erin said as she started to cry.

"Don't worry about it," Jermaine said, now feeling guilty about ignoring her calls and all the negative thoughts he had been having about her.

Just then Erin's mother walked in.

"What are you doing here?" she said to Jermaine, her voice heavy with disgust.

"What?" Jermaine asked wearily.

"I said what are you doing here?"

"Mom, not now," Erin pleaded.

"Hush, Erin. I want to know what hole he crawled out of," Mrs. Jones said with her hands on her hips.

"Erin, I'mma wait out in the lobby. I'll check back with you in a few." Jermaine got up to leave.

"No, you can leave the hospital. You think just because you put on a suit and cut your hair you can come in here and win Erin back?"

Jermaine just stared at her, his anger building by the second.

"We'll take care of Erin. That's what we've been doing. Your shiftless behind can't even pick up the telephone to see how she's doing."

"I'm here."

"Not for long. Get out."

"Go to hell, Mrs. Jones," Jermaine said, finally fed up with Erin's mother's obnoxious ways.

"Jermaine!" Erin yelled.

"What did you say to me?"

Jermaine stood and walked toward the door, trying his best to ignore the almighty Mrs. Jones.

"Erin, I'll be in the waiting area."

Mrs. Jones blocked his path. "No, you won't," she spat. "You will leave this hospital or I'll have my husband place you under arrest. I'm sure there's an outstanding warrant out on you for something."

Jermaine looked at Erin, who shook her head no. But he couldn't hold it in anymore. After all the years of this woman's sly comments and sneaky insults, he'd finally had enough. He snapped.

"You know what, Mrs. Jones? You would want to leave *me* the hell alone because unlike Erin and your punk-ass husband, I don't owe you shit. My responsibility is to Erin and the baby. I don't know who you think you are but you need to stay out of my business. Erin is thirty years old and you still treat her like she's ten. But you play that game with her not me, cuz I'm not your fuckin' kid. From this point on, you will treat me with the same respect you would want to be treated with," Jermaine said before the door swung open and Roscoe entered.

"Who are you in here talking loud to, boy?" Roscoe barged in as if someone were calling for his help.

"This boy has lost his mind," Mrs. Jones said, stunned by Jermaine's verbal assault.

Roscoe charged at Jermaine. "You disrespecting my wife?"

"Daddy, no," Erin screamed.

Jermaine didn't budge. He didn't want it to come to this but Roscoe had been warned and since he didn't take heed, it was time he paid the piper. . . .

Roscoe reached for Jermaine's neck but his pugilistic skills were outdated. Jermaine avoided Roscoe's hands and smacked him real hard. Roscoe fell into the wall but came back up with a lazy right. Jermaine swatted it down with his left and came across with a right of his own, catching Roscoe square in the nose. The punch sent Roscoe straight back into a chair with blood shooting from his nose like a faucet.

"What did I tell you about raising your hands at me?" Jermaine growled, stalking Roscoe.

Roscoe was trying to clear his head when Mrs. Jones jumped on Jermaine's back. "Call security!" Mrs. Jones yelled to a petrified Pembrook, who had just walked in and looked like he wanted to be anywhere but there.

"I'm out of here. This is a little too Jerry Springer for me. Erin, I wish you the best," Pembrook said before grabbing his suit coat and running out.

Jermaine removed Mrs. Jones's hands from around his neck and was tempted to give her a taste of what he had just given her husband when Erin let out a scream that stopped all the commotion.

22

Running

od Himself couldn't have convinced Calvin that he'd be in a situation like the one he was now faced with. But here he was pacing the floor of his hotel room like a caged animal, racking his brain to come up with his next move. He knew the proper thing to do was turn himself in and let his lawyer get his bail reduced and his assets unfrozen, but he couldn't chance the flip side. Once he made contact with Jermaine, then and only then would he turn himself in.

The knock on his door froze his heart midbeat. Calvin carefully eased over to the door and placed his eye to the peephole. It was the desk clerk who'd checked him in.

"Yo, man, this is Eric from the front desk. I know you in there but you need to get out of here. The FBI is here looking for you," Eric whispered with his face to the door.

Calvin flung open the door.

"Is there another way out besides the elevator?"

"You can take the service elevator or the stairs. I suggest the service elevator because it's quicker and you better get a move on. They are showing your picture around downstairs and asking a lot of questions."

Calvin ran back into his room and quickly threw his things into his bag. He tossed the gun inside and made a swift exit.

"Aren't you going to ask me what they want me for?" Calvin asked Eric.

"Nope, it's not my business," Eric said, shaking his head.

"Thanks a lot, young man. I'm innocent and this will all blow over real soon. When it does, I won't forget you."

"Don't worry about it. I hate all cops, no matter what organization they hide under. They always trynna keep the black man down. So this one is on me," Eric said as he motioned for Calvin to hurry up.

"Take care," Calvin said as Eric placed his key into the service elevator.

"No, you take care," Eric said, watching the elevator doors close. He turned to see two white men walk past him in a hurry. They stopped and knocked on the door to the room that Calvin had just left.

Calvin exited the building on a side street and was met by a cool March breeze. He hurried down the sidewalk leading away from the Hilton. He fumbled in his pocket to retrieve his ringing cell phone. He flicked it open to answer but paranoia had frozen his tongue.

"Calvin, this is Kelly. Are you there?"

"Who are you?" Calvin asked, feeling betrayed.

"You have to turn yourself in. You're all over the news; you're a fugitive from justice."

"And I have you to thank for that. So you're a cop?"

"Yes, I am, and you have yourself to thank for your situation. I'm not the one that was cheating hardworking people out of their life's savings."

"I haven't cheated anyone out of anything," Calvin barked. "What do you want?"

"Listen, Calvin, turn yourself in, and if you're not guilty then you'll be vindicated. But all of this running is not helping your cause."

"I thought prostitution was illegal?"

"What are you talking about, Calvin?"

"They pay you and you sleep with me to get information. I'm not a lawyer but that sounds like entrapment to me."

"No, everything that I feel for you is real. Calvin, I had no choice. My director found out that you and I had a relationship and he basically forced my hand. There was nothing I could do."

"I didn't even know you had a director. I thought you were a real estate broker. At least that's what you led me to believe."

"I was thinking about a career change when I met you. But when your case came across my desk, that's when things just got out of control. Calvin, I'm sorry," Kelly said. "But you have to turn yourself in."

"Go to hell."

Calvin hung up the phone. He looked around and realized he had no place to go. He called Robin.

"Robin, it's me. How is C.J. doing?"

"He's fine," Robin said with no emotion. "What's going on with you? The FBI has been here all afternoon. They just left with a bunch of papers from your study."

"Did you tell them anything?"

"I haven't said anything to anyone. I told you what you were doing was wrong but you didn't listen, did you?"

"Robin, save the lecture." He sighed.

"Well, whenever you use unscrupulous practices for your own personal gain, someone is bound to get pissed, Calvin."

"I need to meet with Jermaine," Calvin abruptly changed the subject. "Do you have any idea how I can get in contact with him?"

"No, I don't, and it is my understanding that he doesn't want anything to do with you."

"I know that but I think I can change his mind. Just give me a number, an address or something."

"Calvin . . ." Robin sighed heavily. "I don't understand you. First you act like this child doesn't exist but now that your secret has been exposed, you are all up in arms about forming some kind of relationship with him. I don't get it."

"Maybe you'll never get it but I can't keep living this lie. I have to see my son. He needs to know how I feel. I'm trying to do the right thing. Will you help me?" he pleaded.

"Calvin, this is your mess so you clean it up. Please don't call here anymore. Good-bye, Calvin."

"Robin, don't hang up. Please. I'm desperate."

"You're desperate. Well, good. You have no idea what kind of shame you've brought on our family. C.J. just came home from the hospital, and the minute we walk in the door he sees his father's face plastered all over the television set like some kind of criminal. Look, I have to go," Robin said through tears.

"Robin, I realize now that I've been a horrible husband to you, but believe me when I say that I do love you."

There was a click and then he heard a dial tone.

Calvin closed his eyes and leaned against the building. He flipped the phone back on and called Information. It was a long shot, but what did he have to lose?

"I need a number for Jermaine Banks."

"Please hold."

Calvin held his breath while the operator took her sweet time searching for the number. Then he heard her voice.

"Sorry, sir, we don't have a listing for anyone by that name. Would you like to try another name?"

"Will you try Nanette Banks?"

"Hold, please."

Calvin dipped into an alley when he saw a dark-colored Crown Victoria ride by. He recognized the blue windbreaker the passenger was wearing.

"Please hold for the number."

He reached in his jacket pocket and removed an ink pen. He wrote the number down on his hand.

Calvin dialed Nettie's number and hoped that God had placed forgiveness in her heart.

Drama

Jermaine was sitting on the floor of the waiting room when a gray-haired white lady came in with the news.

"Are you Erin Jones's husband?"

"No, he's not," Mrs. Jones snapped as she stood up.

"Are you the father of the baby?" the doctor asked Jermaine.

"Yes." Jermaine stood up and shook the lady's hand.

"I'm sorry, but Miss Jones miscarried," the doctor said. "She can see you in about ten minutes."

Jermaine's heart pounded and he closed his eyes and ran both hands over his head.

"Erin lost the baby?" Mrs. Jones said in shock. She fell back into her chair holding her chest. "Oh Lord, no."

Roscoe sat down beside her and tried to comfort his wife but she swatted his hand away.

"This is all your fault, Jermaine!" Mrs. Jones yelled as she stood and walked over to Jermaine.

"Martha, take that back," Roscoe said, surprising everyone in the room by coming to Jermaine's defense. "If it's anybody's fault, it's ours. Erin didn't need to be around all of that shouting and shit. She was already sick. Now, no matter what we think of Jermaine, he's the man Erin chose to be with."

"How could you fix your lips to say that I had something to do with the death of my grandchild?"

"Martha," Roscoe warned.

"Don't 'Martha' me," Mrs. Jones said, looking at Roscoe as if he'd committed blasphemy.

"I think you owe Jermaine an apology," Roscoe said, folding his arms.

"Apology! I wish I would. He's lucky I'm not filing murder charges against him," Mrs. Jones spat with all the venom she could muster.

"Damn it, Martha," Roscoe yelled. "How would you like it if you lost *your* child? Have you thought once about how this boy must be feeling? It was *his* child too. Not yours."

"Erin is my blood."

"And the baby was his blood. What makes you think your blood is any redder than his?"

"He killed our baby," Mrs. Jones cried, collapsing in the chair.

"Get a grip, woman!"

Jermaine had heard enough. He stood and left the room. Roscoe followed him but not before he shot a scolding look at his wife.

"Jermaine, wait up, son."

Jermaine kept walking.

"Goddamn it, Jermaine, slow down. You know I'm too old to keep up with you," Roscoe said, already huffing from the ten steps he'd taken.

"What, man?"

"Listen, I'm sorry about the way this whole thing went down. I know how you feel."

"Whatever!"

"I lost a child once. It was before I met Erin's mother. Stillborn."

Jermaine stopped walking and looked into Roscoe's bloodshot eyes; he could tell that he was trying. He couldn't explain it but in some twisted way, they were finally connecting.

"I tried to walk out, man, and y'all kept pushing me and pushing me. Why couldn't y'all just leave me alone?" Jermaine said, his voice rising.

"I know. Jermaine, I'm sorry. Emotions just ran high and, well . . . I'm sorry."

"Yeah, well, that's not going to bring my child back, is it?"

"No, it's not, but all I can say is I'm sorry."

"Yeah, well, join the club," Jermaine said, walking off again.

"Sometimes it's hard to let go of your children. You got a son, you'll see, but especially your daughters. No one's to blame here. This is the way God intended for it to be," Roscoe said, struggling to keep up with Jermaine.

Jermaine stopped and leaned on the wall. He slid down to the floor and tried to get it together. Even though he and Erin weren't on the best of terms, she had still been carrying a part of him; now that was gone. He placed his head in his hands and exhaled.

Roscoe placed a hand on Jermaine's shoulder. Nothing else needed to be said.

"I need to see Erin," Jermaine said as he reached out for Roscoe to give him a hand up.

"Yeah, she probably wants to see you too."

"Can you do me a favor?"

Roscoe grunted and rubbed his badly bruised nose. "Yeah, whatcha need?"

"Will you make sure your wife isn't in the room? I can't do her right now."

"Give me a second," Roscoe said as he shuffled down the corridor.

Jermaine looked up to see Roscoe with Mrs. Jones in tow. "Go ahead," he urged.

"Jermaine," Mrs. Jones said, dropping her head. "I'm sorry. I just got beside myself. Erin is my baby and I just wasn't thinking. Will you forgive me?" She reached out for a hug, her way of calling a truce.

Jermaine stared at the chaotic-looking woman with graying hair. Her eyeliner was running down her beige-colored face, and she looked a complete mess. He wanted to hate her for all the evil things she'd said about him, and in a way he did, but today he had seen enough drama. He just nodded his head.

"I don't have a problem with you, Mrs. Jones," Jermaine said as he walked by her outstretched arms, opting against the embrace.

Erin was lying on her side whimpering when Jermaine entered.

"Hey, there. How you doin'?" he asked softly as he walked to her bedside and sat down.

She sniffled and continued staring at the wall.

"Do you need anything?"

"We lost her," Erin said, barely above a whisper. "We lost our baby."

"I know, but everything's going to be all right. We still have you."

"The doctor said I may never have kids."

"Don't worry about that right now. Plus, if I had a dollar for all the times I've read stories about how wrong doctors are, I'd be a rich man."

"I feel so empty inside," Erin cried. "Like I don't wanna live no more."

"Hey, don't talk like that." Jermaine leaned over and wiped the tears from Erin's eyes.

"I feel like I'm less than a woman, Jermaine. I can't have kids. I just don't wanna try no more," she sobbed.

"Erin, don't do this."

"You were right, Jermaine. I'm not a woman."

"Erin, stop being so hard on yourself. You *are* a woman, but life doesn't always work out the way we want it to. Everything's gonna be a'ight."

There was a light tap on the door and Erin's sister, Sharon, walked in carrying a bouquet of flowers and a card.

"Hey, Jermaine," she said politely.

"What's up, Sharon," Jermaine said, figuring Roscoe must've had a talk with her because she was worse than Mrs. Jones when it came to "protecting" Erin from him.

"Hey, baby girl," Sharon said as she placed the vase and balloons on the table and leaned down to kiss Erin.

"I'll give you guys some time alone. If you need me, I'll be out in the waiting room."

Jermaine walked into the waiting room, where he saw his mother consoling Mrs. Jones.

He shook his head. *That lady ain't nothing but drama.*

He kissed his mother on her cheek and took a seat on the far side of the room. He pulled out his cell phone to call Dana.

Closing In

The phone rang four times before the answering machine picked up: *"You've reached the home of Nettie Banks; please leave a message."*

Calvin hung up the phone. He didn't feel right leaving a message. Not after all these years. No, he needed to talk to Nanette. Besides, he had a feeling that his phone call would go unreturned. Calvin stopped the chatter in his head and flipped his phone open again. He was sure Nanette still hated him but this wasn't about her, it was about Jermaine. He *would* leave her a message. And he would keep leaving them until he got what he wanted.

Calvin dialed the number and waited for the machine to pick up.

"Hello?" a female voice said unexpectedly.

Nettie's voice paralyzed Calvin.

"Hello?" she said again.

"Ahh . . . may I speak to Calvin—I . . . I mean Nanette Banks, please? This is Calvin Sharpe."

"Well, look what the cat done drug in. How are you, Calvin?"

"I'm okay. How are you?"

"I'll have to say, you are the last person I expected to hear from."

Calvin didn't have a response for her.

"What can I do for you, Calvin?"

"How have you been, Nanette? It's good to hear your voice," Calvin said, and it was good.

"I'm doing just fine. What can I do for you?" Nettie said bluntly.

"I'm looking for Jermaine," Calvin blurted out before he thought about it.

"Why?"

"I need to see him."

"Why?"

"Nanette, I know I've never been there for Jermaine, but I don't want to die without at least having one meaningful conversation with him."

"Are you dying?" Nettie asked, somewhat distracted, as if she couldn't care one way or the other.

"No, I just have a lot going on." Calvin could tell she was washing dishes.

"I see," Nettie said carefully. "Jermaine is a grown man. He handles his own affairs. The days when he needed my permission to do anything are long gone."

"Will you at least give me his number?" Calvin pleaded.

"I'm sorry, Calvin, but I can't do that. Jermaine is real peculiar about his telephone number. He doesn't like me giving it out to just any ol' body," Nettie said, now rinsing.

"But I'm his father," Calvin said, losing his patience. Couldn't this woman hear the desperation in his voice?

"Wait a minute," Nettie said, shutting the water off abruptly. "Did you just raise your voice at me?"

"I'm sorry."

"That's an understatement. Why now?"

"I just need to talk to him. Tell him how I feel about him."

"How you feel about him? You earn feelings, Calvin, they don't just pop up because you say so. You don't know Jermaine any more than you know the Korean that cleans my clothes."

"He needs to hear my side."

"What side?" Nettie said, finally raising her voice.

All of the anger that Calvin had expected from her when he'd first called surfaced.

"You know what, Calvin? You are full of it. Now that your picture is all over the news, you're running around trying to fix your past. What you did can't be fixed. It may be forgiven but it'll never be fixed. You have a nice day."

"Wait!" Calvin begged. "Please, Nanette, just give me a chance to do what's right for once in my life. I don't know what will happen with this FBI thing. I need to talk to Jermaine. Please put me in touch with him."

"I would rather die a thousand deaths than to let you bring any harm my child's way."

"I'm not trying to harm him. I would never do that," Calvin said, sincerely hurt that she would think such a thing.

"You know, Calvin, it was so hard raising Jermaine on my own. He needed a father so bad, someone to show him how to be a man. Someone to get on his case when my kind of discipline no longer affected him. You know, there was a time when I thought I would lose my child to the streets. He was getting in trouble with the police two, three times a month. But I kept hanging in there. And finally he lost his appetite for destruction. Now Jermaine is finally becoming the man that he was intended to be, and I couldn't be happier. He doesn't need a father now, he needed one of those years ago, but you opted to send a check instead. Now, if you really want to help Jermaine, stay away from him. There is nothing you can tell *my* son," Nettie warned before she hung up the phone.

Calvin stood with the phone still up to his ear. He took a deep breath and looked up to the bright, moonlit night.

"Okay, I'm done trying to do this on my own. I know I haven't been a very good man but I'm sure You've seen worse than me. Have a little mercy on me, will You? Got-damn it."

Calvin stepped from the alley and hailed a taxi.

"Where ya headed?" asked the locked-hair taxi driver with a Jamaican accent.

"I don't know."

"Tell me some t'ing, mon," the driver said, not moving.

"Just drive," Calvin said, fumbling with his Palm Pilot. He called Jacobi, his private investigator.

"Jacobi, this is Calvin. You got anything on that case I gave you?"

"Hey, my friend. I saw your picture on the news. You're hot, man."

Calvin tried to control his anger. He wanted to know why the authorities were showing his picture around like he was a murderer.

"Do you have the information I asked for?" Calvin said, slowly and deliberately.

"Yeah, I got a little something. I haven't had time to really work on it, though. You know, give it that Jacobi-probing that you guys pay me top dollar for."

"Jacobi, please! Just give me what you have," Calvin snapped.

"Okay, okay, calm down. Jermaine Banks, hmmm let's see. He lives in North Philadelphia on the corner of Thirty-second and Diamond. I'm still working on place of employment and his telephone number."

"Thanks a lot," Calvin said, hanging up.

"Driver, take me to Thirty-second and Diamond," Calvin said, anxious at his first sign of hope.

How Sweet It Is

Jermaine loaded the last box into the U-Haul truck then pulled the large sliding door down and locked it. He walked around to the front of the truck and said his good-byes to his longtime neighbors.

"Jermaine, don't forget about me once you get out to the burbs," Vera said with her lips sticking out.

"Aww, Vera. Yo' ass is just mad because you won't be able to talk all that shit no more," Dave said.

"Shut up, Dave," Vera barked. "Me and Jermaine have always been cool. And I still got my gun so I can talk all the shit I wanna talk."

Dave shook his head and turned to Jermaine. "Brah, keep driving and don't look back at this raggedy-ass place. What's the mayor named? Milton Street. Well, he needs to fix these damn streets. Potholes look like swimming pools."

"Yo, J, I appreciate you looking out for me with that job situation." Murphy said.

"No problem. How you doin' in school?" Jermaine asked.

"I'm doin' a'ight," Murphy said, smiling.

"Yeah, you better be, cuz I still got eyes in these streets, boy."

"Yeah, I wonder who that might be," Murphy said, looking directly at Dave.

"A'ight, y'all, I gotta roll. Y'all stay up." Jermaine gave Dave and Murphy brotherly hugs. "Vera, I'll drop by to check on you every now and then." Jermaine leaned down and kissed her on her forehead. He knew she would miss him the most.

"Before you leave, you need to go and sanitize your lips," Dave said, frowning up.

"Fuck you, Dave, you half-breeded bastard," Vera said, holding up her middle finger for Dave to examine.

Jermaine chuckled and walked toward the U-Haul while Vera and Dave bickered like an old married couple. He jumped in the truck and looked around North Philly one more time. Just as he cranked up, Dave walked over.

"I almost forgot about this," Dave said, handing Jermaine a fat envelope.

Jermaine shook his head. "You know I'm retired."

"I know, but this is dough you already made. I got it from your uncle."

"Damn, I'm surprised he still had some left. How'd you get it?"

"Caught him right before he walked into the dope house. I guess his mind was on that blast and not who was watching. Anyway, he stuffed this Crown Royal bag into a brick in the alley. I just slipped up and took it. It's a little over twelve G's in there. I'm surprised he hadn't overdosed," Dave said, shaking his head.

"Did you pay yourself already?"

"Nah, I'm straight, consider it a going-away gift."

Jermaine nodded his head and ran his fingers across the bills. He didn't doubt for one second that Dave was telling him the truth about not taking any money. He counted off a thousand dollars and handed it to Dave. "Do me a favor, man, make sure Vera eats."

"What's up with you and her pippin' ass?" Dave asked.

"She's caught some bad breaks but she's still good people. So buy her a few burgers and make sure her mouth doesn't get her killed. I'll holla at 'cha," Jermaine said as he reached his hand out the window and slapped Dave's.

"That's like a full-time job, but I'll look out for Mouth Almighty," Dave said. "You take care of yourself, big man."

"Will do."

The next day Jermaine woke up to a four-chimed doorbell. He rolled off the air mattress and stretched the kinks out of his back. The doorbell sounded again.

"I'm coming," he said, throwing on a T-shirt.

Jermaine walked over the hardwood floors and opened the door.

"Good morning, Mr. Man," Dana said as she walked in bright-eyed and bushy-tailed.

"What time is it?"

"Ten o'clock."

"I'm running late," Jermaine said as he walked back into his bedroom and looked in a few boxes for a change of clothes.

"Make yourself at home, Dana. I need to hop in the shower."

"I can't stay long. I just stopped by on my way to church. Thought I'd see if you wanted to go."

"Nah, I can't go today. I'm taking Khalil to meet my deadbeat dad's parents," Jermaine said from the bathroom.

"From what you said they seem like nice people. I'm sure he'll love that," Dana said, standing in the bathroom door watching Jermaine brush his teeth. All he was wearing was a T-shirt and pair of boxers.

"You better watch out." Jermaine turned to Dana with a mouthful of toothpaste. "I'm kind of sexy. You'll mess around and miss church staring at me like that."

"Sexy you are, but not so much that I would miss my weekly replenishing of the spirits," Dana said, closing the door. "I'll wait for you out on the stoop. It's a pretty day."

Jermaine rushed through his shower and joined Dana outside and inhaled the fresh air of his new surroundings. The Art Museum area of Philadelphia was nothing like his old Thirty-second and Diamond neighborhood. He waved back at a college-aged white girl who was jogging by his condo.

"So do you like your new place?" Dana said, leaning back against the railing.

"Yeah, it's straight. Thanks for hooking this up."

"I'm just happy you could move in on such short notice. Now all you have to do is make the payments on time," Dana said with a smile.

"I'll do that. Even if I have to hit the block and get my hustle on." Jermaine smiled.

"Oh no, you're among the working class now."

"How could I forget? But I don't know how long I can last with that little bit of money they offered me up at Pace."

"You'll make it happen some kind of way," Dana said, rubbing Jermaine on the shoulder.

"Yeah, I'm sure I will," Jermaine said, looking around his peaceful surroundings. "You know, I already love this place but for some reason I feel guilty."

"Guilty? What, you don't feel like you deserve a wood-burning fireplace and vaulted ceilings?" Dana joked.

"Nah, it's not that. I'm talking about this whole *Leave It to Beaver* scene. White folks jogging with their dogs, birds chirping. You know, Dana, white people have done some major damage to blacks, but here I am at total peace around them. Why don't I feel this way when I'm around my own people? I always got my guard up."

"I know what you mean, but we're getting there. And the more people that step up and shed that ghetto mentality, the better off we'll all be. You should be proud of yourself, Jermaine."

"For what?"

"For taking the first step in exposing you and Khalil to a different world. Philadelphia is a beautiful city—you just have to step outside that ten-block radius in North Philly and experience it a little."

"Yeah, I hear ya," Jermaine said, looking at his watch. "You know what, love, I hate to leave you but I gotta go."

"Yeah, me too," Dana said, reaching out for a hug. "I'll see you tonight?"

"I'll call you when I get in. My little brother is supposed to be teaching me how to play golf today," Jermaine said, taking an imaginary golf swing.

"Look at you. Turning into a true buppie."

"I don't even know what that is but it has a nice ring to it."

"Once you have a few lessons I'll come out and show you a thing or two," Dana said with a smile.

"You play?"

"Yeah, but not as much as I'd like to."

"Black folks and golf. When did that marriage take place?"

"I've been playing all my life. My dad used to take me out to the course every Sunday after church."

Jermaine kissed Dana on the lips. They shared eye contact without speaking.

"Why?" he asked.

"Why what?"

"Why did you hook me up with this place?"

Dana sighed and leaned back against the rail. "Jermaine,

there's just something about you. Trust me when I say I wavered on telling you about this place. Y'all brothers have so much game, but when I saw you up at my office building trying to get a job, I said, This man is for real and he's trying and I'm going to do what I can to help him get there. That's all," Dana said, hunching her shoulders and smiling. "Besides, if us sistas wanna stop saying there are no good black men, it would behoove us to help out when we can."

"You know, Erin used to be on me all the time about doing this or that, but you came along and actually helped me *do* something about my situation. She could've hooked me up with a million places, she sells real estate, but all she ever did was criticize," Jermaine said, staring off into the distance.

"Well, don't be too hard on her. Maybe she doesn't know how to give. Or maybe you weren't in a position to receive. Who knows? But you're in good hands now," Dana said, smiling. She stood and walked down the steps. "I better go or I'll be late for church."

"Okay, and tell your pastor to keep his eyes to himself," Jermaine said.

"I'm all yours, love."

Jermaine knocked on Amani's front door. He looked at his watch and knocked a little harder. He shook his head in frustration and walked down to the end of the block and back up the alley to the rear of her place. He let himself in the gate and stormed up to the back door, but froze in his tracks. It took all the self-control he could muster to contain his temper.

Amani was buck-naked on a sofa with her legs hoisted in the air, and there was some curvy-bottom female with her head stuffed between her legs. Amani's mouth was open, her eyes closed; she was obviously caught up in the moment. But that moment was about to come to an abrupt end.

Jermaine banged on the glass door hard enough to shatter it.

Amani jumped to her feet, knocking her candy licker off balance and flat onto her bottom. Jermaine banged again. Amani grabbed a housecoat and quickly covered herself. Her partner made a beeline to the bathroom. For a few seconds Amani just stared at Jermaine and he didn't break eye contact. He was pissed. She was pissed. Amani slowly walked over to the door and opened it.

"Who in the hell do you think you are, Jermaine?"

"Amani, don't make me slap the shit out of you," Jermaine growled. "Where's Khalil?"

"He's in his room, watching TV." Amani quickly changed her tone. She had seen this look before and wanted no part of it.

"Oh, and you just had to have your little pussy licked right now. This couldn't wait until he was gone?"

"Go get your son, Jermaine," Amani said, trying to remain calm.

"Yeah, that's exactly what I plan to do. I'm not bringing him back. You can call whoever in the hell you feel like calling. Yo' ass is unfit."

"Okay," Amani said, abandoning her cool role. "Now I know you've lost your mind. Just because you get a job and move doesn't make you Cliff Huxtable all of a sudden. Now, I might be a little out of line but . . . no, fuck that, this is my house and what I do in the privacy of my own home doesn't concern you. So I'll see you tomorrow at six when you bring my son *home*." Amani stepped aside to let Jermaine pass.

"Nah, you can stop trying to play that game. I'm totally legit now and whatever it is that you think you got on me is some bullshit. I'm not playing with you no more. I give you a thousand dollars a month and you can't even pay the day care."

"Khalil has to eat, he needs lights, clothes, transportation, and all kinds of other shit that your measly thousand dollars doesn't even begin to take care of. So don't you dare come at me with that nonsense."

"Correction! You need all of that and I'm not responsible for you. Khalil's expenses ain't no G a month. I can add, divide, and subtract, and I'm subtracting your freaky ass from his life."

"Get out, you ain't taking Khalil nowhere," Amani screamed.

There was a loud thump upstairs, then they heard Khalil cry out, "Momma!"

Jermaine took off running up the stairs; he jumped over the fire that was quickly consuming the floor. He grabbed Khalil and took him out of the house.

"Stay here, little man," Jermaine said as he sat Khalil on the steps.

"I was cooking like my momma . . ." Khalil cried. "I'm sorry, Daddy."

"Don't worry about it, man," Jermaine said. He went back into the house and grabbed a blanket and headed back to the kitchen.

"Stop putting water on it," he yelled at Amani. "It's grease." Jermaine threw the blanket over the floor and smothered out the blaze.

"Where is Khalil?" Amani asked, scared to death, looking at the big black burn spot in the middle of her kitchen floor. "Is he all right?"

"Yeah, he's fine, but he's not living here anymore. You downstairs getting your freak on and my child—"

"Okay, okay," Amani screamed through her tears. "Fine, Jermaine." She sunk down to the floor crying uncontrollably. Jermaine wanted to smack her but just shook his head and walked away. Obviously her guilt was kicking her ass.

Then he stopped. Jermaine looked at the mother of his child and felt a hint of sympathy for her. He had no idea what she was going through but by the looks of her, it was more than she was letting on.

"Amani, I just trynna do right by my son. You know my Pops wasn't around and all I'm trynna do is be there for Khalil as much as possible. I know better than anybody what these streets can do to him. You can still see him whenever you want, I just need to have him with me."

Amani nodded her head.

Jermaine walked out on the steps and picked up his son.

"Khalil, go in there and say bye to your mom. You coming to live with me."

"I'm not going to see my mom ever again?" he asked, fearful.

"Of course you gonna see your mom. You'll just be living with me. You can see her anytime you want."

Khalil smiled and pumped his fist. "Yeah. I'm coming to live with you in your new house?" he asked, smiling. For him, the fire episode was already forgotten.

"Yep, now go hug your mother and tell her you're sorry for trynna burn up the house."

26

The Other Side

Jermaine looked at the address on the piece of paper and matched it up with the house he was staring at. He did a double take. This place was huge.

"This is some bullshit," he said to himself. "This nigga rich."

"Daddy, I thought you said you were going to stop saying bad words," Khalil said from the backseat.

"Sorry, lil man," Jermaine said, unable to take his eyes off the stone mansion with the long white columns and enough windows to keep Windex in business for years to come.

He punched the call button on the key-code pad at the gate.

"Yes, may I help you?"

"I'm here to see C.J."

"Your name?" the lady said with some sort of accent.

This clown got a foreign maid, he thought.

"Jermaine Banks."

"*Sí, señor.* Señor C.J. is expecting you. Please drive up to the property."

After the gates opened, Jermaine put his truck in gear and followed the curvy driveway up to the house, admiring the expertly manicured landscape. He got out and unhooked Khalil from his car seat.

"Daddy, is this my uncle's house?"

"I guess so."

"This nigga rich," Khalil said, wide-eyed.

"Watch your mouth, boy," Jermaine said, smacking Khalil on the back of his head.

"You said the same thing, Daddy." Khalil frowned and held his head.

"You can't say what I say."

"What's a nigga?"

"An ignorant person." Jermaine grabbed Khalil's hand and led him up the ten or so steps leading to the front door.

"My momma calls you ignorant all the time."

"Yo' momma got issues."

"What are issues?"

"Stop asking so many questions."

"My teacher said I should ask questions."

"Boy, be quiet. We can't be acting all ghetto up in here."

"My momma said you're ghetto."

"Hush."

Before Jermaine could ring the doorbell, the door opened and C.J., Louis, and Edna were all standing in the doorway with big smiles on their faces.

"Hey, man." C.J. shook Jermaine's hand. "Hey there, Khalil."

Khalil hid his face behind his father's leg.

"Don't tell me this is my great-grandbaby," Edna said, crying already.

"Hey there, big fella," Louis said, reaching out for Khalil.

"Oh, now you wanna act shy? Say hi to everybody," Jermaine

said, trying to free Khalil from his leg. He wasn't letting go. "He'll warm up to you in a minute. Man, y'all living kind of large out here."

"I guess." C.J. shrugged.

"You guess? I don't know any black folks living like this."

"Me either, Jermaine," Louis said.

"So Jermaine, how have you been?" Edna said, giving her husband a warning look not to start in on Calvin today.

"I'm okay. How have you been doing, Grandma?" The words felt natural leaving his lips.

"Man, we were waiting on y'all. We have to get back on the road. But before we go, I got to get a few little things for my great-grand," Louis said before disappearing into a side room.

"A few? That man has lost his mind over you, young fella. Come over here and give your granny a hug."

Khalil looked at his daddy to see if it was okay. Jermaine nodded, then Khalil walked over and wrapped his arms around Edna's neck, causing more tears.

"I hear you a car man, Khalil," Louis said as he maneuvered a remote-control, gas-powered Porsche around the corner.

Khalil leaped from his granny's arms and grabbed the car.

"Whose is this?" he asked with eyes as big as silver dollars.

"It's all yours, buddy," Louis said, still holding a big bag filled with gifts for Khalil.

"Daddy, these people are the bomb," Khalil said, running over and jumping up into Louis's arms.

"Oh boy, I'mma old man," Louis said, grunting. "You trynna kill me?"

"Khalil, calm down," Jermaine said.

"He's all right, leave him alone. He's all boy, just like I like 'em," Louis said with a smile that wouldn't quit.

"Tell your grandparents thank you."

"Thank you," Khalil said, smiling.

"You're welcome. Your grandma got you a few more things," Louis said, removing boxes from the bag.

"Come on in, Jermaine," C.J. said, leading Jermaine down a long hallway. "Have a seat in my father's study. I'll go and grab a few sets of clubs, and we can be on our way. Do you want something to drink, a snack or something? I can have Maria bring something out."

"Nah, I'm cool."

Jermaine took a seat on a soft leather chair and stared hard at the painting on the wall behind the desk. The brown skin, the dark eyes and high cheekbones—he couldn't help but see himself in the man that stood so proudly behind his family.

Baseball cards!

Jermaine couldn't explain it, but his mind drifted to the very first time he'd felt the cold steel of a policeman's handcuffs.

One night he had heard his mother crying about not having enough money to pay something. He was just about to ask her for some money so that he could buy himself a pack of baseball cards so that he could trade with his friends. He stopped at her door and turned around. The next day he went into the corner store and stole a pack. The police were waiting for him to leave the store. They handcuffed him and took him to jail. From that point on, he no longer feared being incarcerated.

As he looked around at the luxurious living quarters that his father was providing, he knew that if his dad had been in his life, he would've had money for those baseball cards.

All of a sudden he didn't feel so well. Every feeling of neglect he'd ever experienced came crashing down on him like an ocean wave. He hated his father now more than ever.

He turned away from the picture, vowing not to let his true feelings ruin the day.

"Well, Jermaine, I really hate to leave you, buddy, but I gotta get on back to the South," Louis said, walking into the study and taking a seat in the chair beside Jermaine.

"I understand. It was nice meeting you."

"When will you be able to get that grand of mine down to North Carolina? We have acres of land with a few horses. He'd love it."

"Sounds like I'd like that myself. We can try to get down there when school is out."

"I guess you heard about your father," Louis said, suddenly sullen.

"Heard what?"

"He's all over the news. He's a wanted man," Louis said, shaking his head with frustration. "Some kind of corporate fraud or something."

"That's too bad. I know he's going to hate to leave all of this for a jail cell," Jermaine said, unmoved. He looked around at all the nice things his father had accumulated and shook his head. *I guess all that glitters ain't gold,* he thought.

"You reap what you sow," Louis said.

"True."

Louis and Jermaine stood and embraced.

"Let me give you my new info. I just moved last night to a new place." Jermaine walked over to his father's desk and wrote down his new address and telephone number. "Same deal as before: don't share it with your son."

"Yeah, I was hoping you would've changed your mind on that. The reason he won't turn himself in is because he's trying to find you."

Jermaine thought about what he'd just heard. He didn't know how he felt about that.

"You found me, and it took you all of twenty-four hours from the time you found out about me. He's known about me all my life."

"I understand," Louis said, throwing his hands up. "Edna. Edna come on round here and say bye to Jermaine."

Edna walked in carrying Khalil.

"I told you he'd warm up to you," Jermaine said.

"Yeah, he's a darling," Edna said, wiping away her tears.

"That woman keeps more water in her eyes than a fish," Louis said.

"Hush up, Louis. I just met my babies and now you rushing me off."

"You the one that has to go to the doctor."

"Oh, forget about them doctors. I'm staying with my baby," Edna said, hugging Khalil tighter.

"Look here, Jermaine, I'll look for you this summer. Khalil, my man, you take care of your daddy, you hear? You only get one," Louis said, more for Jermaine's benefit.

"Where y'all going?" Khalil asked.

"Back to North Carolina. That's where we live," Louis said.

"I wanna go," Khalil said. "Daddy, can we go?"

"Oh Lord." Edna reached out and hugged Jermaine and ran from the room.

"Why is my grandmommy crying?" Khalil asked.

"She cries when she's happy, and she's happy to see you, fella," Louis said. "I'm going to have to stop and get about ten boxes of tissue for the trip home."

"Y'all have a safe trip. I'll call you," Jermaine said, shaking his grandfather's hand. "You're a good man."

"You're a good man yourself." Louis turned to Khalil and said, "Granddaddy loves you," then walked out of the room before his own eyes started to moisten.

"So, Jermaine, are you ready for your first golf lesson?" C.J. asked, walking into the study with two golf bags on his shoulders.

"I guess so," Jermaine said, trying to snap out of his funk. He hated to see his grandparents go; he was just getting used to them.

"Is everything okay?"

"Yeah, what about you? How've you been holding up?"

"I'm okay. A little weak, but I need exercise and my doctor said I can't play tennis, so golf it is."

"Well, let's go."

Jermaine sat lost in his thoughts as C.J. babbled on and on about something. He couldn't get his mind off that face in the picture and how different his life could've been if the man that had helped create him had been more of a man and stuck around to raise him.

"Hey, slow up, man. Your turn is coming up," C.J. yelled.

"You talk funny," Khalil said from his seat in the rear.

"Oh yeah? I fight funny too." C.J. reached to the backseat and tickled Khalil.

Jermaine watched the two boys playing. Then he took a deep breath and decided to let it go. There was nothing he could do about the deadbeat his father was, and nothing would come from hating him.

I still don't want nothing to do with him, he thought.

They unloaded the truck and walked out onto the greens.

"Hey, man, we have to get you in the right kind of gear. Golf is all about the look," C.J. said as he led the way into the pro shop. "Find a few pair of pants and a few shirts. What size shoe do you wear?"

"An eleven."

"I'll get you a pair of those new Tiger Woods. Don't let me forget to get you a glove."

"Man, I don't need all this stuff," Jermaine said, looking at the price tag on a pair of pants. "I might not even like the game."

"You'll love the game and you'll be glad I introduced you to it."

"If you say so," Jermaine said, shrugging.

"Khalil, try this hat on," C.J. said, placing a Temple University cap on his nephew's head.

"C.J., what's up, man?" the young cashier said as he rang up all of the items they placed on the counter.

"What's up?"

"We missed you at the state this year. You know we lost in the semis."

"I heard. Maybe next year," C.J. said, placing a platinum credit card on the counter.

"Your total is five hundred and thirty-two dollars." The cashier swiped the card and bagged the items.

"C.J., the card has been declined. I'll run it again."

"Yeah, something must be wrong."

"Nope, it declined again. I'll just put this stuff on your account."

"Go ahead. Jermaine, will you grab this stuff? The dressing room is over there. I need to call my mom and find out what's going on with this card. She probably canceled it and didn't tell me."

"My mom does that all the time. Don't you hate that?" the cashier said.

Jermaine shook his head at the privileged kids and grabbed the bag and headed to the dressing room. Khalil stayed with C.J.

"You look cool, man," C.J. said as Jermaine emerged from the dressing room looking like a PGA participant.

Khalil took one look and cracked up. He was pointing at his dad, laughing so hard that Jermaine had to join in too before they headed for the golf course.

"Okay, Jermaine, golf is a game of finesse. Remember, it's all about the grip and form," C.J. said, showing Jermaine the proper way to hold a club.

Jermaine took a swing and missed the ball. Khalil laughed again.

"How did I miss that ball?" Jermaine asked with a smile.

"Poor form, too much power. Watch this," C.J. said as he positioned himself toward the center of the ball. He loosened his grip slightly and closed his eyes. He took a swing and smacked the ball about two hundred feet.

"How did you do that?" Jermaine asked in amazement.

"You can do it too," C.J. said, adjusting the club in Jermaine's hand.

Jermaine took another swing and took a nice chunk out of the grass but the ball was still sitting on the tee.

Khalil couldn't stop laughing.

Jermaine realigned himself with the ball and took a deep breath. This time he made good contact with the ball. He felt like a kid making his first jump shot. "Did you see that?" he asked, excited. "What about that, Khalil?" Jermaine said, chasing his son for a congratulatory tickle.

"I saw it," C.J. said, making his way over to the cart. He didn't look well.

"Yo, you a'ight?"

"I'll be fine, just give me a second, Jermaine. I'm starting to feel light-headed."

"Are you okay?"

C.J. shook his head. He was starting to sweat. Then he staggered over to the cart and took a seat.

"Do you need some water, man?" Jermaine asked, concerned about his little brother. "C.J.? C.J.?"

C.J.'s eyes were starting to swell, then he laid down across the seat and passed out.

"Daddy, what's wrong with Uncle C.J.?" Khalil cried out.

"I don't know, buddy, but we gotta get him to a hospital." Jermaine called 911 from his cell phone.

Jermaine strapped Khalil into the golf cart and drove his little brother back to the clubhouse. He took C.J.'s cell phone and pressed the last number dialed. Robin answered.

"Mrs. Robin, this is Jermaine. C.J. just passed out. The ambulance is on its way."

"Oh my God. Are you guys still at the golf course?"

"Yeah."

"I'll meet you at Chestnut Hill."

27

Can I Get a Witness?

rs. Sharpe, C.J. is going to need a kidney transplant. His body is just not responding to the treatments that we chose as an alternative to dialysis," the doctor said, showing Robin a chart. "He's reached end-stage renal disease. That's when the kidney is malfunctioning to the point where a transplant is the only option. Now, we've tested his father and he's a perfect tissue and blood match. Is he still willing to go through with the procedure?"

"Of course he is," Robin said, wiping away her tears.

"I'm sorry, but I have to ask. I've seen some strange things occur when it comes to donors. We'll need to get Mr. Sharpe in here as soon as possible."

Robin snatched her purse from the floor and tore through it looking for her cell phone but it wasn't there.

"Jermaine, may I borrow your phone? I need to get in contact with Calvin. I must've left mine at home."

"No problem," Jermaine said, handing her the phone.

Robin dialed and waited for what seemed like hours for Calvin to answer.

"Jermaine, is this you?" Calvin said eagerly.

"No, this is Robin and—"

"My caller ID said Jermaine Banks. Where is he?"

"Calvin," Robin yelled. "C.J. is sick and we need for you to get down here right away. He needs a transplant."

"A transplant? I thought—"

"I don't care what you thought. Get down here now," Robin said before becoming hysterical. Jermaine took the phone from her.

"This is Jermaine. Do you think you can make it on over here and help this boy get on with his life?" Jermaine said flatly.

"Jermaine, is this really you?"

"Listen, man, this is not our time. It's C.J.'s," Jermaine said, already frustrated with Calvin.

"Will you be there when I get there?"

Jermaine shook his head in amazement. This man's son was in desperate need of his assistance and he wanted to play catch-up.

"Yeah, I'll be here. You just get here."

"I'm on my way," Calvin said to a dead phone.

"He said he's on the way, Mrs. Robin. Everything is gonna be fine," Jermaine wrapped his arm around Robin while she sobbed.

"Thank you, Jermaine."

"Hey, anything for lil bro."

Robin shook her head and excused herself.

Jermaine sat in the waiting room chair going through the names in his cell phone book. He came across Erin's name. It had been a little over two weeks since her miscarriage and he felt obligated to check on her so he pushed the "send" button.

"Hello."

"What's up, Erin?"

"Hey, Jermaine. How are you?"

"I'm cool, sitting here at the hospital."

"Are you all right?" Erin said flatly. It was more out of courtesy than concern.

"Yep," Jermaine said, picking up on the disinterest in her voice. "I was just calling to check on you."

"I heard you moved."

"News travels fast."

"I bumped into your friend Dave this morning at Pathmart."

"I see."

"So now that we're no longer an item, you're doing all the things I ask you to do, huh?"

"Why does it have to be because you asked me to? You just don't get it, do you? I'm a grown man and the changes I'm making in my life have nothing to do with you. If anything, I moved because of that damn rat."

"What?"

"Nothing! Look, I need to go. You take care of yourself."

"Why do you hate me so much?"

Here we go! Jermaine thought.

"I don't hate you at all."

"You have a birthday coming up. Do you wanna do dinner?"

"I have plans."

"Oh," Erin said, taken aback. "You're going on a date?"

"Erin, our time has passed. Let it go!"

"I've been thinking about you a lot lately. I miss you and I don't want it to be over."

Jermaine sighed and shook his head. "Erin, I can't deal with you, your mother, your daddy, and your sister. Y'all wear me out."

"I thought they apologized for everything."

"They did and I'mma leave it at that."

"So you're leaving me?"

"Nah, you left me. I'm just holding you to your word."

"I see. Well, if you change your mind I'll be here," Erin said in her best "take me back" voice.

"Take care of yourself, Erin."

Jermaine hung up with Erin and called Dana.

"Hey, love," she answered.

"The wonderful world of caller ID. How you doin'?"

"Waiting on you."

"Yeah, looks like I'm going to have to cancel."

"Is everything okay?"

"Nah, my little brother needs a kidney transplant. He passed out on the golf course today. I had to get an ambulance to get him here."

"I'm sorry to hear that. You need me to bring you anything?"

Damn, this girl is sweet, Jermaine thought. *I hope she stays that way.*

"Nah, I'm good. Maybe we can do lunch tomorrow."

"Sounds like a date. Call me if you need me," Dana said.

"Will do. Talk to you later."

"Okay! Keep your head up."

Robin walked over to Jermaine. "C.J. wants to see you," she said.

"Are you okay?"

"Yeah, I'm fine."

"Hey man," C.J. said with a weak smile as Jermaine entered his room. "Sorry I flopped on you and Khalil."

"Don't worry about that. How you feeling?"

"Not too good. Where's Khalil?"

"I dropped him off at my mom's. Your dad is on the way up here now so you can get that transplant."

C.J. looked surprised. "I thought he was in jail."

"No, I just spoke with him. Unless you rich folks can just walk up outta jail when you have something else to do, he's still a free man."

C.J. looked disappointed. "He was never there for me either, Jermaine."

"What do you mean?"

"We lived in the same house but that was about it. Then he hit my mother. That's when I made the call."

"What are you talking about, C.J.?"

"I called the FBI and told them everything I knew about his shady accounting books."

"Man, you're fifteen. What do you know about your dad's accounting books?"

"I heard him and my mom fussing one night about his company cheating people out of their life's savings. That made me want to do some research of my own. People invested in him, they believed in him, and some of them lost everything they had. I don't want his kidney. I'd rather die."

Jermaine sat speechless. He heard a knock on the door and the man in the picture that hung behind the desk in the study of the mansion in Gladwyne walked in.

"Jermaine!" Calvin said, walking over to Jermaine and extending his hand. "How are you, son?"

"I'm fine but don't call me son," Jermaine said, staring Calvin straight in the eyes. He never touched his hand.

"I know you hate me. And I know that nothing I say may matter, but I never meant for things to turn out this way."

"Oh yeah, how did you expect for them to turn out?"

"I don't know," Calvin said, dropping his head.

"Damn right you don't know because you didn't stick around long enough to see," Jermaine said, pointing a finger in Calvin's face. "Man, talk to your son cuz just like you didn't want anything to do with me, I don't want shit to do with you," he said through clenched teeth. "C.J., I'll holla at you later."

"Jermaine, don't leave," C.J. pleaded.

Just as Jermaine turned to leave he was met at the door by two men wearing dark suits and sunglasses.

"Calvin Sharpe, you're under arrest."

"Wait a minute," Calvin said, looking around for an escape route. "I need to give my son a transplant."

"Will you place your hands behind your back, please?" one of the agents said firmly.

"My son needs a kidney transplant, and I'm his donor. Officers, please, my son's life is at stake."

Just then Dr. Talmage walked in. "What's going on here?"

"We are here to place Mr. Sharpe under arrest," one of the agents declared.

"Can this wait? We were two seconds away from transplant preparations."

"I'm afraid not," the agent said.

"Do you want to be responsible if something happens to this patient? You literally could be walking out of here with his only chance at life."

"Sir, we have orders."

"Screw your orders, this is my son you're talking about here," Calvin said, trying to pry his hands loose.

"Dr. Talmage, how long does it take to see if I'm a match?" Jermaine said, walking back into the room. "I'm his brother."

"You're his biological brother?"

"Well, yeah. Half-brother. We have that in common," Jermaine said, tossing Calvin a disgusting look.

"I could rush the results and we could have them in an hour, tops," Dr. Talmage said. "But we'd have to brief you, and you'd have to sign a waiver."

"Let's do it. I don't want to keep these guys from upholding the law," Jermaine said with a smirk.

"Jermaine, please. This is my responsibility, son," Calvin pleaded.

"Responsibility?" Jermaine frowned and stared at Calvin. "What would you know about responsibility? You don't pick and choose when you're gonna be responsible. I've been to hell and back all because you were *irresponsible*. I have a son of my own now and I would rather die than to leave him for these streets to raise, and that's exactly what you did to me. I hope you get a lot of time in jail to think about how fucked up you are."

Jermaine stared at Calvin, who was looking at the floor.

"I . . . I tried, but your mother wouldn't let me—" Calvin started.

"You sound like a bitch. People don't *let* men do a damn thing. Especially take care of their children. *Real* men demand that role," Jermaine stared at Calvin.

"Okay, Jermaine. You are right. I wasn't a man back when you were born. I didn't have a clue as to how to be a father."

"You still don't," C.J. chimed in.

"You shut up." Calvin turned to C.J. "Jermaine has a right to be angry, but you're just spoiled as hell. Now, I'm sorry I didn't make it to sit in the stands at all your extracurricular activities, but I was out working. Working to provide you with a lifestyle that most of our people could only dream about. So you just shut your little ungrateful ass up."

"Look, man, I don't hate you. I just don't want anything to do with you," Jermaine said, for once agreeing with Calvin.

"Jermaine, can we start over? I just want to be your friend."

"A wise old man told me, if you raise your kids right, when they grow older they'll be your friends. We can never be friends, Calvin. Doc," Jermaine said as he turned away from his father, "I'm ready when you are."

28

Jermaine

appy birthday to you, happy birthday to you. Happy birthday to Jer-maaaaine, happy birthday to you!"

My mom and Dana got together and called themselves giving me a surprise party for my thirtieth birthday, but I knew what they were up to because Khalil told me. He tells me everything, cuz that's my little man.

I don't know why, but standing in my new home, surrounded by family and friends, made me think about all the times I could've been dead. I thought about all the times I've been shot at and all the times I retaliated. All the times I've been in and out of jail. I looked at my mom and thought about all the sleepless nights she spent worrying about me. Damn!

I blew out my candles and made a wish. What did I wish? None of y'all damn business. Nah, I'm just kidding. I wished for Khalil to have a long and trouble-free life. I needed a minute to myself, so I excused myself and headed out to my front stoop.

I took a seat on my rail and became overwhelmed with a feeling of joy. Real joy, not the kind of joy I was used to when I was operating in the streets. Nah, this was pure. The feeling of knowing I was going to be all right. It was a feeling that I've never experienced before. Ain't that something? Thirty years old and I have never known happiness. Speaking of thirty, that was a number that I never thought I'd see on a cake with my name on it. Just looking back at the life I was living and the fact that most of the people from my old element didn't care about life or death, I realized how fortunate I am to have made it this far. It's crazy how the kids raise the adults sometimes because everything I do or have done to make my life better is because of Khalil. Because that's my little man.

"Is everything okay?" Dana asked, peeking her head out the door.

"Yeah, I'm straight," I said, motioning for her to join me. She walked out and slid into my arms. "You know, I've never felt as good as I feel right now. I wish I could bottle this feeling up."

"You seem happy."

"I am, and I owe a lot of this to you."

"Well, you know, I do what I can," she joked. "Like the old saying goes, behind every good man is an even better woman."

"Yeah, well, after we get rid of all these people, this good man is going to get behind this good woman and break her off a little something. Butt naked!"

"You so nasty," she said. "Can you at least wear your Timberlands?"

"Only if you wear them hooker boots."

"Ohhhh," she said, taking a bite at me. "Let me get back inside and finish beating Khalil on that PlayStation. Do you want me to fix you a plate?"

"Yeah, but give me a few minutes."

"Okay, sweetie," she said, giving me a peck on the lips.

Damn, I'm feeling that girl. I think she's the one, but I'm going to take it slow, because I once felt that way about Erin, and y'all know how that turned out. Speaking of Erin, she's been calling and I've been using the hell out of caller ID to ignore her. She swears she's responsible for this so-called change that I've made. And to be honest, I don't see the big change. I mean, I'm still the same old Jermaine with a new address and a job. I'll still slap the taste out of someone's mouth if they rub me the wrong way, so I don't get it.

Anyway, Dana and my mom did manage to get one surprise in: my grandparents. They came up for my big day. The more time I spend around them, the more I want to kick Calvin's ass. I keep wondering how different things would've been if they'd been involved in my upbringing, but I'm trying to let those thoughts go, because things aren't that bad now. I got a lot going for me, and maybe I needed to go through everything I went through. Who knows?

I wasn't a perfect match to donate a kidney to C.J., so some judge gave Calvin emergency bail so he could go through with the operation. The surgery was a success and C.J. is recovering quite well. I told him once he's all better we'll finish out our golf game. I've been to the driving range twice with Dana and I'm going to be ready for him. Tiger, Tiger Woods y'all!

After the surgery Calvin was allowed to stay out of jail until his court hearing. He's still begging me for a little of my time. Every time he calls he sounds so damn pitiful, but he'll be a'ight. About the only thing I've learned from him is the importance of cherishing your family. That's why I'm glad I didn't shoot my uncle Herb the other day. He's in the house talking loud and saying nothing. Yeah, I've forgiven him for his thievery, but I haven't forgotten, and I don't trust him as far as I can spit, but he's family, so what can you do? I had Dana hide all my valuables when my mom told me she was bringing him with her.

The big surprise was how well Robin and my mom are getting

along. I didn't tell my mom about hooking up with my father's family because I knew she had some ill feelings about Calvin, but guess who told? That's right, Khalil! I will say Calvin has good taste in women because he chose two of the best in my mom and Robin. They are in my kitchen right now laughing like two Cheshire cats.

ust as I stood up to go back in the house, I heard a horn blow. I turned around and stared at the driver. Gotta hand it to him, he's persistent.

I leaned back on the railing and folded my arms. The car door opened and out stepped Calvin. He didn't look like the polished CEO in the picture. His eyes were bloodshot and his hair was in dire need of a comb. Whatever was going on inside of him was kicking his ass.

He walked up to me and stood at the bottom of the steps.

"I just wanted to say good-bye."

"Bye."

"Before I go, I want you to have something. Consider it a birthday gift," Calvin said, handing me a briefcase. "Inside are the deeds to two apartment complexes. You are the sole owner. You can do whatever you wanna do with them, but I suggest you hold on to them and pass them along to Khalil one day. Right now each one nets a little over one hundred thousand dollars per month. I put some savings and treasury bonds in there for Khalil so when he turns eighteen he won't have to worry about paying for college. Granddaddy took care of that," he said the word *Granddaddy* like I couldn't take that from him.

Then he walked off.

I sat there for a moment and I thought, *What do I have to lose?*

I stood and walked behind him.

"Calvin," I called out.

When he turned around, I noticed the gun.

He stopped and pointed it to his head.

"Yo, don't do that, man," I yelled. "Think about C.J."

He was serious. He didn't say a word.

"Calvin, we can move on from here. Why don't you come in the house and have some cake." I know that sounded weak, but damn, I've never worked on a suicide hotline before.

I slowly walked up to him and he took a step back. Just as he closed his eyes I reached for the gun.

Bam!

Oh shit! Blood went flying everywhere. I jumped back as Calvin's body hit the ground twitching. I couldn't move. The thunderous gunshot called everyone from out of my house. My grandfather was the first one to my side.

"Call an ambulance," he yelled back at the crowd.

My grandmother screamed when she saw her only child laid out on the concrete. She ran as fast as her seventy-four-year-old legs could move her and collapsed on top of her son.

"Edna, no," my grandfather said, pulling her up. "Jermaine, get your grandmother back in the house," he screamed, but he seemed to be in total control.

I snapped out of my shock and grabbed my grandmother by her arm, but she pulled away and tried to run back over to her son. I caught her and wrapped my arms around her waist.

"Calvin!" Grandma screamed as I led her over to Robin and Dana. It took all the strength I had to lead her away.

Robin opened the car door and she and Dana managed to get Grandma in the passenger seat.

Calvin was on his back, eyes fluttering, clinging to life.

Uncle Herb straddled Calvin with a hand over the gunshot wound to stop the flow of blood.

The paramedics showed up in less than five minutes.

"What happened?" one of them asked me as he moved a thousand miles per minute. "Talk fast."

"He had a gun to his head and I slapped it down just as he pulled the trigger. The bullet went in his chest or neck. I can't tell. Is he going to make it?"

"I don't know."

They put Calvin on a stretcher and wheeled him to the ambulance. My grandfather got in with them.

I watched them work on my father and realized he was human just like me. He had made mistakes just like I had, and he deserved forgiveness. "Hey, Gramps, won't you stay here and make sure Grandma is okay?"

"I need to go with Calvin."

"I got him," I said and climbed in the back. Calvin looked at me and I patted his hand. "Hang on in there, Pops."

Maybe I have changed.

Acknowledgments

First, I must thank God for continuing to bless me. I was at a book signing in Dallas, Texas, at the fabulous Black Images Book Bazaar with the wonderful Mrs. Emma Rogers when a lady came up to me and told me that I was her son's favorite author. I thanked the lady and went on with my book discussion. When I returned home, there was a letter from a young man in a juvenile detention center who said his mother had met me and told me all about him. He asked me if I could adopt him once he was released. I wrote him back and told him that he was already my son. Those weren't just words to appease the young man. I really feel an obligation to every young person I meet. Therefore, I hope you find what I write entertaining as well as enlightening.

I do what I do because of my son, Rashaad Hunter. He is the little light in the wind that keeps me sane.

I must send out major love to my mother, Linda J. Hunter—your love just grows and grows and I already have a job. ☺ A book just isn't a book without me thanking my wonderful family: Carolyn B. H. Rogers, and by the time this hits the stands it will be Ph.D.— do your thing, auntie. Donna Moses, you know you are sooooo sweet. Ethel Hunter, I miss you more and more each day. Uncle Dick, you are still the man. My father, Louis N. Johnson—we've turned out to be the best of friends. My uncle Clifton Johnson— I'd like to make my appointment now for my dental cleaning. My uncle Fred Rogers, my road dog. My uncle James Charles, Jr. Ernest Myers—you're all right with me. Sherry Johnson. Little bro's Jibade, Ahmed, Ayinde, Brandon. Lil sis Shani. My cousins are just like my brothers and sisters since we all grew up together. Barry, my big little cousin, Anne and David Gilmore, Sharon and Chris Capers, James (Ray Ray) Moses, Lynette Moses, Tony Harrison (R.I.P.), Ron Gregg, Gervane Hunter, Amado and Hunter Rogers, Darle, Anthony, Keith, and Mike Charles. Monica Thaxton for giving me the best gift anyone could ever give, our son. Willie and Schnell Martin. Michael J. A. Lewis for all the behind-the-scenes police info.

My entire literary family: my agent, Elaine Koster—thanks for handling my business. Eric Jerome Dickey—thanks for all that you've done for me personally and professionally; you're a true friend. Carl Weber—year after year you keep it real and I appreciate that. Kim and Will Roby, and Gloria Mallette, Jihad, Pearl Cleage, Timm McCann, keep your head up. R. M. Johnson, Mary and Willard Jones, thanks for the hospitality. My Random House family: Melody Guy—not only are you a wonderful editor, I consider you a good friend; Brian McClendon, let's do it again; Kelle Ruden, thanks for keeping me hydrated; Steve Messina, Dan Rembert, and Bruce Tracy.

I have met so many friends over the years that it would be impossible to name you all, so I'll holla at a few of you: Ebony Stell, Dwayne Dancer, Pam Gibson, and Porshe Fox. Tammy Martin. Cicely Tabb—thanks to you, The Hearts of Men Foundation is in good hands. Moe and Dionne Kelly, Daphne Morrison, Sharon Smith, Jamise, Carla, Kelly, and all the folks at Reflections Bookstore in Connecticut. Toni Gadsden, Tiffany Murray, Craig and Erica Grant, Leonard and Liz Gary, Rodney Baylor, all of my people in and from Florence, South Carolina, and last but not least, much love to all the independent booksellers who push my titles.

TROUBLE MAN

A Reader's Guide

TRAVIS HUNTER

READING GROUP QUESTIONS AND
TOPICS FOR DISCUSSION

1. When all else in Jermaine's life is going wrong, Khalil seems to give him hope. Why is this? Without his son, would Jermaine's choices in life have been any different?

2. Jermaine knows he can't last on the streets forever. Why does he find it so difficult to let go? Why does he allow Buster to join the game? Is he responsible for Buster's death?

3. In the end, Jermaine finds his life is going in a direction he never imagined. What is responsible for this change?

4. When Calvin says he feels leaving Jermaine out of his life was one of his biggest mistakes, is he telling the truth? Why couldn't he commit to being in his son's life from the start? Was it really Nettie who drove him away?

5. Erin wants Jermaine to be the kind of man she can be proud of, but she seems to encourage him in all the wrong ways. Why? Have they outgrown each other? What is different about Jermaine's relationship with Dana?

6. In different ways, C.J. and Jermaine were both abandoned by Calvin. Are there any similarities in their very different childhoods and lives?

7. C.J. feels his father was a bad husband, father, and business-man. Is he right to turn his father in?

8. Robin doesn't believe in divorce, yet her husband is a man she neither respects nor loves anymore. How does this influence her behavior toward her husband and her son?

9. Jermaine's newfound relationships with Dana, his grand-parents, and C.J. help draw him out of his drug lifestyle. Is it his new family that causes the changes in his life or his own growth as a person?

10. Erin's parents and sister know almost everything about her life and are quick to give advice. Are they too involved in her life? Is this Erin's fault or her family's?

An excerpt from bestselling author
Travis Hunter's latest novel,

A One Woman Man

Dallas Dupree is a one woman man. A handsome and successful
teacher, he is both worshipped and envied in his Atlanta neighborhood, and he chooses to live and raise his daughter, Aja, in the
ghetto he grew up in rather than desert his roots.

The only problem is that the one woman for him—his beloved
Yasmin—passed away giving birth to his daughter. Now Dallas
struggles through a string of empty relationships, unable to commit
his heart because no woman can measure up to Yasmin. However,
when Dallas plays with the wrong woman, he finds the consequences may cost him much more than he can afford.

Are You My Daddy?

"Are you my daddy?" a soft voice asked. Dallas Dupree felt someone standing over him. He popped up in the bed and looked around the strange room for the voice. His naked body was covered with sweat.

Where in the hell am I?

Dallas felt someone stir beneath the covers. His heart raced. Joy and fear took over. "Yasmin," he said softly. Then he looked down at the naked woman beside him and jumped. He rubbed his eyes and his head throbbed.

Things started slowly coming back into focus and he promised himself that he'd never take another shot of tequila for as long as he lived.

Last night, he and his coworker Kenya went to Café Intermezzo in downtown Buckhead to have a few drinks. Dallas ordered a round and tried to keep the conversation from venturing too far into his personal life because he wasn't ready to go there. But he knew the inevitable question would come.

Why is a man like you single?

And when it came, he shrugged his shoulders and said, "Don't know."

But he did know and that knowledge hurt like hell. He started throwing back shots of tequila right and left and before long Kenya didn't exist. Every so often he'd nod his head or grunt, but his mind was on Yasmin. The more he thought about her, the more shots he threw back.

The next thing he remembered was waking up buck naked to a child's voice.

Dallas glanced back at Kenya, who was still sleeping peacefully.

They'd met two weeks ago when she walked into the teachers' lounge at Alonzo Crim High School. He was sitting alone at the lunch table reading a book called *The Pact*, about three young men who made it out of the inner-city projects to become doctors, when Kenya walked in wearing a dress so tight he could see her heart beat. Dallas was convinced that she was a former stripper. He introduced himself and knew within the first thirty minutes of their conversation that she wasn't his cup of tea but her body, now that was another story.

Dallas hated the dating scene. All of this bed-hopping and trying to get to know someone was supposed to be over when he found Mrs. Right, but now Mrs. Right was gone and he found himself right back where he'd started. He took a deep breath, stood up, and walked into the bathroom. He quickly washed up and then looked around for a towel and when he couldn't find one, he dried himself with some hard toilet tissue, which he was sure she had stolen from the school. He put a pinch of toothpaste on his finger, ran it across his teeth, and rinsed. He looked around the bathroom and grimaced.

She's a filthy li'l something, he thought, looking at urine stains on the floor around the toilet and the dirty bathtub.

Dallas walked back into the bedroom and quickly jumped into his clothes. When he reached down to put on his sandals, he noticed a used condom on the floor beside the bed.

"Aw, damn! Why the hell did I have sex with her?" he mumbled as he picked it up and checked for leaks.

Strange things happen to unattended sperm, he thought, taking the piece of latex back in the bathroom to flush it down the toilet. After he made sure it disappeared down into the swirl of water, he prepared to leave.

He passed through the living room, which was also messy, when he noticed a little boy with big brown eyes sitting quietly on the sofa with his arms wrapped around his knees. He looked up when he saw Dallas and his eyes showed confusion.

"Hey, li'l fella," Dallas said, surprising himself. He walked over to the little guy.

"Hi," the little boy said cautiously.

"Why are you sitting here in the dark all by yourself?"

"I'm scared," the little boy said in a shaky voice.

"Scared? What are you afraid of?"

"I heard my mommy screaming. Did you hurt her?"

"No, I didn't hurt anyone," Dallas said, wondering if the little guy was talking about Kenya—but she hadn't mentioned that she had a son. "What's your mommy's name?"

"Kenya Latrice Greer."

I've been talking to this chick for two weeks and not once did she mention having a kid. Trifling!

"Your mommy's asleep. Would you like for me to go and wake her up?"

"No. She gets mad when I wake her up."

Dallas knelt down in front of the little boy. "What's your name?"

"Darius Nicholas Greer."

"Well, it's nice to meet you, Mr. Darius Nicholas Greer. How old are you?"

"Four," Darius said, holding up four fingers.

"A'ight, you're a big boy," Dallas said, reaching over to feel Darius's muscles. That got him to smile.

"Are you going to be my new daddy?"

Stunned, Dallas replied, "I'm sure you already have a nice daddy."

"But my mommy told me last night that she was going out with my new daddy," he said, crossing his arms and pouting.

"You know what? It's a little too early for little guys to be up. So why don't you go and crawl in bed with your mom," Dallas said, making a mental note to cuss Kenya out for doing this to her child.

"Okay," Darius said, reaching out for Dallas's hand.

Dallas walked Darius to the bedroom door of the room where just hours before he'd been reintroduced to the freakiness of his past and waited while the youngster snuggled up beside his mom. He waved at the little guy before leaving the house. He knew then that he would never come back.

On the ride back over to his side of town in the West End section of Atlanta, he started thinking about his life and what it had become. With the exception of his daughter, Aja, his life was empty. Yes, he could have the company of a different beautiful woman every night of the week, but after they left he would end up feeling just like he felt now—unfulfilled.

Dallas exited off I-20 at Joseph Lowery and headed toward his house by Clark Atlanta University. He stopped at a red light and took in the grim environment in which he chose to live.

Even at five-thirty in the morning, crackheads, drunks, and all the rest of society's problem children were out in full force getting their hustle on. He furrowed his brows and tried to act like he didn't see the familiar face running up to his truck with a spray bottle of dirty-looking water and some crumpled-up newspaper.

"Can you spare some change? I'm hungry. . . ." The guy in the shabby clothes started his speech but stopped when he recognized Dallas. He abruptly dropped the bottle in the street and pulled his left arm up to his face as if he were checking the time. "Where the hell you coming from?"

"What's up, Baldhead?"

Baldhead still looked at his arm as if he were a scolding parent.

"Answer me, boy," Baldhead said, still inspecting his watchless left arm. "Yo ass out here creeping, ain't cha?"

Dallas didn't answer; he just smiled and shook his head.

"Gotcha self a new truck, huh? What's that, a Cadillac Suburban?" Baldhead said, eyeing the shiny new vehicle.

"Baldhead, you get a job yet?"

"What kind of job I'mma get? Shit, all I know how to do is iron. You know anybody who needs they clothes pressed?"

Dallas laughed. "Can't say I do, Baldhead."

"Dallas, let me hold a li'l sumptin'? A dollar or sumptin'."

"I'm flat broke," Dallas said, showing the palms of his hands.

"Damn, Dallas, you got to be the stingiest rich nigga I know. You buying up all the houses 'round here, gotcha self a brand-new truck, so I know you got some money," Baldhead said as he stepped back and did a little dance. "You ain't think I was up on your business, did you? Boy, I know everything 'round here."

"Then why don't you know how to get a job?"

"Tell your evil-ass brother to give me a job," Baldhead barked.

At the mention of his brother, Dallas bristled. "You tell him," Dallas shot back.

"Hell no. That nigga be done kilt my ass for smoking up all his shit," Baldhead said, smiling and showing off a surprisingly bright smile. "You know Priest ain't used to be that mean when he was a cop. Now he's worse than the devil."

The light turned green.

"Baldhead, I'll see you around," Dallas said, driving off.

Once his older brother, Priest, was a pillar in the community, but he had traded in his police badge for a journey to the other side of the law. The fact that he could do this after the toll drugs had taken on their family ate at Dallas. Their mother died of a drug overdose, their father died of cirrhosis of the liver because he couldn't give up his addiction to the drug called alcohol, and their brother, Antoine, lost his life in an altercation with a small-time drug dealer. Dallas couldn't understand it.

But Dallas owed his life to Priest. At least the Priest he used to know. The Priest walking around now, killing his own people with his poison for profit, was a lost soul. He'd lost his soul when he was fired from the police department for taking money from a drug dealer. After that he stopped caring about his people. When Dallas found out his brother had joined the ranks of the wicked, their bond was forever broken.

But as much as he hated to admit it, he knew it was because of Priest's street reputation that he was allowed to come and go, in the heart of the ghetto, unmolested. Even standing a full six feet three inches and two hundred and forty pounds, he knew someone would eventually try to test him, but it hadn't happened yet and that could only be the work of Priest Dupree. His big brother was still looking out for him.

Dallas pulled into the driveway of the same house he grew up in. But it looked nothing like it did in those days. Gone were the broken windows, rotting woodwork, and dirt driveway. He had completely gutted the entire place, purchased the lot next door, added on a few more rooms, and manicured the landscape. Now his place looked like it belonged in an exclusive gated community rather than next door to a crack house. He pushed the garage button and slid his SUV in beside his convertible Lexus.

Dallas walked into his beautifully decorated home and tossed his keys onto his baby grand piano. He took the stairs two at a time and headed straight for his shower. As he removed his clothes the telephone rang.

He checked the caller ID and frowned. It was Kenya. He immediately became aggravated but quickly calmed himself.

Dallas could kick himself about his new predicament with Kenya. He knew she wasn't any different from any other woman; she wanted a man. And since he was nice to her, took her out for dinner and drinks then obviously sexed her up, she felt like she was on the right track to getting one. Wrong! He decided to let the call go to his voice mail.

Even before he went out with her, he knew things would change if they ever had sex. Things always changed.

Dallas wasn't the find 'em, fuck 'em, and flee type. He was more of the find 'em, see if I halfway like 'em, then fuck 'em type. But he prided himself on not taking people for granted, and when most of his peers were taking full advantage of the disproportionate ratio of women to men in Atlanta, he was proud to call himself a one-woman man. He was always up front and honest and he tried his best to treat everyone with the same level of respect. It didn't matter if the person was a doctor, lawyer, or a straight-up hood rat; they all walked in the door with the same value. He especially knew how to treat women, but he rarely ran across a woman who knew how to treat herself.

The minute the phone stopped ringing, his cell phone rang. Dallas shook his head and groaned. "Aww, damn! I gotta stop dealing with these damn stalkers," he said, not even bothering to check who it was.

Another Monday morning was upon him and he really wasn't looking forward to dealing with a bunch of hardheaded students, petty teachers, and an incompetent principal.

He went into his bathroom and turned on all the jets in his shower. When he had it as hot as he could stand it, he hopped in and let the steam and heat relax him. Ten minutes later he jumped out, dried himself, and took care of the rest of his morning grooming duties.

Dallas walked into his closet and scanned his extensive wardrobe. The way he felt always affected the way he dressed and today he felt like wearing shorts and a tank top but if he did, Mrs. Locus, his principal, would have a fit.

For the last few weeks, every morning when it was time to go to work, he started feeling fatigued. *I'm starting to hate my job*, he thought.

Dallas stood there for a moment and let his newfound reality sink in. He walked over to the window and looked down at the addicts on the corner. Most of them were out prostituting themselves to pay for their habits. He wanted so much more for them, but he shook his head and pulled back the shades.

A simple white shirt and a pair of black pinstriped slacks would do for today. As he dressed, the telephone rang again and he cursed. He walked over, checked the caller ID, and his mood lifted.

"Hello there, little lady," he said, taking a seat on the side of his bed.

"Rise and shine, good-looking. It's time to get up and make the world a better place," Carmen LaCour said to her younger brother.

"I'm tired," Dallas said.

"Well, good morning to you too! Why are you so tired?"

"I don't know." Dallas sighed as he ran his fingers over his closely cropped hair. "Maybe it's my job, maybe not."

"Your job? I can't have the right telephone number. Is this the house of Dallas Dupree?" Carmen said sarcastically.

"Cut it out. I just wanna go someplace where the schools don't have metal detectors. Someplace where the parents take an interest in how their children make out in life. I get so tired of having to do it all myself. I send some parents a note home about their child's behavior and it's never returned. I spend most of my time disciplining rather than teaching. And you know what? I'm getting a little tired of it."

Carmen made some sound that meant "I told you so."

"You know there was a time when teaching was the only thing I wanted to do, but now it just drains me," Dallas said.

"Dallas, honey, I'd be lying if I told you I wasn't sitting over here smiling my face off."

"Come on, Carmen, this isn't funny."

"Change doesn't occur until we get a little uncomfortable. I worry about you over there with those people."

"What do you mean *those* people?" Dallas said, back on the defensive.

"Just what I said," Carmen snapped. *"Those people."*

"They are *our* people. They're human beings just like you and me."

"Humans they are, but they're not like you and me. Those people live by their own set of rules and one day you'll realize that you can't save those who don't want to be saved, Dallas."

"So what do we do, give up on everybody who does not meet our standard of living?"

"I'm not saying that, but you have to realize the difference between black people and niggers."

"Now why you gotta go there?"

"You took it there," Carmen said, standing her ground.

"Carmen, it could've been me out on those streets. I just can't be so quick to judge."

"Dallas, I hear you, but it's deeper than you think. You gotta get out of there."

"I just can't become one of those who make good, then run out to the burbs never looking back. I need for my people to see someone up close and personal who is doing something with his life. That way they know they can do it too."

"Dallas, I truly understand how you feel and I commend your effort, but you're fighting a losing battle, sweetie. You're a giver and *those people* are takers. Eventually you'll run out of gifts," Carmen said.

"Move, Dallas. If not for you, then do it for Aja. I mean, why wait for one of those animals to hurt your daughter in some kind of drug-induced rage?"

Dallas was quiet.

"I don't have to tell you what an addict will do when they can't get their hands on some drugs. And there you are, flashing all that wealth in their faces."

"I'm not flashing it in their faces. I'm showing them that they can have it too. I'm from here. I grew up with most of these folks."

"Yeah, but that's not what they see. All they see is a man with the means to give them what they need. I'm surprised you've lasted this long without something happening," Carmen said. "Dallas, I want you to come down to the hospital when you get a moment because I want to show you something."

"What?"

"That you're not one of them. Even God said the poor would always be among us. You can't change that. It's divine order."

"I hear ya," Dallas said. It was time to change the subject because neither one of them was going to change the other's mind. "So what's up with you?"

"I'm serious, D.," Carmen said.

"Yeah, I hear ya."

"Maybe you need to take the day off. I got somebody I want you to meet anyway," Carmen said, ready to talk about her favorite subject: finding her baby brother a wife.

"Can't! Got a baby to feed and bills to pay," Dallas said as he stood and cracked his neck to help relieve some of his stress.

"Baby?"

"That's right," Dallas said proudly.

"That's an old woman hiding out in a three-year-old's body. I'm telling you that li'l girl done been here before."

"Pull up."

"I'm just kidding. You know Aja is my heart. Is she up?"

"She's visiting with Yasmin's parents this weekend."

"Oh, that's nice. I know I tell you this all the time but your big sister is so proud of you."

"Yeah, yeah, yeah," Dallas said.

"Shut up. Now when do you wanna meet this young lady?"

"Never!"

"Dallas, don't be like that."

"Carmen, you know I don't like your bougie-ass friends."

"Now who might you be talking about?"

"All of 'em."

"You just don't like them because they don't have sex with you on the first date."

"No, cuz most of 'em do. Bougie people are the biggest freaks. Since their whole life is a lie they need to take the edge off when the doors close," Dallas said, cracking himself up.

"Shut up. I can't help it that you're used to dealing with those ghettofied dropouts."

"Whatever! I'd rather deal with someone who knows they need some help than some educated basket case who thinks she has all the answers just because she graduated from some antiquated school system."

"You're intimidated by a sister's education?"

"Please. Blabbing on about their education is why most of them are single. Then they wanna run around here talking about the brothers ain't stepping up. Whatever!"

"Wrong. Most of my friends are single by choice."

"Yeah, cuz they choose to be bougie and after a brother get that ass he don't wanna deal with 'em."

"See, that's the problem. Brothers always trying to get that ass. Hold on a second," Carmen said as she spoke to her husband in the background.

"Tell pretty boy, I mean Sterling, I said what's up," Dallas said.

"Now you pull up. Listen, I gotta run but let's talk soon. Have you spoken with Priest?"

"Nope," Dallas snapped.

"You guys still aren't talking?"

"He's my brother and I love him. And I'll leave it at that."

"Okay," Carmen said, deciding not to interfere with their brother thing. She'd learned over the years that they broke up just to make up. "My friend's name is Monique and I'll give her your number. I'll come by on Friday to pick up Aja. Toodles! Love ya! Bye." Carmen hung up before Dallas could respond.

Dallas shook his head and put the phone back on its cradle. He walked by the mirror to give himself a once-over before he left for school. Over his shoulder he saw the reflection of a beautifully framed black-and-white chalked picture of Aja being held by her mother. He'd cried for a week when the artist he'd commissioned to draw it delivered the piece.

Aja was the spitting image of Yasmin. He took a deep breath. Oh, how he missed Yasmin.

ABOUT THE AUTHOR

TRAVIS HUNTER is the author of the best-sellers *The Hearts of Men, Married but Still Looking,* and, most recently, *A One Woman Man.* He is a motivational speaker and the founder of The Hearts of Men Foundation, through which he mentors underprivileged children. For more about Travis Hunter, his books, his tour events, and other news, visit his website, www.travishunter.com.